No Less than a Marquess

The Night Fire Club
Book 3

KATE MCMURRAY

ARE YOU SIGNED UP FOR DRAGONBLADE'S BLOG?

You'll get the latest news and information on exclusive giveaways, exclusive excerpts, coming releases, sales, free books, cover reveals and more.

Check out our complete list of authors, too!

No spam, no junk. That's a promise!

Sign Up Here

www.dragonbladepublishing.com

Dearest Reader;

Thank you for your support of a small press. At Dragonblade Publishing, we strive to bring you the highest quality Historical Romance from some of the best authors in the business. Without your support, there is no 'us', so we sincerely hope you adore these stories and find some new favorite authors along the way.

Happy Reading!

CEO, Dragonblade Publishing

Additional Dragonblade books by Author Kate McMurray

The Night Fire Club
I Never Forget a Duke (Book 1)
Everything but the Earl (Book 2)
No Less than a Marquess (Book 3)

Prologue

Cornwall, 1800

FLETCHER BASILDON THOUGHT it was a grave injustice that his father insisted on him continuing his lessons into the summer, when by rights, he should have been outside, enjoying this fine weather, and not trapped inside this stuffy drawing room.

The tutor Father had hired was droning on about the history of British relations in Ireland and the Basildon family role in it— "the Greystone title is an Irish one," the tutor emphasized—and it all seemed rather sordid. British monarchs were forever trying to invade Ireland, and some Basildon ancestor had marched alongside whichever Plantagenet king had invaded and built a castle that was now just a crumbling ruin on the Irish coast, and Fletcher was supposed to take pride in this triumph of territorial expansion. Instead, he asked, "But *why* did the king invade Ireland?"

The tutor didn't seem to have a good answer for that, beyond, "It was there for the invading."

When at long last Fletcher was dismissed, he immediately ran outside. It was a warm day, but at least there was a nice breeze. He had a mind to run to the pond at the back of Mother's garden and jump in it, but first, he encountered Lady Louisa and her governess.

The governess—a stern, prim woman named Mrs. Blanchard—sat on a bench, her hawk-like gaze trained on little

Louisa as she was arranging a tea party for her dolls at a small Louisa-sized table.

Fletcher paused. He was too old now to play with Louisa. That was what his mother said, at any rate. He was at the dawn of adulthood, she said, although he was dubious. He was still too scrawny and short to be labeled as anything other than a boy, but Father said any day now he'd grow.

Still, the two of them were often the only children about, and they'd gotten into a fair amount of trouble together over the years. They'd horrified Lady Petty by making mud pies by the pond, they'd once crushed one of Fletcher's mother's rose bushes—and ripped up Fletcher's favorite shirt—after a game went awry and Fletcher fell onto the bush. They liked to catch frogs at the pond together and occasionally leave salamanders for each other by hiding them under teacups at the Greystone formal dining table. And although Louisa in many ways was trained to be a girl—dainty, polite—she'd loved playing in the dirt as much as Fletcher did.

Although now Fletcher was older. Perhaps none of that was appropriate anymore.

"Fletcher!" Louisa said when she spotted him. "Come have tea!"

"We have lemonade, too," said Mrs. Blanchard, which was the main thing that got him to stop. He *was* thirsty. A glass of lemonade might be just the thing.

He sat in a little chair that made him feel like a giant. The other chairs at Louisa's play table were occupied by dolls and Louisa. Louisa was too small to pour anything but air into teacups, but Mrs. Blanchard produced a pitcher of lemonade and poured some into one of the cups. So Fletcher partook. The lemonade was a bit warm, but it was still refreshing. The cook here at Basildon House made her lemonade tart, without much sugar, and Fletcher loved it.

The Petty family—Louisa's parents—were here to visit for a few weeks. They came every summer. Louisa's father had been close friends with Fletcher's father since their days at Eton, so Fletcher generally saw a lot of the Pettys. He was fond of Louisa, and their five-year age gap had mattered a lot less to him before he went off to school, but as he approached his thirteenth birthday, he *was* starting to feel that perhaps he was too old to play with a little girl.

"Fletcher," said Louisa, "my dollies and I have been talking about weddings."

"Oh, no," said Fletcher.

"Sally wants to know who you will marry."

"I don't intend to marry anyone."

Louisa shot him a sardonic look, silently admonishing him for not playing along.

"What?" Fletcher said. "I'm too young to marry." His protest came out with a squeak.

His voice hadn't changed yet. He knew from encounters with older students at Eton that it likely would soon, but he still sounded like a child when he spoke, and he resented it. He could not wait to be grown. To be a taller man who spoke with authority instead of a boy who squeaked.

"Not tomorrow, silly," said Louisa. "I mean, when you grow up."

"I don't know. Maybe I haven't met her yet. I don't need to decide right now, do I?"

"You could *pretend.*"

Fletcher glanced at Mrs. Blanchard, who had a faint smile at her face as she resumed reading the book she had in her lap.

"Who are *you* going to marry?" Fletcher asked.

"You," she said. As if it were obvious.

"You can't marry me," Fletcher said.

"Why not?"

"We've been raised as siblings. Do you not think it would be strange for us to be married?"

"No. I like you. You talk to me like I'm smart. We like to sing songs together and catch frogs and have tea parties. What else is there to want in a husband?"

Fletcher laughed. "You make it sound simple."

"It is. Although I suppose if a handsome prince offered for me, I'd have to say yes."

"Naturally."

"But if no handsome princes are around, I'm marrying you."

"If you say so," Fletcher said. Hopefully, it wouldn't come to that.

Chapter One

London, 1818

FLETCHER BASILDON, RECENTLY made the Marquess of Greystone after the death of his father, stood on the back terrace of the Rutherfords' palatial London home and stared at the stars.

What a shambles tonight had proved to be.

First, Eltingham had managed to swindle him out of a small fortune at cards because Fletcher had counted incorrectly.

Then, he'd had to pour his friend—Larkin Woodville, the Earl of Waring—into a carriage after he drank one too many glasses of brandy. Fletcher had not known it possible to become so drunk on brandy, but Lark had certainly proved it could be done.

Then, he'd watched Owen Thomas, the Earl of Caernarfon and Fletcher's dearest friend, spend the evening dancing with his wife like the besotted idiot he'd become. Fletcher was happy for Owen, but mostly it highlighted how lonely Fletcher had felt of late. Nearly all of his friends had married and had their own families now, and Fletcher found himself too often left to his own devices.

And now he'd had to bear witness to maybe the worst thing of all—the announcement of the engagement of Lady Louisa Petty to the Duke of Rotherfield.

If anyone had asked, Fletcher would have made it clear that he was *not* jealous. He just thought Louisa could have found a better husband.

Alas, no one had asked.

No one else was on the terrace, which was a little bit odd considering it was such a nice night. The cool, crisp air had a bit of a bite, Fletcher's favorite weather. He had a snifter of Rutherford's good whiskey dangling from his fingers as he looked out at their back garden. He took a deep breath and tried to relax his tense shoulders.

The other thing that had been extraordinary about this whole Season was that suddenly, Lady Louisa was the sparkling jewel to which all eligible bachelors were attracted. Fletcher could not quite discern why; at five and twenty—nearly six and twenty—Louisa was old enough to be considered on the shelf under other circumstances. But once Rotherfeld started paying attention to her, suddenly everyone else did, too.

And why not? Louisa was beautiful and clever, plainspoken and witty, and Fletcher had always enjoyed her company. She deserved to have a whole fleet of men to choose from when it came to finally marrying. And, truth be told, Fletcher was not entirely sure why it had taken so long, but he did not begrudge her the happiness she'd found.

All right, fine, Rotherfeld was exactly the sort of man Fletcher had pictured Louisa ending up with. He was young and handsome, absurdly wealthy, and well respected. And Louisa, despite her advanced age, was one of the best people Fletcher knew. She was pretty, with a riot of dark curly hair that combs and pins struggled to tame; she had a heart-shaped face and a warm smile. What Fletcher liked about her, what he'd admired since their childhood, was her intellect and her sly sense of humor. *Of course* Rotherfeld was smitten; what wasn't to like?

Fletcher was *not* jealous. Louisa was a great friend, like a sister to him, but he didn't have romantic feelings for her.

He took a big gulp of whiskey.

The hinge on the door that led to the terrace squeaked, drawing Fletcher's attention. Hugh Baxter, the Duke of Swynford, walked toward Fletcher.

"I wondered where you'd vanished. I thought maybe you'd left with Lark."

"I thought to win back some of my losses at the card table, but luck is not with me tonight."

Hugh nodded. "You are not, of course, avoiding Lady Louisa."

"I am not. I made sure to congratulate her on her engagement before I walked out here for some air."

"Right."

"I wish her all happiness."

"Naturally."

"You don't believe me."

"I do believe you are happy for her. But who will you take to the opera now?"

Fletcher sighed. His not-so-secret love of opera had been developed over the course of many years of accompanying Louisa, who also loved it. They would talk at length about the music, the costumes, the spectacle. But there was something… unmanly about loving opera, so Fletcher had complained, apparently unconvincingly, to his friends about having to attend so often.

"I imagine I will find someone. Perhaps I should. I seem to have become the last man standing. Maybe it's time for me to find a potential wife candidate to escort to the opera."

Hugh chuckled. "You use a tone as if you must now go to the rookeries to contract leprosy. Besides, Lark is still unmarried."

"He's married to a bottle these days."

"Indeed. Quite the spectacle he made of himself tonight."

"I think I managed to get him outside before he did too much damage."

Hugh sighed. "I'm worried about him."

"I know."

"I think I had not considered all the ways love can wreck a man."

Fletcher turned to Hugh, who was looking out at the garden. "What do you mean?"

"When I met Adele, I would have moved heaven and Earth to be with her. Luckily, I did not have to. She and our son are the greatest things in my life. But Lark has not been so fortunate, and he had to watch the person he loves marry someone else last year. I thought he would be better by now, that he'd make his peace and move on, but I'm afraid he's more miserable than ever."

"Yes."

"I am perhaps not making a compelling argument for courtship."

Fletcher laughed ruefully. "I will admit that now that I've inherited the title, I feel a bit more pressure to find a wife." Well, perhaps more accurately, Fletcher's father's death had brought home for him that life was finite, that he could not fritter away his best years on frivolity. Fletcher had been content to live a life of leisure, until recently. He could not put off making his own family indefinitely.

Hugh nodded. "I was young enough when my father passed that I was perhaps better able to resist that pressure."

"You and Owen both seem happy. Louisa seems happy. I'd like to find some of that happiness for myself."

"A worthy endeavor."

"But it's not as easy as saying, 'I'd like a wife now.'"

"Oh, I don't know about that. I think if you walked back into that ballroom and started a whisper campaign that the Marquess of Greystone is ready to marry, a line of eligible debutantes would form rather quickly."

Fletcher groaned. He didn't want an eligible debutante. He wanted a partner in life, someone with some brains and a sense of humor, someone he could have conversations about literature and, yes, opera with. Someone like Louisa, frankly. But... not Louisa.

"Come back inside," said Hugh. "Find some beautiful woman

to dance with. Drink and be merry."

Fletcher downed the rest of his whiskey. "Yes, all right."

LOUISA HADN'T WANTED to announce her engagement in so public a setting. That Daniel insisted on it still puzzled her. It seemed gauche to create a spectacle.

The look on Fletcher's face would be seared into her mind for a very long time.

She was in the center of a crowd of women slowly losing her mind as everyone tittered and congratulated her. Daniel Woodbine, the Duke of Rotherfeld, was one of the most eligible men in the *ton*. Handsome, wealthy, *and* an accomplished scientist. He'd parlayed a hobby of birdwatching into further scientific study and now sat on the board of the Royal Society of Ornithology. He and Louisa had discussed the mechanics of flight at length—the physics of it were fascinating—although Louisa was less interested in the birds themselves. Still, it was an impressive package, everything Louisa wanted in a husband.

She should have been happier.

They'd been courting on and off for almost a year. Sort of. Louisa had spent the summer at her family's home near Bristol, and Daniel had only found time to visit her once, so she felt like most of the hot months didn't really count. She was... fond of Daniel, but she didn't love him. Her mother kept insisting that would come in time. Louisa believed it. After all, Daniel was very nice to look at—an athletic figure, curly blond hair that swept rakishly over his forehead, sparkling blue eyes, and a dazzling smile—but he was also kind and clever, and marriage to him would mean she'd live in luxury for the rest of her life. She didn't really care about the luxury, but it was nice. Daniel owned a well-appointed townhouse in London, but he also had a sprawling estate in Shropshire, near the Welsh border. Louisa had not actually seen it yet, but Daniel's sister assured her that it was beautiful.

But the look on Fletcher's face.

She sipped from a glass of lemonade and looked around the room while accepting congratulations from the women around her. Fletcher and Swynford entered the ballroom.

Fletcher looked nice tonight. He wore a fine blue jacket that she thought might be new. He'd combed his hair into the style that was currently fashionable, forward and over his forehead. Swynford, whose wife had become a close friend of Louisa's, said something to Fletcher that made him laugh.

She didn't think she'd imagined it. When Daniel had banged his pocket watch against his glass to get the attention of everyone in the ballroom and announced that Lady Louisa had consented to be his wife, Fletcher had looked stricken. By coincidence, he was right in Louisa's line of sight when Daniel made his announcement. Fletcher quite looked like he'd been punched directly in the sternum. Then he closed his eyes and left the room.

Louisa had wanted to tell him first. She felt she owed him that. Fletcher was her oldest friend. He must have been upset that he learned news so important when everyone else did, but not from her directly. Unfortunately, Louisa was trapped by well-wishers and couldn't get to Fletcher to apologize. And, sure, now he looked happy enough speaking with… drats, what was her name? Some pretty young debutante who seemed to hang on Fletcher's every word.

But Louisa had seen his face.

Daniel appeared at her side again. She smiled at him, which made the women around them titter. He smiled back and offered his arm. "Dance with me, my love."

"Of course," she said, glad to be escorted out of the crush.

She *could* love him, she reasoned as they waltzed. There was much to love. Even now, he danced like he'd been taught to since birth—perhaps he had, Louisa knew not the way of dukes—and she would have struggled to keep up had he not had a firm hand and the ability to lead her.

She caught Fletcher dancing with the young woman he'd been talking to. A brunette. Louisa could not remember her name. One of the Countess of Caernarfon's friends.

The song ended. Daniel bowed politely, winked at her, and said, "Excuse me, my dear, I have some business to attend to. I'll be back before you miss me." He kissed her hand and left the ballroom.

Fletcher politely left the woman he'd danced with and then approached Louisa. She braced herself for the conversation they needed to have and gestured for him to follow her. They walked off the dance floor and into a slightly less crowded part of the ballroom. When he stood before her, they both began speaking at once.

"You first," said Louisa.

"Congratulations again on your betrothal."

"Thank you." Now that Daniel wasn't hovering, she felt she could speak more freely. "I'm sorry. I wanted to tell you myself. I planned to this week, before the formal announcement appears in the paper, but. Daniel, apparently, could not hold back his excitement."

Fletcher pressed his lips together. "Indeed."

"I hope you are not too cross. I didn't want to make a public announcement. I wanted to tell my friends directly."

"It's all right," said Fletcher. "As long as you're happy. That's all that matters."

"I am."

"Then I wish you the best."

"You say that like this is good-bye."

Fletcher frowned. "Isn't it?"

"I don't see why."

"These days, a lot of our friendship involves going places together. Won't Rotherfeld be the one to escort you places now? Surely he would not approve of his wife socializing with an unmarried peer."

"He knows you and I are merely friends. I've told him many times. He cannot control who I socialize with."

"If he's your husband, I'm pretty sure he can."

Louisa crossed her arms. "Well, welcome to the nineteenth century, Fletcher. Women are allowed some measure of freedom now."

Fletcher looked unconvinced.

"Oh, so you would keep your wife on a tight leash, should you marry? Hide her in your house and not allow her to socialize with others?"

He tilted his head. "No, but if one of her friends were an eligible bachelor, I might take issue with it."

Louisa was surprised Fletcher was being so obstinate. "Yes, but you and I do not have a relationship that Rotherfeld need worry about."

"You and I know that. Rotherfeld doesn't."

"Are you acting odd because you think once I'm married, we won't be friends anymore."

Fletcher let out a breath and let his tense posture go. "I'm not acting odd, but yes. You are one of my dearest friends, and while I understand that a man and a woman being friends is perhaps unorthodox, we are like siblings. I knew this day would come because some handsome lord was bound to snatch you up, and while I truly am thrilled for you and hope you have all the happiness life can afford, I suppose I am sad that you and I will not spend as much time together."

"I shall endeavor to ensure that is not the case."

Fletcher gave her a wary look, but Louisa could not speak on it more because Daniel returned.

"Greystone," said Daniel.

Fletcher gave him a curt nod. "Rotherfeld."

"I suppose you were just congratulating my fiancée."

"I was," said Fletcher. "Congratulations are in order for you as well. You will soon marry one of the best women in the *ton*."

Daniel beamed at Louisa. "Yes. I agree."

"If you'll excuse me." Fletcher stepped away. Louisa wanted to grab him and pull him back, explain to him that her betrothal changed nothing, but she knew that wasn't true.

Daniel leaned over and kissed Louisa's cheek. "Come, my love. I'd like to introduce you to a few of my other friends."

Louisa followed, but she looked around for Fletcher. He was tall and easy to spot; she saw him walk out of the ballroom.

She knew, deep down, that he'd been right, that Louisa's obligations to Daniel would preclude spending as much time with Fletcher as they usually did during the Season. But she hardly thought that should mean their friendship would end. Surely there would be nights when Daniel was busy, and she needed an escort to some event. Daniel didn't care for the opera, so Fletcher could still attend with her. Nothing *had* to change, at least not drastically.

So resolved, Louisa focused her attention on her future husband and allowed him to introduce her to his friends. She tried not to think about why she should feel so sad about Fletcher.

Chapter Two

L ARK WAS IN the middle of writing letters of apology to anyone he might have offended by his drunken behavior of late when a footman knocked on the doorframe of his study and said, "I have today's papers."

"Thank you, Johnson. That will be all."

"My lord, if I may. There is an item on page three that may interest you."

Lark sighed. "All right. I will look later. That will be all."

Johnson looked like he wanted to say something more, but he nodded, placed the newspaper on Lark's desk, and left.

Lark continued writing for a few more minutes, but then curiosity got the better of him. He picked up the paper and scanned the headlines. Nothing dreadfully interesting. Parliament was out of session, the Prince Regent was clearly counting down the days until his father finally succumbed to whatever odd illness was plaguing him, wheat prices were fluctuating. Yawn. Lark turned to page three. Someone, probably Johnson who had been with him for a long time and knew him well, had taken the time to circle the relevant square of text.

It was a birth announcement. The Marquess of Beresford and his wife had welcomed a baby boy.

It was like a knife to the heart.

For two years, Lark and the Marquess of Beresford—Anthony

to Lark—had been lovers. The year before, Lark had ended it, because the pressure on Anthony to marry had become overwhelming. Anthony had talked constantly as if this was not an issue at all, that he could simply pass on the title to a cousin and continue his secret relationship with Lark indefinitely without marrying. And yet, two months after Lark had ended it, the announcement had appeared in the paper that Anthony had married the sister of the Earl of Clairbourne.

What Lark should have done was move on. He should find a wife of his own. He should do everything in his power to forget all about Anthony. He told himself this at least once a day.

He had thus far utterly failed to adhere to this plan.

Instead, apparently he was currently trying to determine how much drink was needed to obliterate his memories of Anthony. He had yet to find a sufficient amount of whiskey.

Now he stared longingly at the liquor cabinet in the corner of the room.

The thing of it was, Lark had been utterly, completely, ridiculously head-over-heels in love with Anthony. But Lark had chosen to end their relationship for valid reasons. He'd gotten spooked when a man had tried to extort him; that man had met his untimely end in a carriage accident before he could be persuaded not to talk to a scandal sheet, but the incident had worried Lark all the same. Then Anthony's mother had given him an ultimatum: Anthony must find a woman to marry by the end of the previous Season, or she would choose bride for him. Lark knew he had done the right thing, that their relationship could not survive much longer. They were at risk of getting caught, and thanks to a new bill that had been passed by Parliament, that could very well mean they would have both been hanged. Anthony had no interest in leaving Lark, so Lark had taken the choice out of his hands, thus freeing Anthony to marry without further obligation to Lark.

And now Anthony had the heir his mother had so desperately wanted.

Johnson appeared in his doorway again. "The Marquess of Greystone is here to see you, my lord."

Lark supposed he deserved that. "Show him in."

Fletcher appeared in his doorway a moment later. "I just wanted to check that you were still alive."

"Barely," Lark said.

Fletcher frowned at him. "The damage should be minimal, although you might want to send a letter to the Duchess of Montford to apologize for spilling wine on her gown."

Lark groaned and made a mental note to add her to the list. "She was wearing something hideous, wasn't she?"

"Her gown was a shade of brown reminiscent of a muddy pond," Fletcher said with a nod. "Undoubtedly you improved it, but I imagine money to pay for the gown's cleaning would not go amiss."

"All right. I will send her a letter this afternoon. Was there something else?"

"Hugh's pretty worried about you."

Lark sighed. He understood the implication was that Fletcher was worried, too. "I know. I've behaved abysmally all Season. I've been unable to shake my melancholy and doing a piss poor job of hiding it."

"You're still upset about Beresford marrying."

"I all but pushed him toward the altar. I don't know why I should feel this way." Lark pointed at the newspaper. "I've solved the mystery of why Anthony has been absent this season." Anthony hadn't attended any large social events, although Lark had assumed, perhaps incorrectly, that it was because Anthony was avoiding Lark.

Fletcher sat in a chair across from Lark at the desk. "Don't torture yourself."

Lark passed the newspaper to Fletcher. As Fletcher read the item, his eyes widened. "I didn't realize it would be so soon."

Fletcher's tone was that of someone who was anticipating the news. "Did you know about this?" Lark asked.

"I did. I received a letter from Anthony a couple of months ago. I apologize for not saying anything, but his letter explicitly asked me not to tell you. All I knew was that his wife was expecting, but I didn't know when the baby would arrive."

Lark sighed. "I had no idea."

"His letter to me implied he intended to tell you himself. I suppose I am not surprised he didn't."

No. Anthony wouldn't have. Too painful. Too confrontational. "He and I have not spoken since his wedding."

Fletcher hesitated, but then said, "Look, I cannot know what you are experiencing right now, but there must be healthier options for managing your feelings than trying to find the bottom of every bottle in your liquor cabinet."

Lark knew Fletcher was correct. He didn't want to feel this way anymore, but there was clearly no amount of liquor on earth that could obliterate Lark's grief and regret, or surely Lark would have found it by now. "I've been acting like a fool."

"Your friends have nothing but sympathy for you, but you make it challenging at times." Fletcher rubbed his forehead. "I'm sorry, I should not have said that."

"You're not wrong. I'm a mess."

"Come with me to the club tonight. Spend time with your friends instead of wallowing in your pain alone."

"All right," said Lark. "But don't let me drink anything more potent than tea. I think I need to stay away from liquor for a while."

"Agreed."

BEFORE GOING TO see Lark, Fletcher had spent a long, dull day meeting with a parade of accountants and solicitors and advisors in an attempt to get a handle on his father's vast business empire.

Somehow, Fletcher had not known the extent to which the

late Marquess of Greystone had his fingers in many pots. Property, farms, various investments in new technology…the holdings were vast. More than Fletcher felt he could manage.

Shortly before his death, he'd started investing in shipping goods between England and the Americas. Fletcher had argued with him about the ethics of importing things like cotton and tobacco from plantations that used slave labor, but the elder Basildon had argued that he was investing in the shipping infrastructure and not the goods themselves. "It is not up to me what people choose to buy and sell, or how those goods are produced." Fletcher disagreed. He generally tried to stay out of political arguments, but he objected to enslaving humans and wanted to see the trade abolished. It was tempting to take up his father's seat in Parliament for that reason alone. Still, finding a way to divest himself of those holdings had been his first order of business, and his advisors assured him he'd made a tidy profit for it.

Fletcher and his father had not been especially close. John Basildon had been an ambitious man who worked hard to expand his family's wealth and power. He was domineering with a short temper, and he had very specific ideas about the exact place each member of his family occupied. As the head of his family, it was his job to be outside the home growing his fortune, so Fletcher didn't see a lot of him growing up.

Upon his death eight months ago, Fletcher had inherited the lot of it and found it overwhelming. Father had tried to impart his business wisdom once Fletcher came of age, but it had not prepared him for *this*. Although once his health started failing, Father had begun lecturing his son on the finer points of his business, Fletcher still felt like he had a lot to learn.

The only saving grace was the small legion of people Father had employed, and whose expertise Fletcher relied on now. Still, he knew he had only a fraction of his father's business acumen, and he walked away from each meeting he'd had today convinced he'd be the one who destroyed the family's fortune.

He arrived at his club that night with all this on his mind, thinking he could perhaps sell his stake in a few more of these business ventures and reinvest the money in something Fletcher understood better than, say, cross-Atlantic shipping.

Lark had followed him to the club but was currently otherwise occupied, speaking to an acquaintance. Instead, Fletcher and Owen sat near the fire, their usual spot in the club, and Fletcher mentioned he'd had business meetings but didn't get into the details. He still thought of all of these men he'd spoken with as his father's employees; he was still wrapping his head around the fact that he'd inherited all this and now all those men worked for him.

"I suppose the good news," Fletcher said, wrapping up his brief description of his day, "is that even if I decided to sell all of it tomorrow, I'd still have enough to ensure that my grandchildren are well taken care of."

"You'd better get on making those grandchildren, then," said Owen.

"Now you sound like my mother."

"Far be it from me to suggest that you get married. I understand your thinking. But one thing to consider is that there is something to be said for waking up next to a beautiful woman every morning. And now that my boy can walk, there is never a dull moment at home."

Fletcher laughed softly. Owen's wife was a ceramic artist, and Fletcher feared for the beautiful vases she made now that they had a small child on the loose in their home.

He supposed part of him wanted that. Owen seemed much more content recently. He'd spent the summer in Wales, and Fletcher had gone to stay with him for a few weeks because Fletcher's country home in Cornwall was undergoing renovations and Owen's home in Wales was near the north coast and the breeze off the Irish Sea kept it from ever getting too hot. Fletcher's impression of Owen's home life was one of deep happiness. Owen and his wife, Grace, were obviously in love and they doted on their year-old son, who had a bit of mischief in his eyes. Fletcher looked forward to being the boy's enabling uncle, wreaking havoc on his well-meaning parents.

"On the other hand," Owen said, "several of Grace's friends have recently become engaged, and the rest of this Season is going to be attending one wedding after another."

"Poor Owen."

"I know. At least Parliament is out of session. If I had to deal with those stubborn old blokes *and* attend every social occasion to which Grace is invited, I'd go mad. I had no idea she was such sought-after company when we married."

"Such a difficult life you lead."

Owen rolled his eyes. "You are fonder of social gatherings than I am."

"Perhaps. What is your next engagement."

Owen stared at the ceiling for a moment while trying to remember. "I think it is Lady Danvers's garden party a few days hence. I don't really keep track. I rely on Grace to tell me where to go."

"When we were children, Louisa and I once replaced the sugar in Mrs. Danvers's tea service with salt."

Owen grinned. "You always were good for a prank. Remember the time at Eton when we short-sheeted all the beds?"

Fletcher shook his head. "Not my best work. I am especially proud of the time I found out Banks had that stash of racy literature and I replaced the lot of it with old math books."

"He was *mad*," Owen laughed. "Or the time you put snowballs in Easton's satchel."

"I haven't done anything like that in years."

"I am glad I was your friend and thus mostly immune from this trickery, although I do recall you once switched the clothes in mine and Hughes's trunks so that suddenly his trousers were too short and mine were too long."

Fletcher smiled.

"Do you ever think about doing things like that anymore?"

Fletcher slowly sipped some very fine whisky and looked

around. He caught a glimpse of Rotherfeld, an unwelcome invasion as far as Fletcher was concerned.

"I'd like to hide a very large spider wherever Rotherfeld stores his pretentious cravats."

Owen followed his gaze. "Explain to me your issue again," said Owen, pouring Fletcher another serving of the whisky. "With the duke, I mean."

"I don't have an issue with Rotherfeld," said Fletcher.

"The hell you don't," said Owen.

Fletcher was somewhat comforted by the warmth of the fireplace. Lark and Hugh were across the room, conferring with a third man Fletcher didn't recognize, but the conversation looked lighthearted. Hugh laughed so loudly at something the man said, the sound carried across the room. And Rotherfeld stood with the Earl of Sutterfield, chatting and lighting cigars, perhaps toasting Rotherfeld's betrothal.

At least Rotherfeld was out of earshot and not paying attention to Fletcher. So he said, "I *don't* have an issue. He seems perfectly fine."

Owen let out a breath and shook his head, like this conversation was fatiguing him. "He is marrying your Lady Louisa."

"She's not mine." Still, Fletcher felt willing to concede that Rotherfeld irritated him. "All right. I don't have an issue with Rotherfeld per se. By all accounts, he is smart and good with money and women seem to think him handsome. I've heard no gossip to indicate he's a gambler or that he's angry or cruel or irresponsible. I'm sure Louisa will be perfectly happy with him."

"I can see your mind churning, though."

"Would I be sad if he were to be bitten by a large insect and develop an extremely itchy rash? No. I cannot really articulate why he bothers me so much, aside from the fact that I am a little sad because I am certain marriage will mean I will see less of Louisa."

"She is your friend."

"Yes."

"Why should that change?"

Fletcher rubbed his temples. He knew Owen was making conversation. He surely must have seen the impossibility of this situation. But Fletcher said, "How shall I put this? Had Grace a male friend before she married you, and he remained unmarried, would you allow her to socialize with him still?"

"Not unless I was also there and kept him within punching distance." Owen gave Rotherfeld an assessing look. "I suppose I do see your point."

"Nothing untoward has ever happened between me and Louisa, nor would it. But Rotherfeld does not know that, and I suspect he will keep her from me, or at least insist she see me less. So if you must know, I am sad about potentially losing my friend to this marriage. But that is my issue to cope with, not Louisa's or even Rotherfeld's."

"It's not like you won't see Louisa. She and Adele have become close, so any party Hugh and Adele throw would include an invite to the Rotherfelds. They will be regulars at major events during the Season. I don't see how Rotherfeld could be so distrustful as to not allow you and Louisa to accompany each other to various public events, such as the opera on evenings when he is not available. Not much has to change."

"I understand, but I do not agree."

"Perhaps the thing to do is befriend Rotherfeld. Prove to him that you're someone he can trust his wife with."

Fletcher would have rather jumped in the Thames, but it wasn't a terrible idea. If Fletcher could get Rotherfeld to trust him, then maybe little would change with his relationship with Louisa.

"Would you trust Grace to be alone with me? You know me," Fletcher asked.

"Yes, but I know for certain that you are not interested in Grace and that Grace only has eyes for me." Owen shrugged. "Fletcher, you and I have been friends for a long time. I trust you. But that trust does not develop overnight. Have you and

Rotherfeld even had a conversation that lasted longer than a minute? You don't know each other, so you can't trust each other. If he trusts you, he won't see you as a threat. Until that time, as far as he knows, you could be trying to steal Louisa. You aren't, are you?"

"No, of course not."

Sutterfield walked away, leaving Rotherfeld alone.

"Go talk to him," said Owen. "Make nice."

"Fine, fine."

Fletcher stood and approached Rotherfeld, who looked startled when he noticed Fletcher.

Fletcher extended a hand and said, "How are you, Rotherfeld?"

"Ah, greetings, Greystone. I did not realize you were a member of this club."

"A long-time member. I don't recall seeing you here before."

"I have not been. Mason's is renovating their building after a small fire last week, so I am in need of a new place to spend my evenings. Sutterfield invited me to see it tonight. I've only ever been here as the guest of other members. But the membership here is quite elite. How long has Swynford been a member?"

"Oh, a decade or thereabouts. As long as I have."

Rotherfeld nodded. "I don't mind saying, Swynford impresses me. My father knew his. Great man, the late Swynford."

"Yes. That is, I didn't know him well, but I dined at his home a few times. Swynford and I are old friends."

Fletcher was unsure of how to make an impression here. Dropping Swynford's name likely helped. He opened his mouth to say something inane, but Rotherfeld said, "I imagine that now that Lady Louisa and I are engaged, you and I will be seeing more of each other. She tells me that you and she are like siblings."

"Yes," said Fletcher. "That is, our parents were close friends, and we played as children. I have often served as her escort to social events, although I expect now that you are getting married, you will take over that role. But yes, Lady Louisa and I have long been friends, and I care about her a great deal. I am honestly thrilled that she has found such an upstanding man to be her husband. She seems happy and I am happy for her."

"Kind of you to say." Rotherfeld smiled. "I hope…that is, it would please me if you and I were to become friends. I know we do not have much in common aside from our mutual affection for Lady Louisa, although I hope you can assure me that your affection for her is brotherly."

"It is."

"Good, good. Perhaps we can have you to dinner in the coming weeks."

"I would like that a great deal." This almost felt too easy. "Louisa did not tell me. When is the wedding?"

"Oh. Next month. I believe we have secured the fifteenth for a wedding at St. Paul's."

"Lovely." The fifteenth was five weeks away. "I look forward to it."

Rotherfeld nodded. "Yes. Good. I believe we understand each other, then."

"You have no reason to trust me, but I want to assure you, I only wish for Louisa's happiness. I hope that is clear."

"Yes. It is. I…thank you, Greystone. Your relationship is a bit unorthodox, so I am glad to hear you clarify it. Louisa has insisted there is no romantic spark between you, but as you are not blood related and you are still unmarried, I did worry. Perhaps I need not."

"I endeavor to prove that you can trust me."

Rotherfeld shook Fletcher's hand again. "I do hope that turns out to be the case."

Another gentleman approached and asked for Rotherfeld's attention, leaving Fletcher to retreat to his friends. Hugh and Lark and joined Owen at the fire.

"Well?" Owen asked.

"He seems amenable to friendship. Invited me to dine with him and Louisa."

"All right. Good first step."

"What is happening?" asked Lark.

Owen explained the friendship scheme. Fletcher mentally promised to try, although even now, he felt annoyance creeping up his spine as he watched Rotherfeld move through the room.

Lark let out a sigh. "The politics of gender are really something."

"This is just how it is," Fletcher pointed out. "At any rate, I intend to be Rotherfeld's greatest friend."

Lark saluted him. "Godspeed."

Chapter Three

DANIEL WOODBINE, THE Duke of Rotherfeld, had done everything right. He'd courted Louisa in the most formal, polite way possible, taking her for walks in the park or slow rides around London in his carriage, always with a chaperone present. He kept conversation to safe topics—news of the day, books Louisa had read, art she liked. Their engagement would last about six weeks, overall, which felt hasty, but Louisa's own father insisted it was all right.

Nothing inappropriate had happened.

Was it wrong for Louisa to have wanted it to?

She had needs and desires, after all. She knew it was unladylike to express them, but she'd spoken with her married friends and knew some of their secrets. The small ache in her chest whenever Daniel walked toward her, when he smiled at her...that was something important. She was fond of him, yes, but he was attractive, too, and if sometimes she wondered what it would be like to kiss him or what he looked like under all his layers of clothing, well, that was perfectly natural.

But he'd been the perfect gentleman.

Today, he'd accompanied her to an art show put on by the Countess of Devonshire, who was an avid art collector. Her son had just returned from his tour of the Continent with several important pieces, including a Caravaggio and a striking Rubens that depicted Venus in all her nude glory.

"It seems inappropriate for young ladies to see art like this," Daniel said, his posture tight as he looked around.

"It is fine art," Louisa pointed out. "The Venus is…that is, if it makes you uncomfortable, I'm also very interested in the Gainsborough paintings Lady Devonshire has collected and we can go look at those, but please know, Your Grace, that I am not so very young, and I am in fact in possession of a female body and know what they look like in the nude."

Daniel frowned at that. "Yes, of course." He gestured at the Caravaggio. "There is something… raw about this painting, too, though."

Louisa looked at it. Daniel had said *raw* like it was a bad thing. The painting was of a young man, perhaps one barely past being a teenager, holding a basket of fruit. He wore an open white shirt that was falling off, such that it revealed a nude shoulder and a muscular arm. The man's lips were parted in a way that Louisa found sensual. Like perhaps he had some sexual desire for the viewer, or for the man painting him.

Louisa may not have had much physical experience herself, but she understood desire.

Still, she said, "Perhaps we should move on."

Daniel seemed relieved to be leaving the presence of Lady Devonshire's racy new paintings and into the safer world of her collection of portraits. One of the Gainsborough portraits was of the Dowager Duchess of Swynford, back in her youth, perhaps immediately after her wedding. In it, she wore a pink gown under a heavy-looking fur-lined coat and had her hair teased up into an elaborate powdered coiffure with feathers decorating it. Louisa found it curious that the portrait was here and not in Swynford's house, but it was also widely known that Lady Devonshire loved to collect Gainsborough portraits, and that she and the dowager were cousins.

"This is an impressive collection," Daniel said to Lady Devonshire, who'd been hovering as they perused the portraits.

"Thank you, Your Grace. And Lady Louisa, you are an appreciator of art. What did you think of what my son brought back from the Continent."

"He has a fine eye, my lady," Louisa said. She looked down the corridor and spotted a marble statue. "Oh, is that the Apollo?"

"It is! Would you like a closer look?"

"Lord Devonshire has such exquisite taste," Louisa said, mostly to Daniel. He seemed unconvinced.

"This man is naked," Daniel said.

"He is nearly two thousand years old," Lady Devonshire said. "My son bought him in Greece. Is he not spectacular?"

Daniel looked wary. "Should this be on display with all these young ladies about?" He looked around at the small gathering of women who had come to appreciate Lady Devonshire's collection. "It seems questionably appropriate—"

"Oh, I will try to steer the unmarried ladies from the sight of young Apollo's manhood, but I know Louisa to be a great appreciator of art and mature enough not to swoon at the hubris of this statue."

Louisa laughed. "Thank you, my lady."

"It just seems—"

But Daniel was cut off by the arrival of Adele, the Duchess of Swynford, and Grace, the Countess of Caernarfon. They walked in, arm in arm. Daniel must have recognized them as Louisa's friends, because he muttered something that sounded like, "Oh, thank god," and then smiled at the new arrivals.

He looked at his pocket watch. "I am afraid I have an appointment with my man of business and must depart. But I'd hate to deprive Louisa of her time spent with fine art. Can you ladies see to it that she makes it home?"

"Of course," said Adele. "There is plenty of room in our carriage. She can ride home with me, Your Grace."

"Then I leave her in your capable hands." He turned toward Louisa. He lifted her hand and kissed her knuckles. "When shall I see you next, my love?"

"The opera tomorrow night. You agreed."

"Indeed I did. Mozart, I believe." His tone indicated she'd asked him to eat rotten fish, and he was steeling himself for it.

"Yes," she said. *"Le Nozze di Figaro."*

Daniel nodded, albeit without much enthusiasm. "Then until tomorrow, my lady." He bowed, gave Lady Devonshire a cursory bow, and then departed.

"Did he leave…hastily?" Louisa asked her friends.

"A bit," said Grace.

Louisa let out a sigh. "The art here… it seemed to make him uncomfortable."

Adele glanced down the hall at Apollo. "Is he bothered by male nudity?"

"He seems to think I should be."

Grace laughed. "You *should* be, but he should know by now how much time you spend around fine art. I know some museums have added fig leaves, but that was not what the Greeks intended."

Grace was a sculptor who sold her pieces under a male pseudonym, and although clay was her medium, she had an encyclopedic knowledge of all kinds of sculpture. She and Louisa had gone to the British Museum a few weeks before to look at some new marbles in the collection, nude sculptures all, and Grace had also seemed unfazed by the art. It seemed she had many books in her personal library with sketches of some of the same statues; she claimed the sketches did not do the real things justice.

Louisa looked at the Apollo again. "Why, do you think, did they make so many nude statues?"

"The Greeks had less shame about the human body, I suppose," said Grace. "They wanted to celebrate the body beautiful. We want to cover it up, lest any weak-willed individual be overcome with lust and act in a way that is unbecoming. Social mores change over time, I suppose."

"I suppose if I were your future husband, I'd want to shield your eyes from depictions of the male physique, should my own physique fall short of the ideal," said Adele. "I don't think Rotherfeld will have that issue."

"This is just…" Louisa gestured toward the statue. "All right. You two are married ladies and you both have children, so you have of course seen your husbands in the flesh, while I have only ever laid eyes on marble men, but I guess I don't feel any shame, even if I probably should. I don't think my looking at a statue will affect me much in any way."

"Apollo is not driving you wild with lust?" Grace asked, a glint in her eye.

Louisa looked over the statue. "No, not really."

"That is men's fear, too. Both that they will prove inadequate, and that somehow seeing another man will corrupt their women."

"I do not think that is the case."

"I'm not disagreeing with you, I'm just explaining what men tend to think."

Adele laughed. "Men are foolish creatures."

Louisa, not for the first time, wondered if she was making a mistake with Daniel. "Do you think Rotherfeld is so insecure that he'd want to shield me from art?"

"*Did* he shield you?" Grace asked.

"I suppose he didn't. He just seemed extremely uncomfortable."

"Perhaps he's the one who feels shame."

Louisa wondered what that said about Rotherfeld's character. Women were supposed to be sheltered and protected from the horrors of the world outside the home—or so Louisa's father had said on more than one occasion, although this was not something he enforced with much vigor—but it seemed like Rotherfeld was the one who had been sheltered. Was Grace correct? Was Rotherfeld worried about inadequacy? Was he worried looking at art would warp Louisa's mind.

"Rotherfeld is a very handsome man," said Adele. "I doubt

you would find him wanting."

Louisa laughed. "This whole conversation is absurd."

Adele looked around. "Oh, dear. Is that my mother-in-law?" She was looking at the Gainsborough.

"I'm afraid it is," said Louisa.

"She was pretty in her youth. I suppose pure evil hardens a woman's features."

Louisa laughed. "The dowager is not evil."

"She is a little bit. Hugh building her a home of her own was the greatest gift he's ever given me, especially now that she has stopped calling on us so incessantly. I only have to see her at luncheon after church on Sundays, and these days, mostly she ignores me, which I suspect is for the best."

"You've been married for almost three years," said Grace. "Has she not melted a little?"

"A tiny bit. She dotes on my son. He's two and has the attention span of a house fly, but she still likes to lecture him on the importance of carrying on the grand Swynford name."

"Seems like a good use of her time," said Louisa.

"At least she is not lecturing *me*."

Lady Devonshire had wandered off somewhere but now returned and said, "Would you ladies like to see the new paintings?"

"Are they scandalous?" asked Adele.

"One is a female nude," said Louisa.

"Then yes, please, my lady," said Grace. "Show us the paintings."

AT THE CLUB a few nights later, Fletcher told his friends, "I called on Rotherfeld today and he invited me to luncheon."

"And you broke bread with him?" asked Lark, looking horrified.

"I am trying to follow Owen's advice, which was to befriend Rotherfeld so that he knows he can trust me in the company of his future wife."

Lark wrinkled his nose as if he found this whole business distasteful.

"Do you take issue with Rotherfeld?" Fletcher asked Lark.

"Not as such, I just find him rather dull."

"I'm right, am I not?" Owen said, mostly to Hugh. "Rotherfeld's instinct will be to prevent his wife from spending time with her unmarried male friend, but if Rotherfeld understands that Fletcher's intentions are brotherly, then he may allow their friendship to continue."

"I would trust my wife in the company of any one of you," Hugh said.

"Precisely," said Owen.

"But I have known you all since we were boys," said Hugh. "Fletcher is unlikely to engender that kind of trust in, what, a month?"

"Let us talk about everyone else's problems!" Fletcher said, probably too loudly. He was tired of going in circles about this.

Owen laughed. "Well. Since you are *not* in love with Lady Louisa—"

"I am not!"

"—we'll let it slide this time. And I don't have any problems."

"Of course you don't," said Hugh, laughing.

"What can I say? Life is good. Dafydd is very close to saying his first word." Dafydd was Owen's son, who was just over a year old. "He's been saying *mmm* a lot lately, which I think means he's about to say *Mama*. I'd feel insulted, but since Grace is also my favorite person, I'll allow him to bestow the honor upon her first. And he's terrorizing our nanny now that he's on foot, but I find that entertaining more than anything else."

"Children are small terrors," Hugh said. "My Edward is a chatterbox. Never stops talking and most of it is nonsense. Adele seems charmed by it, though. And she has been making noise about having another, but I am yet to be convinced. She was so ill with Edward."

"Women forget," said Owen. "Apparently it's nature's way of tricking them into having more children. That is, according to a book Grace made me read."

"Perhaps we are not the best judges of what women are capable of," Fletcher said.

"Probably true," said Owen.

"What is happening in Parliament?" Lark asked Owen, seeming eager to change the subject.

"Not much. It's not officially in session, but Lords is in a lather about that assassination attempt on Wellington, and the only real bill on the horizon right now is one to build more churches, a cause about which I have no feelings one way or the other."

"This is what our government is spending its time on?" asked Fletcher. "Churches?"

"Take it up with the Prince Regent."

"I've read," Lark said, leaning forward like he had some good gossip, "that the mad race for an heir is on. With the royals, I mean. Cambridge is marrying some German princess."

"Indeed," said Owen. "The rumor is that Queen Charlotte has ordered her unmarried sons to find wives and get to fathering an heir as swiftly as possible, now that Princess Charlotte has departed this world and Prinny has essentially put his wife out to pasture."

It was publicly known that Prince George loathed his wife, so no one expected them to have any more children. Thus the king's other sons were expected to beget heirs with all possible haste to prevent the collapse of the monarchy.

"There is a running bet going among the Lords in Parliament," Owen went on, "about how long Prinny lasts once he ascends to the throne. I've got money on five years." By all accounts, the king's health was failing, and the Prince Regent was not exactly in peak physical condition.

"That's terrible," said Lark. "How do I get in on that bet?"

Owen laughed.

It was true, after Prince George's daughter passed, there was new pressure on his siblings to beget heirs with all possible haste. The Duke of Cambridge, one of the king's younger sons, was the first to marry, it seemed, but the rest wouldn't be far behind.

"Perhaps the real bet," Fletcher said, "is which of the king's sons succeeds in fathering an heir first."

"We have a pool on that, too," said Owen.

"The oldest sons have wives they are either estranged from or who are too old to bear children," Lark pointed out.

"Wasn't Clarence married to that actress?" asked Fletcher.

Lark's eyes practically sparkled. He'd always been a terrible gossip. "They were never married but the king allowed their relationship to carry on, and all of their sons have titles even though they are not legitimate and cannot be in the line of succession. But the relationship ended some years ago, I think. And Clarence is apparently on the hunt for some European princess or wealthy heiress to marry now, too, even though he's no spring chicken. He's in his fifties, I think."

"That is hardly an age of infirmity," said Hugh. "I hope to still be able to make love to my wife regularly when I am in my fifties."

"Godspeed," said Fletcher.

"I know Lark is a sad sack now," said Owen, "but do you, Fletcher, intend to find some beautiful heiress to marry this Season?"

"I suppose I must eventually. I currently have no prospects."

"Why didn't you marry Louisa again?" asked Hugh.

"That is not the nature of our relationship."

"Surely there are worse outcomes than marrying a friend," said Lark.

"Yes, but as we've just discussed, the begetting of heirs is an important aspect of marriage, and I've never viewed Louisa in that light."

"You've never imagined her and… bedsport?" Owen asked. "Never."

Fletcher sighed. To say *never* would be an exaggeration. "All right, fine. I have eyes. I can see she is a beautiful woman. So not *never*. But definitely not seriously. It is possible for men and women to be friends with each other without there being sexual attraction between them. And even if I did find her attractive, she clearly doesn't find *me* attractive, because she's marrying *Rotherfeld*."

"Hence the luncheon today," said Owen. "And how did that go? You didn't tell us."

Fletcher frowned. How to describe it? "Do any of you know Rotherfeld?"

Everyone shook their heads. Owen said, "Not well."

"Not well?"

Owen shrugged. "Our paths have crossed but if I've ever had a conversation with him about anything more substantive than the weather, I've forgotten it."

"See, this is my issue. Rotherfeld is…boring."

"As I said," Lark said, lifting his hand.

"Boring?" asked Hugh.

"Dull. Uninteresting. He does not care for culture. Dislikes the opera. Thinks theater is vulgar, even Shakespeare. Doesn't read much beyond newspapers and the occasional history but nothing so uncouth as a *novel*. He mentioned that he escorted Louisa to the Duchess of Devonshire's gallery a few days ago, but he found the art troubling."

"Troubling in what way?" asked Hugh.

Lark raised an eyebrow. "I was there yesterday to see her new Caravaggio. It is a sensual depiction, I will grant you, but I didn't find it troubling."

"*You* wouldn't," said Owen. "I heard it was a male nude."

"It is not. The painting depicts a young man with one shoulder exposed. I daresay, I see more in the mirror when my valet dresses me in the morning. The younger Devonshire has acquired a nude Venus, a depiction by Rubens if I remember correctly, and it obviously is meant to titillate, too, although Rubens had a type that is not to all men's tastes. I thought the painting was lovely, though. Perhaps the Caravaggio is not the sort of thing prudish young dukes want their fiancées to see, but it is hardly a scandal. It's art, after all."

"Well, the Duke of Rotherfeld does not approve of *art,*" said Fletcher. "He does not approve of much. I found him quite puzzling. And boring. Did I mention that? The luncheon felt like it went on for five years. I can't imagine what he and Louisa talk about."

"He's a good-looking gent," said Lark. "That's all most women are looking for."

Fletcher bristled at that. "Louisa is not most women. She'd be dissatisfied in a typical *ton* marriage. She'd want a marriage like you fellows have, with a spouse who loves her and wants to spend time with her. Not some oaf who… God!" Just the mental image of Louisa enduring a husband who was the sort of man who only rutted against his wife a few times a year for the purposes of conceiving an heir…it made Fletcher nauseous.

Owen gave Fletcher a curious look, but said, "And you don't think Rotherfeld is that man?"

"I suppose I don't know, but luncheon today was not encouraging."

When Fletcher arrived home an hour later, this was still on his mind. His butler, Gerald, took his coat and then held out a silver tray with a letter on it. Fletcher disliked this level of formality, but his late father had insisted, and Fletcher hadn't had the nerve to make things more relaxed at home. He picked up the letter with a sigh.

It was from Louisa. Fletcher scanned it. *…alas, Rotherfeld has plans elsewhere Thursday night. It would please me if you accompanied me to the opera in his stead. Rossini's new opera,* La Cenerentola. *I'm told it's a comedy…*

Fletcher walked into his office, scrawled a reply that he would absolutely accompany her, and told Gerald to send it first thing in the morning. This, at least, Fletcher could do. He could spend as much time with Louisa as possible before her marriage, because undoubtedly everything would change after the wedding.

Chapter Four

ON THE ONE hand, Lark reflected, it was good to go to the club, if only to leave his house. He felt like he'd become a hermit in the last year. Things felt more like the old days, less bleak.

For months, he'd barely left his home. He was too devastated, too unfit for company, too unwilling to put on a happy face and pretend his heart wasn't broken. When he did go out, he tended to make a fool of himself, as he had at the Rutherford ball.

The news that Anthony now had a son had not helped, but after the lecture from Fletcher, he was trying. He was trying not to wallow in misery, to spend time with people so as to not be tempted to wallow, to begin reading gossip sheets and scandal pages again, to reengage with his life. It was an enormous challenge, especially now that Anthony was a father and thus completely lost to Lark, but he knew he had to move on.

It was a few days since he'd last been at his club. He'd refrained from invading his store of liquor, at least. He was tempted to drink himself into a stupor and then go to sleep early, because he hadn't had occasion to leave the house in a few days and he was deep in his grief. He missed Anthony terribly, but he was also becoming pathetic, and his self-loathing felt like he was digging a deeper hole. He *had* to find a way to move on, for his own health and well-being, he just didn't know how.

It wasn't like Anthony was dead. Anthony was, apparently, alive and thriving. It was Lark who was home alone and losing his mind.

Johnson appeared at his study's doorway.

"I'm not in to callers," Lark said, glancing at his clock. It was midafternoon. Had he been in better spirits, he might have called for high tea. As it was, he was wearing old clothes and a dressing gown because he hadn't bothered to dress for company that morning.

"The Duke of Swynford is here, my lord. He says it is quite urgent."

Hugh pushed into the room. "You're in to me, Lark," he said. With a quick gesture, he dismissed the butler.

"Hugh, I cannot—"

"The Marchioness of Beresford is dead."

Well, that certainly had Lark's attention. "She's…what?"

"She died, Lark. After childbirth, she caught some kind of infection and passed last night. It's not common knowledge yet, but the news will hit the newspaper tomorrow and the funeral will likely be Saturday. And I found all this out less than thirty minutes ago, so do not ask why I did not tell you sooner."

"Oh, god."

"For what it's worth, Anthony sent me a note. I imagine he sent it to me so that I would get word to you, so that you did not find out from the paper."

"He succeeded."

Lark had no idea what to do with this information. Anthony's wife was dead. Of all things, that was among the last Lark had imagined. But there was nothing to be done about it. Lark was trying to move on with his life; he and Anthony were no longer friends.

He sighed. "Well, thank you, I guess."

Hugh started at him, his hands on his hips. "You've been a right honorable bastard for months, Lark."

"I know. And you are hardly the first to berate me for it."

Hugh stood there for a moment, looking frustrated. He took a deep breath. "I came here because I thought you might want to act. I know his marriage devastated you, but can you pull yourself together and see that he might need you right now?"

"He does not want to see me."

"I beg to differ. If he did not want to see you, he would have let you find out his *wife* is *dead* from the newspaper."

Lark looked up and met Hugh's gaze for the first time. Hugh looked uncharacteristically disheveled. Normally, the best valet money could buy made certain Hugh never left the house looking anything but impeccable—if a bit old-fashioned; Hugh was not a man who cared much for the latest modish trends, but right now, his hair was mussed and his cravat was askew.

"Is it raining outside?" Lark asked. "Your hair—"

"Did you not hear me?"

"Did you rush over here?"

"In fact I did. I received the note from Anthony and then immediately dressed to go out. I thought you should know as soon as I did. And yes, it is raining out. It is London, after all. When is it not raining?"

Anthony's wife was dead. He'd wanted Lark to know before the rest of society did.

"Should I go to him?" Lark asked.

"I can't answer that for you. It's been less than a day. He may not be ready for visitors yet."

Lark didn't know anything about what might have been between Anthony and his wife, but he imagined that Anthony would still struggle with such an abrupt change. A new baby and the death of his wife inside of a week was quite an emotional jolt. Lark could picture Anthony struggling with everything and knew he needed help. Lark stood. "I will go."

"All right. Do you want my help? Shall I come with you?"

"I have not seen Anthony in nearly a year. I believe this is something I must do on my own."

"If you insist. But if you need anything, please call on me.

Anything you need, Lark."

Lark was touched. "Thank you, Hugh. Your haste is much appreciated." He went to the hallway and called to his butler. "Ready my carriage, Johnson, if you please. And find my valet. I should like to make myself more presentable."

"Yes, my lord." Lark may have imagined it, but Johnson almost looked relieved.

FROM THE OUTSIDE, none would know anything out of the ordinary had happened inside Beresford's London townhouse.

His official residence, that was. Beresford had once had several homes, one of which was reserved almost entirely for his assignations with Lark. Lark had seen an advertisement for that house's sale about eight months ago, and he'd mourned the home more than was rational. But that was the past. The Beresford home, where Anthony had lived with his wife, was a four-story monstrosity that was far more ostentatious than it should have been, and Lark realized suddenly that he'd only been inside it a couple of times.

Because his relationship with Anthony was a well-guarded secret. It was never meant to be public. That was how a sodomite found himself at the end of a noose, after all.

Lark alighted from his carriage and ran to the front door hoping to dodge the rain. Beresford's butler, Rollins, opened the door as Lark arrived, and Lark pushed his way inside.

Rollins was the butler from the home Lark had visited most frequently, someone Beresford trusted to be discreet. Seeing him was a bit of a relief, although the man looked deeply unhappy to see Lark.

"Beresford is not ready for visitors," said Rollins with a heavy sigh, as if he were already resigned to this.

"Let me see him. Where is he?"

"The study, my lord. Second floor, on the left."

Lark found Anthony in his study, sitting in a wingback chair and sipping from a snifter of whiskey. His face was pale but red around his eyes, as if he'd been crying.

He was so deuced beautiful, even in this state. It pained Lark to see Anthony without the customary smile on his face, the glint in his eye, but as for the rest of it, Anthony's curly auburn hair had been trimmed but was still unfashionably long, his skin was still soft and pale, his body was still something that pulled at the baser parts of Lark. Lark had not laid eyes on this man whom he'd loved so well in nearly a year, and yet he was still utterly besotted.

But now was not the time to think on that.

"Lark!" Anthony said, sitting up.

"Don't bother with ceremony. Stay seated."

"What are you—Hugh passed on the news."

"Yes. We assumed that was your intention."

Anthony looked miserable. He downed the rest of the whiskey in his glass, set the glass aside, and then wiped a hand over his face. "I won't lie. It's been a difficult week."

"I'm so sorry for your loss."

"You aren't, but all right."

Lark had never seen Anthony look so sad. It was like all the light had been drained out of him. Lark walked close and knelt beside the chair.

"I am! You are in mourning. Hugh thought you might need some support, so I came here to offer it."

Anthony closed his eyes slowly and then opened them again and gazed at Lark. "So here you are."

"Anything you need, Anthony. I will do everything in my power to give it to you."

Anthony's face crumbled. "I can't believe you're here."

"If you tell me to leave, I will."

"No, stay." There was something plaintive in Anthony's tone.

"Do you need something? Shall I fetch a servant, or do you

need tea, or—"

"Would you mind just…sitting with me for a bit."

"All right." Lark stood and moved over to the nearest chair. He perched on the edge.

Anthony was silent for a long time. Lark had never really dealt with grief such as what Anthony seemed to be experiencing. His parents and sister were all still alive. An acquaintance from Oxford had died at Waterloo, but Lark hadn't known him well enough to feel more than a pang of regret when he'd gotten the news. He felt ill-equipped to help Anthony and certainly had no idea what to say. So he waited, as patiently as he could, for Anthony to speak.

"I did like her, you know," Anthony said at last. "Matilda, I mean. Not in the way a husband normally comes to love his wife, but I did care for her, and we became friends of a sort. And to watch the life seep out of her body…"

Anthony stared unfocused at something on the floor, clearly in the throes of some sort of shock. Of course something like this would be stunning. Lark had never doubted he would find Anthony mourning, because that was his nature. He wouldn't have married someone he didn't think he could get along with, so of course they'd forged a friendship, even if Anthony could not offer her his whole heart.

"And now I have a son I have no idea how to take care of," Anthony said. "That is, I've hired a nurse, and she is up with him now. But I do not know how to be a father. I always thought, you know, Matilda and I would figure out how to be parents together, but now she is gone, and I… I have no idea what to do, Lark. Not the foggiest clue."

Lark was glad he hadn't partaken of drink today, because Anthony was in a bad way, and Lark would need to keep his wits about him. He tried, "What is his name? Your son, I mean."

"Henry." Anthony smiled softly. "Perhaps not the most original name, but Matilda was named for England's first queen. Henry I's daughter, who would have been Queen Regnant if her cousin Stephen hadn't made a claim on the throne. So I had the thought to give the boy a good Plantagenet name. It suits him."

"That's lovely."

"Yes, well."

Anthony was clearly hurting, and understandably so. His life had just irreparably changed. Lark tentatively reached over and put what he hoped was a comforting hand on Anthony's arm.

Anthony looked over at Lark. "I don't know what you're doing here or what you expect to happen, but—"

"I only came to see if you needed assistance or support. My intent is merely to offer you anything you need."

"Lark."

"I know we've barely seen each other since your wedding, but you are and always will be my friend. So whatever you need, tell me and I will provide it. That is what a friend would do."

"Will you come to the funeral?"

"Of course, if you want me there."

Anthony nodded. "I'm afraid I am incapable of rational thought right now, so I can't even think of what to ask of you. But I fear I cannot face the funeral on my own."

"You are mourning and not expected to think rationally. I can accompany you to the funeral if that is what you need."

Anthony let out a breath. "I honestly do not know what I need. I am glad to see you, though."

Lark smiled. He wanted to weep. "I cannot know what you are experiencing, but all I want to do is take your pain away."

"I know. That is how you would feel." Anthony shook his head. "Can you tell me about something trite and stupid? Gossip, parliamentary business, something to get over this overwhelming feeling I have that my life is ending."

It was perhaps advantageous that Lark had recently taken to reading the scandal sheets again. "Certainly, I can do that. The Duke of Cambridge just married. The race is on to see which of the king's children will be the first to give the country an heir."

"What a godawful mess," Anthony said, clearly happy for the

distraction. "The king has been in the grips of some madness for nearly a decade, and his oldest son, who is supposed to be ruling in his place, is a ridiculous dilettante who apparently only lay with his wife the one time, but now his daughter is dead, and somehow none of the king's, what, twelve children has managed to produce a legitimate heir? What is wrong with that family?"

Lark laughed. "Is this a sufficient distraction?"

"Lark, if *I* could find a way to father a child, surely one of those seven Hanover men can discern the mechanics of it."

"One would think. I guess we are about to find out."

Anthony rubbed his eyes. "Well, thank you for that. Look at me making a joke."

"I don't love seeing you this way," Lark said. Anthony had almost laughed, but it was clear he was deeply upset. "Your sadness is palpable."

"I am in a bad way," Anthony admitted. "The shock is too fresh for me to understand what I need, but I could use a friend right now."

"I can be that for you. Truly."

Anthony nodded. "Thank you, Lark. Would you like some whisky?"

"I am trying to refrain."

"I've heard that you basically live in a bottle now."

Lark supposed word would have reached Anthony, even if they had not been at any of the same events all Season. Anthony had barely attended anything. And yet. "Near the truth," Lark said. "Hence refraining. Or trying to."

"It's unlike you to overindulge."

"I suspect you know why."

Anthony sighed. "I reckon I do."

"Let us not talk about that now. I could use some tea."

Anthony tugged on a nearby cord to summon a servant. A maid appeared in the door.

"Mary, could you please bring Lord Waring a tea service?"

She curtsied. "Of course, my lord. I will see to it."

"Thank you," Lark said.

"The staff is also mourning the mistress of the house, so I cannot guarantee that tea service will come with anything other than tea."

"That is fine. A cup of tea is all I'm asking for."

"Under normal circumstances, Cook would send up some little cakes or sandwiches or something."

"It's really fine. I understand."

"Let us just sit for a few minutes then, hm?"

"Yes. Let us sit." And Lark did not mind the quiet one bit, not now that he was in the same room as Anthony again. He knew things would never be the same, that they could not just resume their relationship, but Lark *could* help Anthony now when he needed it. That was what one did for loved ones, was it not?

Chapter Five

"ARE YOU SURE this is appropriate," said Louisa's mother. They stood in the family's sitting room as Louisa waited for Fletcher to pick her up to head to the opera.

"Mother. Fletcher and I will sit in the family box, well in view of hundreds of people eager to report any wrong move to the scandal sheets, and so Fletcher will act as he always does, which is as a gentleman."

"You couldn't go to the opera on a night when your future husband was available?"

"This is a one-night-only performance with this soprano from France, and Rotherfeld doesn't like the opera much anyway. Fletcher has long been my opera companion, and no one has ever thought ill of him for it before. I don't see why that should change."

"You are engaged to Rotherfeld now."

"As everyone ceaselessly reminds me. Yes, Mother, I am aware."

"I suppose if Rotherfeld does not object…"

"He does not." Likely because Louisa did not tell him.

"Then fine. But do not do anything to get yourselves in the scandal sheets. It would be terrible if your engagement to Rotherfeld ended."

Louisa was not certain that was the case, but she nodded. "I promise to be on my best behavior."

The Petty butler appeared in the doorway. "The Marquess of Greystone."

"Show him in," said Louisa.

Fletcher appeared a moment later. He was dressed in a dark-blue coat and breeches, one of his finer suits, with a crisp white cravat and a white waistcoat with little blue flowers embroidered on it. He looked quite handsome, in fact, although as was his wont, he'd combed his short hair away from his face instead of over his forehead, as was the mode. Fletcher would never be a paragon of fashion, but he wore a suit very well.

What a ridiculous thing to be thinking about a man she would not be marrying.

"Good evening, my lady," Fletcher said to Louisa's mother. "'Tis a pleasure to see you."

"Take care of Lady Louisa tonight. Do nothing to jeopardize her engagement."

"I would never," said Fletcher, looking alarmed.

"Indeed."

Louisa rolled her eyes. "Come, Fletcher. The carriage is waiting. We don't want to be late. Some of us go to the opera to *see* the *opera* and I want to be there for the first note."

In Fletcher's carriage, Fletcher said, "What was all that about?"

"My mother is concerned that, even though you and I have attended the opera countless times without incident, me being seen with you will end my engagement."

"Surely anyone who cares about such things knows about our sibling-like relationship."

"One would think." Louisa grunted.

Fletcher looked at his pocket watch. "We have plenty of time. The curtain won't rise for another forty minutes."

"I know, but my mother was being overbearing."

Fletcher raised an eyebrow. "Right."

Louisa let out a frustrated sigh. "I'm sorry, but I hate this. I should be able to go to the bloody opera with my friend without it creating speculation about the health of my engagement, especially since I actually like the opera." It was fashionable to go to the opera just to be seen, and many in the *ton* tolerated the art without truly loving it, but Louisa loved music, and she loved the drama of opera, and she always gave the performances her whole attention. Or as much of her attention as she could, depending on the company.

"I don't disagree, but you'll recall I had this same concern. I'm still an unmarried man escorting an engaged woman to a public event."

Louisa looked Fletcher over. He did look very nice tonight. Handsome. Attractive, even. Fletcher's eyes looked intense in the dim light of the carriage. He smelled alluring, too, come to think of it. Louisa wanted to lean closer to get a better whiff but couldn't possibly without looking strange.

She shook her head. "It is not fair to put women in these boxes in which we must always be at our best behavior when men… when *men* can just do whatever they want. There is nothing inappropriate about this. You and I are attending the opera. That is all. But if I should spend three seconds with you without a chaperone, I will be irrevocably compromised? But *you* could spend all night in a pile of women, and no one would bat an eyelash. It is all so dreadfully unfair."

Fletcher stared at her when she stopped ranting. "Feel better?"

"Yes, thank you."

"A pile of women. Is that how you think I spend my spare time?"

"I don't know what you get up to when I'm not around."

Fletcher chuckled. "I appreciate the depths of your imagination."

"But you see my point."

Fletcher picked up his hand. He reached over and moved something off Louisa's forehead. She held her breath as he did it.

Which was all wrong because the entire *point* of this conversation was that there was nothing inappropriate about their relationship, and so Louisa would not read anything more to this than was there. No matter how handsome Fletcher was or how good he smelled tonight.

"Sorry, you had a loose bit of hair. I've restored it to its proper place." He smiled. "I do see your point, though. I also think it grossly unfair that we cannot attend the opera as friends without your mother, who has known me since I was in short pants, thinking something could happen between us. She knows that is not the relationship we have and that I want you to marry Rotherfeld, if that's what you want."

The caveat struck Louisa as odd. *If that's what you want.* It was what she wanted. Wasn't it? What would Fletcher do if she suddenly decided it wasn't?

No sense in worrying about it now. "Well, thank you."

"And I agree that the way society treats men and women differently is unfair."

Louisa nodded, the wind going out of her sails. Of course she wouldn't have to convince Fletcher. He'd always treated her like an equal.

Something else occurred to her. She really *didn't* know what he got up to when he was not with her, and she felt like this might be information she needed. She didn't know much about what men did at night, for example, aside from what she'd heard from her friends in the form of oblique references to sex and liquor. But Fletcher would know what the gentlemen of the *ton* did when gently bred ladies were not about. What did her future husband do without her?

"Can I ask you a question?"

"Of course."

"Have you been with many women?"

Fletcher choke-coughed, clearly surprised by the question. "I don't see how—"

"I am curious about what is normal for men to experience

before they commit to marriage. How much knowledge and experience my husband may have gained prior to asking me to marry him. You see, the only men I've been… familiar with are sculpted of marble, so I am not certain what to expect, but I imagine Rotherfeld does, and I…"

Fletcher gave her a wary look. "This does not feel like an appropriate conversation to have."

"Just tell me, Fletcher. We've never kept secrets."

He frowned. "I can't speak for Rotherfeld. I don't know the man, really. Some men arrive at their marriage beds without having bedded a woman before. Some leave a string of conquests in their wake. For most it's something in between. You won't really know unless you ask him."

Louisa's face was suddenly on fire. "I couldn't do that."

"But you can ask *me?*"

She shrugged. She trusted Fletcher in a way she did not trust Rotherfeld yet. "I see your point. I will ask him when next I see him, but now I'm curious. What about you, specifically?"

Fletcher's eyes went wide. "I don't see the relevance of that."

"You are an average man, I would say. Well, perhaps *average* is the wrong word. I think you are a fine man. But you are typical of other lords of the *ton*, from what I can tell."

Fletcher sputtered. "We cannot…that is, it is inappropriate to discuss—"

"Come on, Fletcher. We're *friends*. Surely you discuss things like this with your male friends."

She knew she was pushing him, and he looked utterly terrified, but now she really wanted to know. Likely Fletcher's level of experience with women and sex would not shed any light on what Rotherfeld had gotten up to in his misspent youth, but Fletcher and Louisa never talked about these things, and now she needed to know.

"Yes," Fletcher said. "I do talk about these things with my *male* friends. *You* are a woman."

"Did we not just finish establishing that we that we are

friends, and, dare I say, equals, of a sort?"

"I do not go into details with my male friends, either."

"I have no experience with men and am not shy about telling you. I've reached this ripe old age still pure as the driven snow…"

Fletcher rolled his eyes. "All right, all right. No need for dramatics."

"You have been with women, yes?" Louisa decided the direct approach might yield more results.

"Yes," Fletcher said, with some reluctance.

"Anyone I know?"

He frowned. "I doubt it."

That meant *yes.* She leaned closer to him. "Who?"

"If I tell you, it can't leave this carriage."

"Who would I tell?"

Fletcher shook his head. "I can't believe I'm telling you this. But it's possible I had an affair with Lady Richelieu."

Louisa gasped. Lady Richelieu was a much older woman—nearly fifty now. "You didn't."

"It was after her husband passed, in my defense."

"How long did it last?"

"A few months. And this was two years ago. It wasn't…it was not romantic. It was… No. I can't talk about this with you."

"Fletcher." Louisa was growing increasingly frustrated by his reticence. Usually, he was candid with her. "Do you think I do not understand? Do you think I do not also have desires?"

"I'm certain you do and that I need not know about them. I don't want to talk about any of this, but you asked."

"So, you had a purely physical relationship, just pleasure and gratification, with the widow Richelieu, who is, what, twenty years older than you?"

"Something like that."

"And other women?"

"Yes, but you definitely do not know them."

"Prostitutes?"

Fletcher recoiled. "What? No! Just not women of the *ton.*"

"I don't know how these things work. I'd like to go into my marriage informed."

"Then talk to your mother or your fiancé. My personal history has no bearing on your marriage. But I do not pay women like that. Just for posterity."

Louisa huffed. She was surprised Fletcher was being so prudish. "I'm just trying to establish that what I've heard is true. That men tend to come to their marriages with experience."

"Yes. As I said, most do."

She leaned close to Fletcher, who flinched. "Why are you so uncomfortable?"

"Because this is not proper conversation."

"That has never stopped you before." Louisa found herself intrigued by whatever Fletcher was keeping with her, and even though she knew this was not proper, she enjoyed pushing him, and now her mind was at work imagining what he must do or be like in bed, and that was a wholly improper thing to think about *Fletcher* of all people, but now her mind was racing.

But before she could say anything further, Fletcher said, "Oh, look, we've arrived at the opera house." He broke land-speed records getting out of the carriage.

Once Fletcher's driver had helped Louisa alight from the carriage, Fletcher was already halfway toward the entrance to the theater. Louisa raced—as well as she could in her delicate shoes—to catch up.

He looked at her warily when she hooked her hand around his arm.

"You need not be embarrassed."

"I'm not embarrassed."

"Then why won't you talk about this with me? And don't tell me it's inappropriate."

Fletcher stopped walking and wheeled on her. He lowered his voice so as not to be overheard and said, "Because it's intimate. Because this is a topic you discuss with your spouse and not your friends. Feel free to discuss this with whoever will listen, but you and I are not having this conversation anymore."

That certainly surprised Louisa. She took a step back from him and they stared at each other.

Fletcher let out a breath. They were surrounded by wealthy opera attendees, so they couldn't have this out here. He offered his arm to Louisa again and said, "I'm sorry. I'm not cross with you." They began walking toward the theater. "You, my dear Louisa, are this remarkable combination of bold and naive, and I love that about you, but I cannot be your tutor, especially when that is the role your husband is supposed to fill. And I will not do anything to disrupt your wedding."

Louisa suspected she deserved that. "All right."

Fletcher patted her hand where it rested on his arm. "All right. *La...* what are we seeing?"

"*La Cenerentola.* It's the story of Cinderella. A comedy. The French soprano is supposed to be very good."

"Then let us focus on that, shall we?"

As the first act ended, a few things crystallized in Fletcher's mind.

First, Louisa looked lovely tonight. He'd thought that the moment he walked into her house. *Lovely* was perhaps too soft a word, in fact, because she'd looked...beautiful. Splendid. Alluring. She wore an emerald-green evening gown that hugged her bosom with a delicate gold necklace with some purple jewels— quartz? sapphire? Fletcher knew nothing about gems—that seemed to point right toward said bosom, and thus Fletcher had been helpless not to look at it, and he felt lecherous for doing so. Louisa was his friend. He should not be admiring her bosom.

But Louisa *was* a beautiful woman. Fletcher had eyes. Tonight, her brown curly hair was piled atop her head with tendrils dangling artfully around her face. She had big eyes and pink lips, and he loved looking at her face. Louisa was one of his favorite people in all of England, and her face was his favorite to gaze upon.

And now she sat primly next to him, her hands folded in her lap, clearly trying to avoid giving the gossip hounds anything to talk about.

Second, he hadn't been paying attention to the opera at all. He knew the rough outlines of the Cinderella story, so he hoped to be able to improvise when Louisa inevitably asked for his thoughts during the intermission. But he had no idea what had happened because he'd spent the entire time replaying their conversation from the carriage in his mind.

He was ashamed to say that he found talking about sex with her arousing. The problem, though, was that he shouldn't have had that conversation with her at all. He should have shut it down earlier. He understood that Louisa was curious about sex, and that he was hardly a virgin himself. He liked sex a lot, in fact, and most of his partners had been actresses or widows or women whose reputations did not rely on staying pure. Lady Richelieu was one of his fondest memories, and though their affair had been short, she'd known her way around his body as few of his lovers had. But there'd been no emotion there. Lady Richelieu— Diane was her given name—was among the sexiest women Fletcher had ever seen, and he liked her company and her lively conversation, but he'd known from the start that she'd discard him when she was through, which indeed she did, and there were no hurt feelings.

He generally did not become aroused around Louisa, but he had tonight, and he didn't know what to do with that information. It was just the topic, he told himself. So he'd ended the discussion.

But Louisa was, of course, a woman, even if she hadn't experienced any kind of sexual congress. She would soon, though. Much to Fletcher's dismay.

Picturing her with Rotherfeld made Fletcher want to put his

fist through a wall.

That was a new feeling. He didn't know what to do with that, either.

The lights in the opera house came on and Louisa clapped delightedly. "This opera is a great deal of fun. The soprano has a voice like an angel. I'm glad we were able to come tonight."

Fletcher had some regrets, but he said, "Yes, I agree." He did generally like attending the opera, although he liked Louisa's company more. And he wanted to get her off the topic of the actual opera, so he said, "Did you see Lady Winter's hat? Do you think she plucked the feathers from an *entire* peacock or…?"

Louisa laughed. "I think that might be an actual taxidermized peacock."

Fletcher picked up his opera glasses and made a show of looking toward Lady Winter. The hat was quite ridiculous, although it did not look as though any birds had been grievously harmed in its construction. "I wonder if we could train a bird to sit on a hat and stay still until an opportune moment, at which point it would come alive and terrify everyone."

"I have no doubt that if anyone could accomplish that, it's you."

"I know the opera is a serious and sober art, but I can't help but think we could liven it up. Live animals, perhaps."

"Oh, certainly. And then as soon as a horse gets spooked, he gallops off the stage and into the audience."

"That certainly would have made that production of *Lucio Silla* we saw last month. I think I slept through part of it."

"It was a rather lackluster production. Tonight is much better. What did you think of the changes the librettist made?"

Well, devil take him. Fletcher had no idea what to say to that. He opened his mouth to say something, anything, but he was blessedly saved by Lady Cheshire suddenly joining them in their box.

Lady Cheshire was another opera regular, one of Louisa's friends, and the two women spent the rest of the intermission discussing the opera. Fletcher excused himself, walked up and down the hall outside the boxes, greeted various acquaintances, and managed to steal a feather from Lady Winter's hat before he returned to the box to find Louisa and Lady Cheshire still discussing.

When the house lights dimmed to signal the second act was about to begin, Lady Cheshire excused herself to return to her seat. So Fletcher sat next to Louisa and said, "My lady, I have a gift." Then he brandished the peacock feather.

"Fletcher, you *didn't*."

"There was an excess of feathers in Lady Winter's hat. I doubt she'll miss this one."

Louisa took the feather and secured it in her hair. "How do I look?"

"Breathtaking." And she did look especially beautiful with that mischievous sparkle in her eye, but Fletcher had added a little mocking to his voice to not give himself away.

Louisa laughed. "I'm sure I look as ridiculous as Lady Winter's hat. I shall try to ignore that you're a thief."

The second act didn't go better than the first in terms of holding Fletcher's attention. He could not make himself focus on the performance. About halfway through Act II, Fletcher gave up and watched Lady Louisa instead. Her attention seemed rapt on the performance, but at one point she turned toward him and whisper-hissed, "What?"

"Nothing. The feather is drooping a bit."

Louisa plucked the feather from her hair and then slipped it through Fletcher's cravat. Fletcher found his breath catching as her knuckles briefly tapped his skin.

Later, as Fletcher escorted Louisa back to his carriage, he supposed he'd done his job to not compromise Louisa in any way, feather-related shenanigans aside. He hadn't so much as touched her while they'd been in the box, aside from that moment she'd touched him. And yet, he felt out of sorts.

"You've been quiet," Louisa said on the ride back to her home.

She absently played with the peacock feather, slipping it through her fingers, and Fletcher was helpless not to watch her long, delicate fingers move.

There was traffic from the stream of people leaving the opera, so they were moving slowly. Fletcher glanced out the window and thought snails might make better time. They'd be in the carriage for a while, unfortunately, which meant Louisa would make Fletcher talk.

"I'm sorry," he said. "Suddenly my mind is on other things. *La Cenerentola* was lovely, but I didn't absorb all of it, I will admit. I'm afraid I don't have much to say about it."

"What other things?"

"Nothing of import. I just found myself becoming easily distracted by stray thoughts tonight. I apologize for not being more attentive."

Louisa nodded. "It's all right. But surely you must agree the soprano was spectacular."

"She was *very* good." Fletcher had no idea if she was, but Louisa seemed satisfied with her answer.

"Do you have any engagements this weekend?" she asked.

"I suppose like most of the *ton* I will be attending the funeral for the Marchioness of Beresford."

"Oh, I nearly forgot. How dreadful."

"Did you know her?"

"No. Well, we may have met in passing, but I cannot recall ever having a conversation with her. How devastating for Beresford, though. He has been a friend to you, no?"

"In a way. More a friend of Lord Waring's. But I promised I'd attend."

Louisa shook her head. "What a dreadful story. She was so young. Beresford must be heartbroken."

"I have not spoken to him myself, but Waring has said he is devastated."

Louisa gazed out the window. "Marriage is…it feels fraught."

It definitely did. But Fletcher said, "I wouldn't know."

"I understand, but…you see so many different kinds of marriages. My parents weren't a love match, but they get on well."

"Same for my parents. Or they did until my father passed."

"Yes. And then you have the Swynfords and the Caernarfons, who all seem so happy."

"Yes. They are blessed in their unions. Swynford's was a love match. But Caernarfon barely knew Lady Grace when they married."

"But they've grown close. I suppose that is the kind of marriage I'm after."

"And do you believe you will find that with Rotherfeld."

"I suppose I can't know for certain, but I do hope so. At least, I should like to avoid the fate of my friend Eleanor. She and her husband barely tolerate each other. And poor Lady Beresford. Oh, my heart aches for that family. Her son growing up without a mother!"

"I know." Fletcher agreed the situation was tragic and hoped not to dwell on it. The funeral would be bad enough.

"Anyway. I don't know what kind of marriage I am to have, and I suppose that bothers me. But you cannot offer much insight."

"I have spoken to Rotherfeld several times since your engagement. He seems agreeable." That was a nice way to put it.

"Agreeable? Is that the best you can say of him?"

Truthfully, Fletcher would be perfectly happy to never occupy the same space as Rotherfeld ever again, but he said, "I had hoped we could be friends, but we do not appear to have much in common. But I shall keep trying for your sake."

"Oh. Yes, of course. I should like it if the two of you were friends."

Fletcher began to doubt that was possible, but if pressed, he wasn't certain he knew the exact reason why. He found Rotherfeld dull, yes, but there were several people of his acquaintance who were not that interesting. Surely he could figure out a way to connect with the man. For Louisa's sake, if nothing else.

He took a deep breath, anxious to be home, but not wanting to show his irritation to Louisa.

"I suppose I was rather forward on the way to the opera," Louisa said. "It's just...no one ever tells women anything. I've had a few conversations with my mother about what to expect once I am married, but, aside from you, men are generally a mystery to me."

"Men are just...humans."

"Yes, but the way they are raised is different from women. You got to go away to school. You can go wherever you want without a chaperone."

"Yes, yes," Fletcher cut her off. He knew all this. "But I think the key to your relating to your future husband will be to have a discussion with him. I am a poor stand-in. I can't know what's in his head or his heart. And you speak frankly with me all the time, and I am a man. Rotherfeld is not much different."

"All right." Louisa seemed disappointed in that answer. "I will take that under advisement."

They rode silently for a moment, and then Louisa said, "How did you manage to extract a feather from Lady Winter's hat?"

"Cunning and guile," said Fletcher with a wink. "Nice to know I've still got them."

Chapter Six

MATILDA WAS BURIED on a sunny Saturday afternoon, in the crypt at St. Paul's Cathedral, and the ceremony was somber and a bit ostentatious.

Anthony still wore a look like he'd been terrorized by her ghost since her death.

Anthony had invited a handful of people over for luncheon after the funeral, but only Lark lingered after everyone else had left. He didn't know what made him stay, aside from a sense that Anthony needed him.

Indeed, Anthony held up a bottle of wine. "A gift from Clairborne," he said, "straight from a vineyard he owns in Bordeaux. Shall we partake."

"I probably shouldn't."

"A single glass, Lark."

Lark sighed. "All right. I will. Unless you want me to leave."

"I do not. Drinking alone at home is too sad to do for one more night. If you are here, I am not alone."

He led Lark to his sitting room, a gaudily decorated but lushly appointed room that had Anthony's touch all over it. Anthony loved over-the-top decorations. Everything he did had always felt just this side of *too much*. In fact, most of the house looked as it had the last time Lark had seen it, at Anthony's wedding breakfast. It was like the marchioness had never lived here.

Lark was intensely curious about all of it, but he didn't dare ask. Had Anthony undone her feminine touches already? Had she made those touches to begin with? They'd spent the summer at his country home, Lark knew that much, so perhaps the late marchioness had not lived here long enough to redecorate. But the whole house was covered in evidence of Anthony's predilection for ornate decorations.

Anthony gestured at a pair of chairs near the fireplace and went about opening the wine. He poured a bit into two glasses and presented one to Lark as they sat down together.

One of the maids was arranging flowers in a vase, which prevented Lark from speaking his mind. He kept an eye on her as she fiddled with the arrangement.

"The vase is new," Anthony said, "a commission from a favorite sculptor. I ordered it months ago, but it only just arrived a few weeks ago. Did I tell you of my suspicion that the artist is not a handsome recluse, as I had imagined, but in fact your dear friend Owen's wife?"

"What?" The accusation struck Lark as absurd. Grace dabbled in pottery, yes, but she couldn't have made anything that pretty. The vase itself was much more to Lark's taste than most of what was in Beresford's house. It was a tall vase, maybe eighteen inches in height, and it was pale blue with little purple flowers painted on the belly of it. The top was made to look like the bloom of a flower and the handles looked like ivy vines.

"I don't know if Owen knows or not, but he has a few pieces in his home that the countess made, and they are remarkably similar stylistically to the artist I like. In fact, I thought Owen had also discovered said artist when I saw a vase in his dining room and remarked that it looked like a Makepeace, and he corrected me and said his wife had made it."

"Hmm."

"I guess I see some reason for subterfuge, because surely if the public knew those vases were made by a woman, there'd be much less clamor for them, but I don't see why Owen couldn't have just told *me*. Unless I'm wrong, of course."

The maid finished fiddling with the flowers, briefly bowed to Anthony, and then left the room.

Lark sipped his wine and thought about what he should speak with Anthony about. Not vases, surely; Lark cared not about the vessels Anthony stored the copious flowers around his house in.

But before Lark could come up with a topic, a footman appeared and said, "Mrs. Church would like a word, my lord."

"Oh. Yes. Send her here."

"Mrs. Church?" Lark asked after the footman left.

"The nurse."

A woman who was perhaps in her mid-thirties appeared at the door a moment later. "I hope the funeral was not too dreary, my lord."

"Difficult for it not to be. Mrs. Church, this is my old friend the Earl of Waring."

"Yes, my lord."

"Did you need something?"

"Just to say that Master Henry has been a bit fussy this evening and may be coming down with something. No fever, though, and he is sleeping peacefully. I wonder if he just misses his mama."

"We all do," Anthony said.

"Yes, my lord. If he does not improve on the morrow, consider summoning a doctor."

"I will. I appreciate it, Mrs. Church. Please alert me if there is something I should worry about."

"Yes, I will. Good night, my lord."

After she left, Anthony turned to Lark. "Should I worry about Henry?"

Lark knew even less about children than Anthony did, but he said, "She said no fever."

"Bless Mrs. Church. I don't know what I would do without her."

"I'm glad you have help."

Anthony nodded.

"I admit, this situation is not what I imagined."

"In what way?"

"Well, I only found out you were a father about eight days ago. This is a terrible situation. I don't know. You truly cared about Matilda."

"I did."

"I feel like a heel for feeling jealous of that." And he did. Clearly, Anthony had managed to have sex with his wife; the baby upstairs was proof of that. That she'd had Anthony's attention—and his body—for the last year made Lark intensely jealous, even though he knew that was ridiculous, especially since he'd pretty much pushed Anthony at his wife. Not to mention she was no longer here.

"No, it…" Anthony looked right at Lark and met his gaze. "It wasn't like that. I was fond of her, yes. But not in the way you're implying."

"Then explain it to me. Since we were not speaking much when you married, tell me about how it all happened."

Anthony sighed. "Can I be frank?"

"I wish you would."

"I had a thought to find some young miss in trouble. To find a bride who was already with child because of some foolish affair, and thus spare me from the duty. I met a woman in just such a state shortly after you left me, but I knew the math was too suspicious. That woman gave birth to a perfectly healthy baby five months ago, you see. It would have been suspect. I know, because she was a dear friend of Matilda's. She moved in with her aunt in Shropshire."

"All right. I suppose I am impressed you managed to follow through with your wife, then."

"She knew."

"What?"

"Matilda. She knew everything. I could not in good conscience go into a marriage under false pretenses. Shortly after we became engaged, I took her on a carriage ride in the park, and we managed to get far enough away from her chaperone that I just told her everything. That I am a man who prefers the company of other men, that I'd recently ended an affair with a man, and that I was not entirely confident I could be a full husband to her. She agreed to marry me anyway."

"Why?" Lark asked. "That is, I mean no offense. You are obviously a handsome, wealthy, and accomplished man and a desirable husband, but I am curious."

Anthony nodded. In the past, this would have earned Lark a snide comment, but Anthony just carried on speaking. "It seems that since her father passed, she has been under the care of her uncle. Said uncle is…not a good man."

"Oh."

"That is to say, he hit her. Never in a place where her bruises would be obvious to the public. And just before our wedding, she told me he'd gotten a look in his eye that made her feel acute danger, that he might try to take advantage of her. She felt trapped in that house where she felt she was in danger daily, so when I offered for her, she said yes immediately because she saw me as her escape. I think…that is, I was happy to help her, to provide a safe home for her. So we began our marriage with an understanding."

"That is kind of you."

Anthony shrugged. "I do have some good qualities, I suppose."

"And now you have a son."

"Yes. She desperately wanted children, so I agreed to try. I played some mental games and managed to do the deed. And once we were certain she was expecting, it was almost a relief to be done with it, although I do not mean to say I was repulsed by her. She just did not…arouse me the way a man would have." He sighed. "She was good company, you know? Held her own in a conversation. Had a fine sense of humor and knew her way around a good jest. Tolerated my eccentricities. Teased me relentlessly, but in a loving way. Read the newspaper in the morning with me the way you used to. I did like her. I keep expecting her to appear in the doorway to tell me this last week has been a joke."

"Your mourning is genuine. No need to convince me of that. I can tell."

"I thought, well, if I cannot have Lark, I will make this situation the best it can be. And then Henry was born, and we were briefly so happy, but within a day, her skin turned yellow. The doctor said it was an infection, which I suppose is quite common. And now I am alone."

"You are *not* alone."

"No?"

Lark reached across the space between the chairs and took Anthony's hand. "I do not know what we are to each other now, but I've missed you desperately and I do not wish to be apart anymore. If you need a friend, I am here. You are not alone."

"Thank you." Anthony sighed. "What changed?"

"What do you mean?"

"What has changed between us that you are willing to sit with me now?"

"You need me."

Anthony shook his head but then leaned back in the chair. He squeezed Lark's hand. "I suppose I do. But I am... I barely recognize myself right now. The sadness and fear I feel are overwhelming. My mother tells this will get better with time, but I cannot...that is, I really do need a friend right now. I am not sure I have anything else in me."

"I understand that. I am not asking you for anything. I just want to help. Honest."

Anthony nodded. "I blame myself," he said, sounding a bit watery. He took his hand back. "I was the one who...but she told me, toward the end, that she wanted Henry more than anything and that it was not my fault. I am trying to take that to heart. I am trying not to feel like the bloody worst man on Earth for drinking this wine. Clairborne lost his sister, after all. He does not seem to blame me, either, but it's hard not to think..."

"Please do not do this to yourself. Sometimes the universe... Random things happen."

"Do you believe in God, Lark?"

"I don't know."

"I never gave it much thought, you know? I suppose I always assumed there was some higher plane of existence we all ascend to when we die, that there is a benevolent being overseeing our time on Earth, but I do not know how he could let something like this happen. She was a good person, Lark. She did not deserve to have her life cut short. She may not have been the love of my life, but she was my friend, and I miss her. I wake up in the morning and I don't know what to do, and this sadness, it is crushing. How will I ever...how can I ever be myself again?"

Lark found his own eyes stung. He stood and offered his hand to Anthony, who took it but stood up on his own. Then Lark wrapped Anthony in a hug. Anthony buried his face in Lark's neck and took a heavy sigh. His body seemed to relax into Lark. Lark rubbed his back and then just held him.

"Anthony," Lark said. "I want you to know, I love you more than I love my own life and I wish I could take away all of your pain. I can't, but I can hold you and support you and help you in any way I have the capacity to help you. You may never fully recover from the events of the last year, from your grief from this loss, and you may never fully forgive yourself, although you should. But I think you will rediscover who you are. It could also be that you've changed, and that's all right, too."

"Lark."

Lark could feel the moisture from Anthony's tears against his neck. Anthony clung to the fabric of Lark's coat, grasping it as though he were holding on for dear life.

Anthony pulled away slightly. He wiped at his tears with one hand. Lark swatted that hand away and wiped away Anthony's tears with his thumbs.

"I have missed you every day since you kicked me out of your house that night," Anthony said. "I think of you daily, and it sits like a weight in my chest. If you are back in my life, I am glad for it, but I am a wreck right now."

"It's all right. Take the time you need to mourn."

"I still love you, too, for what it's worth. I am not capable of acting on that right now, but I will take anything you have to give."

"I will give it freely. No need for reciprocation."

Anthony closed his eyes. "Thank you for coming back to me."

Lark pulled Anthony back into his arms. "I've been miserable without you. I don't think I was wrong to send you away, but every day without you has been brutal."

"Let us not dwell on that now."

"All right."

"Just...hold me a while longer."

"I can do that."

Chapter Seven

AFTER FLETCHER EXPLAINED to Owen in some detail what had happened at the opera—omitting a few salient details about the question Louisa had asked him in the carriage and the information he had volunteered—Fletcher concluded, "I felt out of sorts afterward, but I am not sure why."

They sat at the club. Lark was absent tonight, and Hugh was currently tied up in a conversation with Devonshire, so it was just Fletcher and Owen sitting by the fire.

"Let me summarize," said Owen. "Louisa has been your friend since before you understood the key differences between boys and girls."

"Yes."

"You are fond of her but in a friendly way."

"Yes."

"She is now engaged, and you feel out of sorts about that."

"Perhaps, but only because—"

Owen held up his hand. "You find her fiancé boring."

"Right."

"I don't think it is so much that you are worried Rotherfeld will take away your sisterly friend. I think you have feelings for Louisa, and you are worried about him marrying her when it should be you."

Fletcher scoffed. "Don't be ridiculous."

"It *should* be you."

"What are you talking about?" But somewhere deep in his chest, Fletcher knew. In the same way he couldn't stop looking at Louisa on their night at the opera, he knew his feelings for Louisa were not, in fact, entirely friendly. But what was he to even do about it?

Owen rolled his eyes. "You and Louisa speak the same language. You have similar interests and enjoy each other's company. You've been good friends for most of your lives. You confide in each other and care about each other. The only missing component was a physical spark, but I reckon that, since before Louisa became betrothed to Rotherfeld, you've felt that spark."

"I will admit to…admiring her figure."

"Fletcher, you are being foolish. You love this woman. I know you do. You keep making all this noise about her being like a sister to you, but she's not. It's all there. You know her better than most men know their wives, and you love what you see. You find her attractive. Maybe her betrothal to Rotherfeld is the kick in the head you needed to realize that. You feel out of sorts because you're in love with her and don't know what to do now because you're an idiot and she's engaged to someone else."

"I'm not…"

But he stopped talking abruptly. Of course, Owen was completely correct. Fletcher loved Louisa. It *should* have been him marrying her, not Rotherfeld.

Louisa was *his*. She was his friend, yes, and he understood their friendship was a bit unorthodox for the *ton*, but it worked for them. And no, he did not like that Rotherfeld was taking her away from him. That was what had bothered him since her engagement was announced.

Because Louisa was beautiful. She had a laugh like a bell that had always charmed Fletcher. She was smart and funny, and she loved art, and she understood Fletcher well enough to call him on things when he was acting like an idiot, just like Owen was now because Fletcher had, indeed, been acting like an idiot for months.

"Devil take me," Fletcher said.

"There it is," said Owen.

"I love her."

"Yes."

"But she's marrying Rotherfeld."

Owen nodded. "That is a bit of a predicament, but it's an engagement. Engagements can be broken. She hasn't married him yet."

"What should I do?"

"You could tell her."

Fletcher shook his head. "No, I can't. Her mother made me promise not to do anything to jeopardize her engagement to Rotherfeld, and I intend to keep my word. Plus, she's made her choice."

"You never gave her the option to choose you."

"Why didn't I notice I felt this way *before* she got engaged?"

"I don't know. I've been trying to tell you for at least a year."

Fletcher looked at Owen, who had a smug grin on his face. Owen really had been teasing Fletcher about his relationship with Louisa for a long time, but Fletcher had refused to see it. Why had he refused to see it?

They were interrupted by Lark, who came in and plopped into a nearby chair. He looked upset.

"Are you drunk?" Fletcher asked.

"No, alas."

"Why do you look like someone kicked you in the shin?" asked Owen.

"I've been spending time with Beresford again."

"Is that a good idea?" asked Owen.

"Probably not, but I believe I'm done caring. I've spent nearly a year without him. All it's gotten me is misery. He's in no better shape. We've not…that is, he is still mourning and thus he is not in a position to offer me anything right now, so I am trying to just be his friend, and I'm finding that spending time with him is infinitely better than…not."

Oh, god. Spending time with Louisa was also far better than not spending time with her. The reason Fletcher was so out of sorts about Louisa marrying was that the time not spent together was bound to increase, and Fletcher found the notion of that unbearable. Because he wanted Louisa to spend all of her time with him, and not with Rotherfeld.

This was love. And it was terrible.

"I'll come to your hanging," Owen said to Lark.

A soft smile played across Lark's lips. "I don't believe it has come to that yet. This situation is complicated. He has a child now, and even if he didn't love his wife, her death has upset him greatly. He's…he's like a shell of himself. I haven't asked him to be with me again, I am merely acting as a supportive friend, and I am content with that for now."

"You have been rather unhappy," Fletcher said, feeling foolish as soon as he said it, stating the obvious. *Of course* Lark had been unhappy; the person he loved had married somebody else. What a stupid, frustrating predicament they'd both found themselves in.

Lark merely nodded. "I've been a right miserable bastard. I contend I was right to end the affair, but being right does not make things easier. I think I did not realize the depth of my own feelings. If I do end up with a second chance, I do not intend to squander it. Hell, maybe Beresford and I can buy a farm in Scotland and hide there for the rest of our lives. That would certainly be an improvement over living without him in London."

"I do not care for this love business," said Fletcher.

"I know, it's terrible." Lark gave Fletcher an appraising look. "Who are you in love with?"

"Lady Louisa."

Lark laughed. "Ah, finally."

"You knew as well?"

"Everyone knew," said Owen.

"*I* didn't know."

"Are you going to tell her?" asked Lark.

"I've only had a few minutes to really think on this, but I think not, because she's marrying Rotherfeld."

"Does she love Rotherfeld?" asked Lark.

"I don't know, but she is fond of him."

"When is the wedding?"

"A little over three weeks from now."

Lark nodded slowly. "Do you want her?"

Fletcher truly did. He hadn't let himself feel that way, he realized now, but yes, he wanted Louisa. The way she'd looked night at the opera, those loose tendrils of hair and the way her gown dipped to display her décolletage, the creaminess of her skin and the plumpness of her lips… He'd been thinking about all of it every night since. He wanted to touch her, to run his hands through her hair, to peel off those beautiful gowns she wore.

"I want her," Fletcher said.

"Then maybe what you need to do is present an alternative to Rotherfeld," said Lark. "If you don't want to tell her how you feel directly, then show that you're husband material. That you respect her and care about her and desire her and all of that. Show her that Rotherfeld is not the only man in her life who is willing to marry her. But you'd better act fast if she's getting married in three weeks."

Fletcher looked at Owen. "Should I take advice from this fella?"

"It's not a bad idea, but I still think you should tell her frankly. Don't wait for her to intuit your intent. You're enough of an idiot that you didn't realize you're in love with her until now, so it's plausible that she loves you but isn't fully conscious of it, either."

"You think?"

"It's possible." Owen drummed his fingers against his chin. "I like Louisa. I like the two of you together. I think you can make each other happy. It's both of your stubborn adherence to this idea that you're basically siblings that has prevented you from marrying earlier. Rotherfeld may prove to be an obstacle here. He has more money and power and clout than you do. But if you don't at least try to show Louisa how you feel, I think you will regret it forever. You have to at least try."

Owen had some good points. "Perhaps I will talk to her."

Owen laughed. "That's the spirit."

THE ODD THING about being engaged was that suddenly Louisa's mother's hawklike gaze had vanished.

When Daniel came to call, Mother was suddenly nowhere to be found. She didn't send in a maid to keep an eye on Louisa, either. So Louisa and Daniel now sat in the Petty sitting room, completely alone, albeit with an open door.

Daniel kept a safe, appropriate distance from her. She wondered if this was an act of willpower or just his personality. That was, Louisa thought him handsome and had been thinking about running her hands over his shirt for the entirety of this conversation, but Daniel never gave any indication if he desired her one way or the other. He must have, or he wouldn't have offered for her, but would it hurt him to push the boundaries of propriety a little?

"I attended the opera with Greystone the other night," she said.

Rotherfeld raised an eyebrow. "Did you?"

"*La Cenerentola*. A take on Cinderella."

"The folk story? The one about the woman who acts as a servant and then marries a prince?"

"Essentially, yes, but the opera makes some changes to the story. She has a wicked stepfather instead of a stepmother, for example. And there are some genuinely funny moments."

"Is it in German?"

"Italian."

"Then how can you recognize the humor?"

"I speak some Italian. I understand enough. But the actors also played their parts quite broadly, and—"

"I always thought the opera was more a place to see and be seen. Half the *ton* couldn't tell you the plots of the operas performed each night."

"That may be true, but I've always liked opera as an art. Fletcher—er, the Marquess of Greystone—used to accompany me just to indulge me, but then he grew to appreciate it, too, which is why we go so often together. I like to discuss the particulars of the production with him at intermission."

"Yes. I've been trying to get to know Greystone, since he is a friend of yours. He mentioned the opera last time we spoke."

"Oh?"

"We…it was awkward. We do not have much in common."

"Well, tell me what interests you. Maybe I can find some bit of common ground between all of us that we can discuss should he, say, come to dinner."

"Birds," Daniel said. "As you know, I am an avid student of ornithology. For example, did you know that a flock of tawny owls has been spotted in Hyde Park. Well, not a flock. Officially, a group of owls is called a Parliament, which I think is quite astute."

Oh, no. Bird talk was sure to bore Fletcher to tears. Louisa said, "Birds, yes, of course I know of your passion for birds. I don't think Fletcher knows much about birds, though."

"I like athletic pursuit. I did a bit of rowing at Cambridge, and I enjoy riding."

Fletcher was strong and a decent horseback rider, but not so much athletically inclined, from what Louisa could tell. He'd gone to Oxford but had not pursued athletics there. If Louisa remembered correctly, he'd studied literature. "What else?" she asked.

"I've been reading about farming techniques of late. I'd like to implement some changes to my estate, try planting some different crops and moving the sheep to a better part of the property for grazing."

Louisa was certain someone found farming techniques exciting, but she and Fletcher were not among them.

The concern Louisa had now, though, was not so much that Fletcher had little in common with Daniel, but that *she* didn't. Had she been so blinded by his charm and good looks that she hadn't looked far enough under the surface?

Well, yes.

She frowned. "Yours and Greystone's interests may be incompatible. I know that he enjoys opera and art galleries and garden parties and reading novels, and you do not really care for any of those things. He knows a bit about horses, but perhaps more out of necessity than interest, although he's mentioned he likes to watch races."

"I lost a good bit of money on a race last year," said Daniel with a chuckle.

It wasn't encouraging that the only common ground she'd found so far between them was gambling.

Perhaps none of this mattered. Perhaps she and Daniel could get along just fine talking about their families or society gossip, and Louisa would focus on raising their children while Daniel focused on whatever married men did.

Then she thought of something Fletcher had said about how intimate conversations were meant for one's spouse. Louisa was fairly certain that if she asked Daniel about sex, he'd demur. But she could ask an easier question. "Tell me, Your Grace, once we are married, how do you intend to spend your days?"

"I imagine not much will change from my current routine. Oh, you and I will spend more time together, of course. But I am considering a few investments, so I have been spending time with my man of business and at the bank to see that my money goes toward pursuits that will have a good return."

"Such as?"

"A lot of my work has gone to rescuing businesses that are struggling and then seeing if I can help them turn a profit. For example, I bought a textile mill in Shropshire last year that was mostly lagging behind because it was using outdated equipment. So we replaced all the machinery, and it worked well enough that fewer workers were needed, and now the mill is turning a profit."

"I read about the business with the Luddites last year."

"Yes. That was a difficulty. Luckily, the rebellion did not come to my mill and the equipment remained intact."

Louisa had attended a dinner party at the Caernarfons' a few months before at which the earl had discussed the Luddite Rebellion at length. His sympathies were more with the workers, who were losing their jobs as machinery improved and could run on things like steam instead of human power. Angry workers had destroyed some of those machines, and the government had sent troops to put the rebellion down. Caernarfon thought that the workers should be trained to do new jobs, instead of being left without employment now that they were no longer needed. Louisa thought that a more humane approach to the problem.

"That is interesting," Louisa said now. "Will you keep the mill?"

"Undecided. It is turning a healthy profit now, but I've considered selling it and investing the money in something else. That is the current dilemma facing my colleagues. But are you sure you want to discuss all this? Women care not for talk of finance, do they?"

Louisa sighed and tried not to feel offended. "I will admit, I care not for the particulars of your business ventures. I was just curious if you had invested in a business that might make for an interesting conversation topic."

"Textiles are interesting, are they not? We've been importing a great deal of silk from the East, but it would be nice if we could also manufacture fine fabric here that could be used to make the gowns you like so much. Silk is difficult to manufacture domestically, but muslin, linen, broadcloth can all be made here."

Was it possible that Louisa's future husband was boring? Was she making a terrible mistake?

"You look troubled, my dear," he said after a few minutes of silence.

"It's just… I've been thinking a lot. About our wedding."

"Oh, of course. The arrangements are coming along, I trust?"

"Yes, yes. There is little left to plan. But I suppose I meant not the wedding itself, but what comes after."

"I figured we'd stay in London for the rest of the season and then perhaps adjourn to my country estate for the summer."

Bother. Rotherfeld was never going to get there on his own. Louisa tried one more time. "Right, a sensible plan. But I meant more…you know. What will happen between us? Physically."

Daniel shot her an alarmed look, close to the same panic she'd seen on Fletcher's face when she'd brought up the topic the previous week. Were all men terrified of sex? "That seems a better discussion for your mother."

"Not the…" She sighed. "I am not expressing myself well. I apologize. I understand the basic mechanics of relations between men and women, even if I have no firsthand experience. I just thought, since we are to be married, it might be nice to have a conversation about expectations."

"Expectations?"

"I know little of your past, for example, but I know how men of the *ton* are."

Daniel frowned at that. "Oh. Well, certainly I…that is…" He let out a breath. "This is embarrassing, but I'm afraid I have little experience with women."

"Oh." Louisa did not know if she should find that comforting or alarming.

"I was waiting for marriage, I suppose."

That was a surprise. "Noble of you."

"Thank you. Anyway, as you said, I understand the mechanics of the act, but I suspect you and I will be learning a great deal together."

Louisa supposed she should have found that comforting. That Daniel had no other lovers lurking in his past who could rear their jealous heads, that he'd be bringing no disease to their marriage bed. But then she thought of Fletcher and his widows and actresses, or whichever women had enjoyed the pleasure of his (naked) company in the past, and the idea of spending her wedding night with someone with no experience at all felt a bit terrifying. They'd just be flailing. That Fletcher knew his way around a woman's body was…thrilling, in a way. Arousing.

"We shall learn together," Louisa said, but suddenly she had doubts.

"Glad you agree." He smiled. "It is my intent to make this a good marriage, Louisa. I'd like for us to be happy together, to have as many children as nature will give us, and to live out our days in comfort and style. You want the same, do you not?"

"Well, perhaps only one or two children, but otherwise, yes."

Daniel laughed. "Then do not worry about any of it. We shall…take things as they come. Learn as we grow together. That is what I want, and I hope it is what you want, too."

Louisa smiled at him and nodded but suddenly wanted none of this.

Oh, why had she asked Fletcher all those questions? Why had she allowed him to put ideas in her head? Why was she now picturing Fletcher's big hands on her body and not Daniel's? Fletcher, who was passionate and thoughtful and easy to talk to. Whom she never had to search for conversation topics with. Whose big body was strong, even if he didn't have the same wiry strength as Daniel. Why was she suddenly thinking about licking Fletcher's neck to see if the stubble there was rough like sand?

She covered her eyes with her hands.

"I apologize if all this is embarrassing for you," Daniel said softly.

"It's not that," she said. "I've always been someone who likes to know what she is getting into, so I hoped to have a clearer idea for what to expect from marriage to you. But I suppose taking it as it comes will be a kind of adventure."

"I apologize, but I do not know what to expect myself."

Louisa had a thought to drum up some anticipation. Based on things her friends had told her, it was normal for couples to...experiment with each other before the big day. If they touched or kissed and Mother walked in, what could she even do? Force them to get married? The wedding was three weeks away.

"You and I have not so much as kissed," Louisa said, standing. She wanted to banish thoughts of Fletcher from her mind. He had no business there, not while she was engaged to Daniel. "Perhaps a kiss would have been improper before our engagement, but our wedding is just a few weeks hence. Surely you can kiss me."

Daniel stood, too. "I admire your passion, Louisa."

"Then kiss me."

Daniel took a step forward, closing the space between them. He put a hand on the side of her face. She leaned into his touch. Then he leaned forward and pressed his lips to her.

She'd read about kisses that were full of sparks or fire. This had...none of that. Daniel was cold. His lips were...wet. Slimy almost. It brought to mind kissing a fish. Louisa had never kissed anyone before, but surely *that* was not what it was supposed to be like.

When he pulled back again, he smiled at her. "There. Now we've accomplished that."

She smiled back, but inside, she was struggling not to panic.

Chapter Eight

THE DUCHESS OF Buckingham was a consummate host, even though her husband was fairly useless. Fletcher had gone to Eton with Buckingham and found him entitled and arrogant, the sort of man who came from a long line of dukes who lived off their family's fortune and good name without needing any particular skills or ambitions. But he had succeeded in marriage, because his wife was widely beloved by the *ton* and she threw a good party.

Fletcher circulated on the periphery of her garden, where several of his social peers partook of the fine spread of food placed on tables about the duchess's garden or sat on strategically placed chairs and indulged in conversation.

Lord Harding's daughter, whose name Fletcher could not remember, stood with a friend sipping lemonade toward the middle of the garden. Fletcher knew she was about twenty years old, pretty with dainty features, fond of the color pink, and also that she had a reputation for being interested in science and mathematics. Her father tinkered with telescopes, and Fletcher had heard she also knew quite a bit about astronomy, so he had a thought to engage her in conversation. Perhaps it would cover the scent of his desperation to get to Louisa.

But before he could make his way across the garden, Louisa paused before him, because of course she did.

"You look like a cat who has spotted a mouse," Louisa said.

"I intended to go speak with Harding's daughter."

"Eliza?"

"*Eliza!* Yes, that is her name."

"You wanted to go talk to a woman whose name you do not know?"

"I wanted to talk to a pretty lady who I've heard has a few intellectual pursuits."

Fletcher could sense that he was about to be mocked, and indeed, Louisa said, "Intellectual pursuits."

Truth be told, Fletcher was not completely certain what he was doing. Did he intend to pursue Eliza Harding? No. Start a conversation? Yes. Marry? Definitely not. The way Louisa was staring at him now made him think he could possibly make Louisa jealous, though. Or test her a bit to see if she had feelings for him the way he had feelings for her.

So he said, "Hypothetically, if one were desirous of pursuing a courtship with an intellectual equal, she is a fine specimen, no? Pretty. Knows about stars and things."

"Stars and things."

"I've never studied astronomy, but I did read a book last year about constellations and Greek mythology. Fascinating stuff. So I had a thought to strike up a conversation with Lady Eliza."

"Whose name you did not know until a few seconds ago."

"I'm terrible with names and faces. You know that." He smirked at her. "What's it to you, anyway? Now that you are headed for wedded bliss, should I not pursue happiness for myself?"

"Of course you should, I suppose, I just…" She looked toward Eliza. "No, never mind."

"Never mind?"

Louisa swatted a fly away from her face. "I just came over here to make small talk."

"Is your fiancé here?"

"Yes, but I've lost him. He was speaking with Devonshire

about the mechanics of erecting a hedge maze at his country estate, and there was a detailed explanation of the exact species of hedge or some such and I lost interest."

"So in truth, he lost you, since you wandered off."

She sighed. "I am not opposed to hedge mazes, but I do not care to know how they are made."

"I've never given it a second's thought."

She smiled. "That is what I like about you, Fletcher. So few thoughts in your head."

"You jest, but I did not know a certain species of hedge was needed to make a hedge maze, although I suppose that makes sense. Is it a certain shrub? No, you know what? I don't care. The point of a hedge maze is to, you know, solve the maze, or to perhaps to steal time alone with the object of your affection—or so I've heard—and not to be concerned with the species of plant used to compose the maze."

"Or so you've heard?"

"We could ask the Duchess of Buckingham if she has a hedge maze we can borrow so I can show you what I mean."

But of course, there was no property large enough to hold a hedge maze in London, and this was just a clumsy attempt at flirting on Fletcher's part, and Louisa wasn't even paying attention now. Rotherfeld suddenly appeared fifty feet away. And Fletcher wished there was a hedge maze he could get lost in. Preferably one full of bees.

Louisa frowned. "I'd like to discuss the mechanics of shrubbery with you further, but I suppose I must now get pulled into a conversation about, I don't know. The species of silkworm the Chinese use to make the silk we import or more efficient ways to harvest grain."

"Sounds scintillating."

Louisa grunted. "Indeed. These are all things I have had to pretend to be interested in today, incidentally."

Fletcher frowned at that. Was it possible Louisa found Rotherfeld as dull as Fletcher did?

Rotherfeld approached them, held out an arm for Louisa—which she took—and gave Fletcher a once over. "Ah, Greystone. Nice to see you again."

"Likewise."

"Greystone was just telling me that he is going to start courting Eliza Harding," said Louisa.

"That is not what I said," said Fletcher. "I mean only to start a conversation. Let us not get ahead of ourselves."

"The lady astronomer!" said Rotherfeld. "I've heard she studies the stars with her father."

"Precisely what I intended to start a conversation about."

"I suppose she is pretty," said Louisa. "In a *conventional* way."

"What does that mean?" asked Fletcher.

"Her looks are pretty but expected."

"The devil you say," said Fletcher. Was Louisa jealous? He laughed, suddenly delighted. "I find her striking, and if I do court her, I'm the one who has to look at her, so if you'll excuse me."

Fletcher crossed the garden, still not entirely sure what he was doing. He felt goaded by Louisa and also a bit pressured to prove to Rotherfeld that he had no designs on Louisa.

Even though he did. After all, he was going to talk to Lady Eliza in order to make Louisa jealous.

What a mess.

"Lady Eliza, how are you?" he found himself saying.

"It is a lovely afternoon, my lord. And it is a delight to see you again."

"We did not have a chance to speak much when last we met." Fletcher had no idea when that was. The Rutherford Ball? Three years ago? Who could say? "I have heard you study astronomy, though, and I think that is fascinating."

"Oh! Yes, I do. It *is* fascinating."

They spent a few minutes discussing the book Fletcher had read, but as they talked, Fletcher kept an eye on Louisa, who was letting Rotherfeld escort her to various clumps of gentlemen with whom she pretended to engage conversation that was clearly boring her to tears.

Eliza's father appeared and shook Fletcher's hand, but then someone snagged Lord Harding's and Eliza's attention, leaving Fletcher alone in the garden.

He wandered over to one of the food tables and partook in some small sandwiches. He was eyeing some little cakes when Louisa appeared again.

"Did you know," she said, "that a group of owls is called a Parliament."

"I did not."

"There's a joke there, but I don't have it completely formed yet. Owls are known for wisdom, but that is hardly something you can ascribe to Parliament."

"Definitely not."

Fletcher picked up a plate with a little cake on it that was decorated with a pink frosted flower. He picked up a fork and took a bite. He was disappointed to find the cake was dry.

"A group of crows is called a murder," said Louisa.

"To what can I attribute this vocabulary lesson?"

"My fiancé, the amateur ornithologist. He may not be passionate about much, but he can talk for hours about birds, which he is doing right now with Claypoole."

Fletcher followed Louisa's gaze to where Rotherfeld seemed to be enthusiastically gesticulating in front of Lord Claypoole, who looked on with amusement.

"I can't tell a starling from a magpie," said Fletcher.

"I know."

"You can't either."

"The little ones are starlings."

"Thanks." Fletcher rolled his eyes and finished his cake. Just as he was looking for a place to put the plate, a servant appeared and relieved him of it.

"How was the cake?" Louisa asked.

"It looked prettier than it tasted."

She nodded. "The Duchess of Buckingham seems to think

food is ornamental more than anything else. Little here tastes good."

"I liked those little sandwiches."

"How was your discussion with Eliza Harding?"

"Enlightening." Fletcher had a thought to get a rise out of Louisa now. "We discussed Hercules in both his constellation and mythical form at length."

Louisa patted his arm. "Have you proposed yet?"

"No, but I can be quite charming. I believe if I bring up telescopes and the planet Mars, she'll be putty in my hands."

"You do have your charms, Fletcher."

Fletcher smiled and decided to take the compliment, even though he thought Louisa was mocking him again.

"This party is a bit underwhelming, though," Fletcher said. "What can we do to liven it up?"

Louisa shook her head. "I don't care for the look in your eye."

"These cakes are not really edible. We could put them to better use. Perhaps leave one on a chair for an unsuspecting lady or gent to sit on."

"That is a child's prank," said Louisa, although she was smiling.

"You're right, I can do better." Fletcher looked around, assessing. His desire to put one over on Rotherfeld was great, but he struggled to come up with something that would work. "We could hide a cake in a shrub and tell your fiancé that it's a rare bird."

"That does seem rather harmless. These cakes are an unnatural shade of pink, though. I don't see you mistaking one for a bird."

"Or I could just spill some lemonade and see if someone slips in the puddle."

Louisa laughed and shook her head. "The Buckingham servants are too alert for that. I do appreciate your attempts at levity, but I do not think this party can be saved."

"I shall spend the next several minutes thinking of better uses for these cakes. Perhaps as some sort of building material. Maybe I can build your fiancé a very pink birdhouse."

"Well, while you do that, I am going to subject myself to some very dull conversations."

LOUISA SAT IN a profoundly uncomfortable chair and listened as Daniel regaled several other gentlemen with tales of his exploits birdwatching in the country.

Louisa liked birds, but not to this level. She liked waking up to birdsong or spotting a little group of sparrows hopping around in the park, but as Daniel explained his hunt for some rare bird that was not commonly spotted in England anymore, Louisa found her attention waning.

"One of my colleagues at Oxford has acquired a rare dodo bird skeleton," said one of the gents. "This animal has been extinct for at least one hundred years and was only found on one island off the coast of Africa, but it is a marvelously odd-looking creature. Larger than a swan, physiologically closer to a pigeon, with a very odd beak."

And so on.

She watched Fletcher idly build a tower out of the little pink cakes, which a Buckingham servant quickly disposed of, and then circle back to Eliza Harding, hand her a glass of lemonade, and engage in conversation. Louisa didn't bother to hide that she was staring at him, and after a few minutes, he seemed to notice and looked her way. He finished what he was saying to Eliza, kissed her knuckles, and then proceeded across the garden to Louisa.

That hadn't been her intent, but if he wanted to come speak with this lot of dullards and not Eliza, that was fine with Louisa.

Fletcher said, "May I sit?" gesturing at the chair next to Louisa.

"Please do."

Fletcher sat and then leaned toward Daniel. "What are we discussing?"

"Rare bird skeletons held in various collections around England," said Daniel. He turned back to the group. "I had heard a rumor there was a taxidermy dodo held by an ornithologist in London, but I suppose that is too much to wish for."

"Rare bird skeletons?" Fletcher said under his breath to Louisa.

She shrugged.

"Tell me, Greystone, what do you think of all this?"

"About rare bird skeletons?"

"Sure," said Daniel. "Or collecting specimens. Scientific study. Any of that."

"Well," Fletcher said, sitting up a bit straighter. He paused, probably trying to formulate a response. "'Tis a shame that the rare birds are mostly confined to private collections. Should not some of these specimens be available for the general public to look at and learn from? For example, the British Museum displays antiquities that have been collected over the years, so could they not also display scientific specimens?"

"An interesting idea," said Whitson, the Oxford professor. "I'm of two minds because I like having specimens on hand when I teach, but it might be useful to have a broader catalogue of specimens all in one place. I am especially interested in extinct species, and since those are no longer available to us to see in the wild, it might be useful to have a place to display them for the public."

"Indeed," said Fletcher. "I'm no expert on ornithology, but I have a lot of interests, and I like to read. Sometimes books just cannot do justice to a thing, and it is helpful to see it with your own eyes."

"Indeed," said Whitson. "For example, there is a species of blue pigeon in Africa that I would very much like to get my hands on. There is some speculation that last year's volcanic eruption disrupted its mating journey, and few have been seen this year, and I'd like to see one before it is gone."

"Does the extinction of bird species not bother you?" Louisa asked.

"It bothers me immensely. But it is the circle of life."

"Is it? Why did the dodo go extinct?"

The men all glanced at each other. Louisa took this to mean she had overstepped.

Daniel said, "We don't know exactly. The dodo was isolated to a specific part of the world. It could be that, once sailors stumbled upon their habitat and took a few back to Europe, this depleted the population enough to limit the number of available mates. It could be a weather-related phenomenon, like last year's volcanic eruption. And I'll remind you, that occurred thousands of miles away, but we still felt it here in that it never grew hot last summer because there was too much ash in the air to let the sunlight through. A much smaller disruption could have ended the dodos. A flood or a fire or something."

"All right." Louisa regretted she'd asked.

"There is a lot in nature that we do not know or understand, which is why scientists continue to study it all," said another gent, whom Louisa did not know.

"Understood," said Louisa. "I was just curious. Especially since, if there is a species of bird you are interested in, would you not also be interested in making sure it does not go extinct?"

"Indeed," said Whitson. "But that is sometimes out of our hands."

"Do you think there are species we don't know about?" asked Fletcher. "That is, this dodo bird went extinct a hundred years ago, you said? We know about it because one hundred years is a long time ago, but not so long in the scheme of things. My ancestral home in Cornwall is older than that, for example. Had a dodo been in England, my great-grandfather might have seen it. That is not so far removed from us that people could not easily pass down information. But what if a species of bird died in, say, the time of William the Conqueror. Or further back during Julius

Caesar or Jesus Christ. Do you suppose there are species of bird or any animal that went extinct without our knowing about it? Especially if it happened in, say, the Americas before humans knew the Americas were there?"

"That is definitely possible," said Whitson. "Likely, even. All animals were rescued in the Flood, but it is logical for some of those animals not to have persisted long after that."

Louisa was not certain there actually was a flood for Noah to sail his ark through, that it was just a parable and not an actually recorded historical event, but she decided not to voice such a concern aloud. She expected Daniel might not appreciate such a blasphemy.

"Greystone, right?" said Whitson. "I thought you were older."

Fletcher kept his expression placid. "You must be thinking of my father. He passed about eight months ago."

"Ah, yes. I met him once, years ago. He donated some money to Oxford."

"Likely to smooth my way there. But alas, I studied literature, not science."

"I will try not to hold that against you." Whitson sounded like he meant it.

A few minutes later, once the discussion of birds got rolling again. Louisa made meaningful eye contact with Fletcher, and he took the hint and offered to get her a lemonade. She followed him over to the refreshment table.

"I don't want to hear one more thing about beak shape," she said.

"This is what your dinner parties will be like. 'Oh, my lady, this chicken is delicious. Did you know that chickens *do* sometimes fly?'"

"No."

"No, you didn't know that about chickens, or no, you do not accept that is your fate."

"Both."

"Good luck explaining that to the Duke of Ornithology."

Louisa let out a huff. "Maybe I can conveniently have other plans whenever the scientists come to call."

Fletcher just raised an eyebrow at her as he poured her some lemonade.

"Is it wrong that I find him boring?"

"He *is* boring."

Louisa was startled by that reaction. Fletcher was supposed to reassure her. "Oh," she said.

Fletcher frowned. "I probably shouldn't have said that. And maybe it doesn't matter. Once you're married, you'll be in your own sphere with him, I suppose. You'll talk about household matters and your children. If his great passion is birds, and you care little for birds, he will find other people to discuss birds with."

Louisa sighed.

"Are you having second thoughts?" Fletcher asked.

"I cannot discuss this here."

His eyebrows shot up. "So you are."

"I don't want to talk about it."

Fletcher poured himself some lemonade. After he sipped, he said, "There are worse things in the world than a boring husband."

"But there are better things, too, no?"

"I wouldn't know, but I would guess yes." Fletcher frowned. He pulled out his pocket watch and looked at the time. "I'll need to depart soon. I have another engagement."

"A romantic assignation?"

Fletcher choked on his lemonade. "No! I have a business meeting and then I'm having dinner with my mother. Nothing scandalous."

"I suppose I shall rejoin my future husband and pretend I know the difference between a goldfinch and a parakeet." The prospect did not excite her.

"Chin up, my friend. And goldfinches are the yellow ones, I think."

"Hmm."

He smiled and patted her arm. "I do need to leave, but we shall talk soon."

"I'm holding you to that."

"You could also…" But he shook his head.

"What were you going to say?"

"I shouldn't."

"Fletcher."

He sighed. "If you don't like him, well, you aren't married yet."

And with that, he handed his glass to a server, kissed her cheek, and walked away, leaving Louisa to wonder what, exactly, he meant.

Chapter Nine

FLETCHER RECEIVED A note from Louisa asking him to meet with her with all possible haste. Worried she had found herself in a spot of trouble—and perhaps hoping, with no reason to do so, that she'd decided to toss over Rotherfeld—he wrote back agreeing but asked where, suggesting his mother's house. She agreed, and so now Fletcher was in his mother's sitting room, drinking cooling tea as he waited for Louisa.

The thought had been that at least here, they'd be chaperoned by Fletcher's mother, but he'd quite forgotten that she'd gone to Bath for a few days, so, aside from the staff, he and Louisa would be quite alone. Perhaps Louisa could tell her parents and fiancé that the dowager Marchioness of Greystone was here; if Fletcher had forgotten she'd left town, society probably had, too.

Not that he had any untoward plans. He intended simply to speak with Louisa, to let her have her say. He worried she'd gotten herself in some kind of trouble. But he knew that if he went to her home or she came to his, anyone who spotted them could talk—and keep Louisa from speaking freely—and Fletcher would prefer not to have to meet Rotherfeld with pistols at dawn.

Although Fletcher was a damned good shot, so maybe he'd be all right.

But, no, he should not be harboring fantasies about doing

away with Louisa's fiancé.

Lord, what a mess.

When Hoskins, the elderly Greystone butler, creaked that Lady Louisa had arrived, Fletcher stood as she swept into the room. Hoskins knew Louisa as well as anyone, had watched her grow up, and understood the nature of her relationship with Fletcher, at least until recently.

"Leave us, Hoskins," Fletcher said, a bit loudly, "but ask Mrs. Stone to send up tea."

"Yes, my lord." Hoskins bowed and left.

Fletcher turned to look at Louisa. She seemed in a tizzy. She was, of course, as artfully put together as she always was, in a lavender day dress, a yellow overcoat, and her hair pinned up in an elaborate design. But the expression on her face looked harried.

This did not stop Fletcher from glancing at her bosom. It was right there, after all.

"I am having a bit of a crisis," said Louisa.

Hoskins came back and helped her out of her coat. He left again, saying he'd hang her coat near the door. Poor Hoskins had, perhaps, gotten too slow to catch Louisa when she was worked up like this.

"Will you sit?" He gestured to the settee.

"Oh, all right." She perched at the edge of it while he took a chair opposite her. She glanced at the open door, seeming agitated.

"I forgot until I found the house empty that Mother is taking in the waters at Bath for a few days."

"Oh."

"She took some of the staff with her. It's just Hoskins, who can barely hear anymore, and the kitchen staff, who are downstairs. I apologize if this feels like false pretenses…"

"No, it's fine. I'd rather your mother not hear what I have to say. Who knows she's in Bath?"

"I barely did, so I suspect not many people. I believe she and the Dowager Duchess of Swynford went together, but I don't think anyone else knows."

"Then if anyone asks, I had tea with your mother today."

"Yes. But in reality, we are quite alone. You can speak freely."

"Fletcher." Louisa wrung her hands. "I fear I've made a terrible mistake."

"Talk to me."

It would have to wait, though, because Mrs. Stone walked in with tea service then. She set the tray on the table at the center of the room, and Fletcher was a bit surprised to see not only tea, but also an array of little cakes, as if Mrs. Stone somehow knew there'd be company today even though the mistress was out.

"Did you conjure these cakes with witchcraft, Mrs. Stone?" Fletcher asked.

Mrs. Stone winked. "As it happens, I'm training the new girl in the kitchen. I'm pleased to see Lady Louisa, because now we will not grow fat eating all these cakes ourselves. Please enjoy. I know the pink ones with the berries are your favorites, my lady."

"Thank you, Mrs. Stone," said Louisa. "I believe one of those cakes will be just the thing."

Mrs. Stone smiled and left.

Fletcher took a moment to marvel that even the Greystone staff loved Louisa. How had it taken Fletcher so long to realize he did?

"What is your terrible mistake?" Fletcher asked, once they were alone.

Louisa busied herself pouring a cup of tea and dropping several sugar cubes into it before she said, "I suspect I have been ruled by my baser instincts and have agreed to marry a man who is not much more than a very handsome empty shirt."

Fletcher tamped down the triumph he felt. Carefully, he said, "What makes you say that?"

In truth, he knew the answer, but he wanted to hear her say it. She sat back on the settee and took a sip of tea. "One could argue that Daniel—Rotherfeld—and I have been courting for nearly a year, but it is much less time than that because we spent the summer apart." She seemed to be working through something as she talked. She kept her hands busy.

"Yes," said Fletcher.

"And in all the time we've spent together, you'll be pleased to know, he has behaved himself impeccably. Always polite. Never inappropriate."

"Why would that please me?"

"I assume you do not want me to marry a cad."

Fletcher could not hide his revulsion to the idea. "Indeed not."

"My point being that…oh, I don't know if I should say this."

"Just speak with me. I promise not to tease or be mocking. You can tell me anything."

"But you got upset when we talked on the way to the opera."

A fair point. "In my defense, you were trying to pry information out of me. And, again, we are alone, so if you need to discuss something, you should feel free to do so, even if it is of a personal nature. But don't feel like you need to tell me something you are uncomfortable with."

"The topic did not bother you?"

Fletcher worried she wanted to talk about sex again. "It did, but again, you were pushing me to tell you things about myself I was uncomfortable sharing. I want you to be able to share your thoughts with me, regardless of the topic. But if I feel you have stepped over a line, I will stop you."

"Okay. That is, there is not much to tell, because as I said, Daniel—that is, Rotherfeld—has never done anything in the same neighborhood as inappropriate. Always a perfect gentleman. Even when we are alone."

Fletcher was not sure what to make of that. "What is the issue, then?"

"Well, I have been feeling for the last week or so that…" She looked off into the distance. "I mean, you saw him at the garden party."

"Birds."

"Yes, birds. And grain futures and balancing ledgers and the speed at which paint dries and any number of completely dull topics. It's like once I learned he was boring, I couldn't stop seeing it. Then he called on me yesterday and I tried again in earnest to learn what there was under his very good-looking surface."

Fletcher's heart pounded. His jealousy was becoming an ugly thing. "May we refrain from commenting on Rotherfeld's looks?"

"They are relevant to my crisis," said Louisa, although the edges of her mouth ticked up.

Devil take him. "Carry on."

"I asked about his interests last week," she said. "Do you know what he said his current keen interest is?"

"The growth of grass on the moors? The land speed of a specific species of snail?"

"Farming techniques."

Fletcher was unable school his face. Rotherfeld truly was as scintillating as the reference books in Fletcher's library—which was to say, not at all. "Farming techniques."

"I had engaged him in conversation with the hope that I could find some topic on which you and he could find some common knowledge. The only time he came close was when discussing horse racing."

"I do like a good race, but we'd run out of things to discuss in five minutes."

"He likes the gambling part of it."

Of course he did. Fletcher was more interested in the horses. "That is almost exciting, at least. A common gentlemanly pursuit."

"Uh-huh. And then there are investments."

"That holds some promise. What has he invested in?"

"Textiles."

Fletcher laughed for lack of anything better to say. "Naturally. Why would he invest in anything risky or interesting?"

Louisa's brow furrowed. "Do you not like Rotherfeld?"

Fletcher hesitated. He wasn't sure how to approach this. He wanted Louisa to know what he really thought, and if she was open to it, he wanted to talk her out of marrying Rotherfeld, but he wasn't sure he understood what she wanted. "Do you want my honest opinion?"

"Yes. Unvarnished truth."

"I've only had an extended conversation with him once, and I'm sure he's a perfectly nice fellow, but I found him boring. Which I'd apologize for saying, but you've said as much yourself."

"I have, yes. I have a similar issue with him."

"The birds."

"Yes, but generally. I find conversation with him difficult to sustain. We swiftly run out of topics to discuss."

Fletcher sighed. He struggled with whether to push or whether to let her get where he wanted her to go on her own. It occurred to him that even if he talked her out of marrying Rotherfeld, that did not mean she'd marry Fletcher, so maybe it was better to let her do the work. "Yes, but I don't really think I should get involved with—"

"I kissed him."

Fletcher's stomach dropped. "You did?"

"You're the one who suggested I enact some kind of intimate conversation with him. We were alone, so I brought up our wedding night. He put me off, but I asked him to kiss me, since we're engaged and all and he's barely touched me."

"Oh." Well, Fletcher really hoped for the chandelier above him to fall on him and put him out of his misery.

"And I've kissed him a few times since to see if the first time was just an awkward moment."

"And?"

"It was terrible. Every time."

Thank God. Fletcher fought back a smile. "How could it have been terrible?"

"I don't know. But kisses in novels are always nice. Is kissing nice?"

"It certainly has been in my experience."

"Did I do it wrong?"

"I do not think that is possible."

Louisa grunted. She looked frustrated.

Naive and bold. That was his Louisa. She wanted things and was never shy about expressing herself, but she was still an unmarried lady of the *ton* who had not experienced much of life outside of her family's narrow world.

"Apparently it *is* possible," she said, "because kissing Rotherfeld was highly unpleasant. But that can't be right, can it? I find him handsome. I *wanted* to kiss him."

Fletcher just shook his head, unsure of what to say. He really didn't need to know about her kissing Rotherfeld, although he was enjoying the fact that Rotherfeld was a bad kisser. On the other hand, if Louisa did not want Fletcher, he did not want to sentence her to a life of dull conversations and unpleasant kisses. "Louisa, this conversation may be straying into territory that is not appropriate for—"

"Bugger off, Fletcher."

He gasped at her use of language, but then he laughed. He adored this woman. He was tired of pretending otherwise. "See, this right here, this is my problem. I want you to tell me to bugger off at least once a day, but instead you're planning to marry the dullest man in London."

"Fletcher. That was unkind."

"I'm sorry, but you were on your way to telling me you think the very same thing about Rotherfeld that I do."

Louisa set aside her tea and began pacing in front of him. Fletcher leaned back in his chair and watched her. She truly was beautiful. He could imagine her figure underneath the layers of her gown, and he wanted to touch it. He wanted to pull all the pins out of her hair until those bouncy curls lay around her shoulders. He wanted to show her what kisses *should* feel like. He wanted her naked and underneath him and…

Well. There was that whole sexual attraction between them that he'd thought was not there. Apparently it was an extremely strong presence in their relationship, and he'd just never noticed it. Somehow. But now that he *had* noticed it, it was all he could think about.

But it shouldn't have taken her engagement to another man for Fletcher to fully wrap his head around how he felt about Louisa.

"All right," he said, because she seemed cross. "I apologize. I'm sure there are other people who are not me who find Rotherfeld to be a very exciting man. I'm sure there are other men who are interested in discussing bird beaks and farming techniques with him."

"And horses. I take it he loses money on races quite often."

"I did see him at the Ascot last year. Lost a fortune on a profoundly stupid bet."

"You see my concern?"

"Define your crisis for me precisely. Are you worried that your future husband is dull?"

"I worry I made a mistake agreeing marry him."

Fletcher could see the agony in her expression. Louisa had always been the sort of person who made a decision and plowed ahead with it, and to see her questioning this one—arguably the most important decision she'd ever make—made Fletcher's heart squeeze.

"I am sorry you are dealing with this," Fletcher said, standing so that he might steer Louisa back to the settee, because her pacing was starting to make him anxious, too. "But why come to me?"

"Because you are my friend. You always steer me straight. Remember when we were young and I wanted to collect frogs, but you stopped me?"

Fletcher nodded, not knowing where she was going with this. When he'd been about twelve and she'd been about seven, they spent a summer together at the Greystone manse in Cornwall. Fletcher did remember an afternoon when they'd been sitting beside the pond and Louisa had piped up to say she wanted to gather all the frogs from around the pond in her dress to keep as pets. Fletcher had talked her out of it—the act of collecting said frogs would involve getting into the mud and frogs did not make for good pets because they could hop away too easily, and Louisa's mother would have been horrified and infuriated by all of it—although she had still persisted in capturing one frog and keeping him in the pocket of her dress for the rest of the day. On returning to the house, her mother found it and screamed like she'd seen a ghost.

"Or the time I thought to be a professional musician, even though my piano skills are decidedly lacking. Or the time I tried to smuggle a little statue from Lady Eltingham's gallery?"

"Yes, Louisa, I remember all of those things." And he remembered every prank they'd planned together and carried out. Most of these involved catching insects or small amphibians and putting them in places they did not belong. He probably should have tried to talk her out of some of those, too, but often, they'd been having so much fun together, he didn't have the heart.

"You were not with me when I agreed to marry Rotherfeld, but now I suspect you would have tried to talk me out of that, too, had you been there."

"I am less certain of that," said Fletcher. "The decision about who you marry should be yours."

"And my mother's, at least according to her."

"But you like Rotherfeld. You wouldn't have agreed to marry him otherwise."

"I didn't know him. I realize that now. I know he's kind and intelligent and unerringly polite. But in the last few weeks, I've tried to understand who he is as a man, and all I have so far is that he likes gambling and boring conversational topics, he hates art…and kissing him is like kissing a fish."

"A fish?" Maybe Fletcher's friends were right. He needed to

give Louisa an alternative. "Did he do it right?"

"He admitted to not having much experience with women."

Fletcher found that a little surprising. A handsome man like Rotherfeld? Was it true or was he lying? Fletcher took no issue with it if it were true—it could have just been Rotherfeld was religious, or that he'd lived in gender-segregated spaces his whole life and hadn't had many opportunities to interact with women. But if he were lying to Louisa…

"What should kissing be like?" she asked.

"I don't know that I can describe it. But in my experience, it has always felt good."

"Show me."

"What?"

"Kiss me, Fletcher."

Fletcher just stared at her. His heart was beating so hard and fast, he suddenly worried it might burst. He, of course, wanted to kiss her, he'd been thinking about it since she first said the word *kiss*, but she was engaged to another man. "What about Rotherfeld?"

"I am not allowing you to compromise me. I trust you anyway. This is an experiment."

"An experiment."

"I just need you to… I need to know, all right? Show me what a good kiss is."

He had a million reasons not to kiss her. She could use this knowledge to teach Rotherfeld how to be a better kisser. She could decide kissing Fletcher was also unpleasant. It was possible some women just didn't like kissing. And kissing another man's fiancée was definitely not how gentlemen comported themselves.

But he really, really wanted to kiss her.

"Louisa, I shouldn't."

Louisa made the decision for him. She practically lunged at him, faster than he could react. He caught her at the waist, but by then, her lips were already on his.

So he kissed her.

And it was spectacular. Louisa's lips were soft and pliant, and she smelled like roses and berries and tea, and though he could feel her stays under her gown, just getting a sense of the real shape of her was sending arousal through his whole body in waves. She put her hands on his shoulders and stood on her toes to get closer to him, so he bent his head and parted his lips and licked into her mouth. He felt her sigh and knew he had her. When her hands came around the back of his neck and held him there, he knew Rotherfeld was the dead fish; it definitely wasn't Louisa.

He and Louisa would be fiery together. His beautiful, hot-headed, amazing woman.

Except she wasn't *his*.

He broke the kiss and took a step back. He panted as he looked at her, unable to get his breathing back to normal.

"Louisa."

Her fingers traveled to her lips, which she touched. "Is *that* what a kiss is supposed to be like?"

"We cannot... You are *engaged*..." Fletcher buried his head in his hands.

"Fletcher," she said softly, but he could not bear to look at her.

NOW FLETCHER WAS going through some kind of crisis.

Kissing him had felt amazing. Nothing like kissing Rotherfeld. Kissing Fletcher had made Louisa feel warm and tingly, and she had enjoyed it immensely, and she wanted to do it again, but now Fletcher stood before her, hiding his face.

"Tell me what's wrong," she said.

"You're engaged. And not to me."

"What just happened... Rotherfeld will never know."

"That's not..." He dropped his hands and eyed her. "I do not behave this way. I do not kiss virginal young women who are engaged to other men."

"Right. You keep your indiscretions to incorruptible women." She said it flatly. She was stating a fact.

"You mock me, but I'm really trying to do right by you. And what we just did, that should not have happened."

She nodded. Fletcher was right, she was putting him in a difficult position. "I'm sorry," she said. "Perhaps I shouldn't have done that, but at least I know now what kissing *can* be like."

"Maybe it was a…maybe the timing was wrong. You should try again. With Rotherfeld."

"Yes. Absolutely." Although she doubted the timing could have been wrong on every kiss attempt, and frankly, she was surprised Rotherfeld didn't recognize how bad their kisses were.

But this was all extremely confusing. Suddenly feeling light-headed, Louisa sat on the settee and took a fortifying sip of tea. The tea warmed her, at least; it was the same vaguely spicy blend the Greystone house had been serving for years, and it tasted like Louisa's childhood. She'd spent many afternoons in this sitting room, in fact, struggling to sit still while her mother visited with Fletcher's, or chasing Fletcher around the furniture, or defeating Fletcher at chess as they sat upon the floor in front of the fireplace.

Fletcher had been a joyful and open child, endlessly curious, often mischievous, but he had always looked out for Louisa. He'd indulge Louisa's whims until they became dangerous or unless he saw them playing out in a way that would make her unhappy. He was older, yes, and like a big brother, he took care of her, but there was something else here, too, now that they were adults. Fletcher had become more guarded, especially since Louisa's engagement had been announced.

Fletcher resumed his seat across from her and looked at her warily.

"So what will you do now?" Fletcher asked.

"I don't know. I suppose I owe it to my fiancé to give him

another chance."

He frowned. "Yes. But say…say he *is* dull. You find no common ground. Say he can't kiss you the way you want him to. Will you still marry him?"

"I don't know. Am I dooming myself to a dull life if I do?"

"I can't answer that."

"I don't think good looks are enough to hang a marriage on. People tell me all the time that he and I make an attractive couple, but if we have nothing to talk about… But then I think, maybe it doesn't matter, if my only task is to produce his heirs."

"That should not be your only task."

"No?"

"No. I may not know much about marriage, but I do know that I have friends in happy ones, and they treat their wives as friends and companions. Hugh still struggles a bit with that head injury, so Adele helps him. When he has memory lapses, she helps him fill in the blanks. And Grace practically runs Owen's estate in Wales, and she still makes art on the side."

Louisa nodded. That sounded more like the marriage Louisa wanted for herself. Not to settle for dullness with Rotherfeld. But if not Rotherfeld, then who?

"I say all this to point out," Fletcher said, "your marriage need not be one where you just put up with a husband who you like to look at. That would be dull and unsatisfying. And maybe I exaggerate Rotherfeld's faults. Maybe he does have interests that are worth discussing. Maybe you'll help him manage his property or take up some interesting hobbies, or…I don't know. But what I *do* know, my dearest Louisa, is that you are one of the best people I know, and you deserve to have a marriage to someone you adore and who adores you, with happiness and good health and, well, physical relations and all of it. Because I know how curious and passionate you are, and you would not do well with a dull husband. I fear it would be a prison for you. But I don't know Rotherfeld well."

In other words, Fletcher did not care for Rotherfeld. And if

Louisa's closest friend did not like her husband, that could be a problem.

Louisa regarded him now. Fletcher was in his typical daytime uniform of a neatly tailored blue coat and close-fitting gray trousers. Not the height of fashion, exactly, although the trousers were more modern than the breeches he often wore with more formal outfits. His black shoes were shined enough for Louisa to see her reflection in them. His hair was combed away from his face, and he was clean-shaven, but Louisa suddenly found herself curious. Did he have hair on his chest? Men did, didn't they? Did he have the sort of muscular figure the Greek statues did? Was his body softer? She didn't think so, based on the cut of his coat, but it was difficult to tell.

And, if he kissed her as he had just done, how would it feel if he…

She squirmed on the settee, an uncomfortable ache forming between her legs.

But she was not supposed to desire Fletcher.

"What are we to do?" she asked.

"We?"

"Did you hate kissing me?"

"No. On the contrary."

Louisa took a deep breath. "You've never…that is, you and I have always enjoyed our friendship, but it never felt like, I never expected of you… I don't know what I'm trying to say."

"Are you asking me something?"

"I'm old. Well, not old, but I'm a fair number of years from being a debutante, and I have somehow escaped the curse of being labeled a spinster, although I know much of the *ton* views me as an eccentric. But the truth is that I've had a few seasons with no proposals, so when Rotherfeld showed interest, I thought, well, here is my future. Here is a man who wants me and is willing to offer for me, even if I may be on the older side, even if I may be a bit odd. But since he proposed, nothing has played out the way I expected."

"What did you expect?"

"I expected… more. I thought I'd be happier. But instead, I have doubts."

Fletcher nodded slowly.

"What are you thinking?" she asked.

"I shouldn't say it."

"Please tell me."

He frowned. "I didn't want to do this, because I don't want you to feel pressure, and who you marry should be *your* choice."

"But?"

"If remaining unmarried is your fear, you have nothing to fear."

"How can you say that?"

Fletcher hesitated, but he said, "Put it this way. I know that you and I have a relationship that is not physical or romantic, but we are great friends and never run out of things to talk about. So if you decide to end your relationship with Rotherfeld, and if you cannot find another husband, I will marry you."

At first, Louisa was excited by the idea. It made a lot of sense. She and Fletcher were fond of each other. That kiss showed they had some sparks between them. She would be willing to bet Fletcher would be able to pleasure her in bed the way Rotherfeld never would. They could make a marriage work.

But then she heard what he'd actually said. *If.* "I'm not…you shouldn't settle for me."

"That's not what I'd be doing."

"I don't need your pity, either." Anger and hurt mounting, Louisa stood back up. She ran to the door and shouted, "Hoskins. I'm ready to leave. Ready my carriage."

He'd been sitting on a chair near the front door, snoozing. He startled awake and said, "Yes, my lady."

"Louisa, wait, what are you doing?" Fletcher said.

"I don't need you to offer for me just because I have no other prospects. I'd rather be a spinster than have you offer for me out of pity."

"It's not pity! I—"

"I heard what you said. *If* I break off my engagement to Rotherfeld, and *if* I can't find anyone else because I'm too homely and charmless to find a husband, *then* you will consider offering for me out of the goodness of your heart."

"That is *not* what I said. I merely meant that—"

"I'm leaving, Fletcher. But thank you for giving me what I came here for." Then she stormed down the hall. Hoskins helped her into her coat, and she walked out the door.

Chapter Ten

Lark moved through his club with deliberately slow speed so as to better listen to the day's gossip. The former Lord Chancellor, also Anthony's uncle, had given a rather over-wrought speech the day before, and that seemed to be the talk of the day. The contents of the speech didn't interest Lark much, but he was reminded again that Anthony had enough wealth and power to be above the gossip fray, something he'd repeated to Lark many times, and yet he'd made decisions based on keeping himself out of trouble.

He'd done so at Lark's urging, though. Lark had been the one to insist they end their relationship so that Anthony marry, and now here they were. Given all that had transpired in the last year, Lark had no deeper regret than pushing Anthony away so that they might not find themselves at the ends of nooses. Perhaps Anthony's powerful family and his money could buy his way out of trouble, but Lark had convinced himself that no amount of wealth, fame, or power would prevent the Crown from hanging sodomites—not if he had enemies lurking about. As he'd learned last year, before his would-be blackmailer met an untimely end, all it would take was someone he'd angered in the past learning his secrets to end everything.

He found Anthony sitting alone by the fire.

Something in his chest seized.

Lark approached slowly. He sat in the chair across from Anthony without saying a word, but the movement must have caught his eye, because Anthony looked over.

"Lark."

"I am somewhat surprised to see you here."

"Henry is with Mrs. Church. I needed to get out of the house and talk to my peers. Slow night, though."

"Rotherfeld is holding a dinner party tonight to show off his fiancée, so Fletcher and Hugh are there. I have not the foggiest where Owen has gone tonight."

Anthony looked surprised. "Rotherfeld is engaged?"

"You are out of the gossip loop, I see."

"I've been otherwise occupied."

"Yes. Well, Rotherfeld is engaged to Fletcher's dear friend, Lady Louisa Petty, and Fletcher is beside himself about it, so that has been entertaining in its own way."

"Rotherfeld is engaged to Lady Louisa?" Anthony tilted his head as if this were mystifying.

"What of it?"

"Lark… I hesitate to say this but…"

"Tell me."

"Rotherfeld…that is, Fletcher has feelings for Lady Louisa? Why did Fletcher not offer for her?"

"I think he did not know his feelings until she was engaged to someone else."

"If he has romantic feelings for her, perhaps an intervention is called for."

"Oh, believe me, I've tried, and Fletcher is quite insistent he merely wants Louisa's happiness. If she loves Rotherfeld, he will not intervene—"

"No, I mean… I do not believe Louisa would be happy with Rotherfeld."

Lark regarded Anthony for a moment. Lark suspected he did not want an answer to his next question, but he said, "What makes you say that?"

Anthony sighed. "It's been…years. Before I had so much as a conversation with you. But he and I…"

"Please say no more."

Anthony nodded. "I haven't spoken to him since we ended things, aside from niceties here and there as necessary, and the affair itself was brief. We never…that is, it was physical but not emotional, our involvement."

Lark rubbed his chest. "I'd really prefer not to hear the details."

Anthony gave him an appraising look. "My point was just that…I find the engagement curious. Louisa is an intelligent, beautiful woman, and Rotherfeld is…"

"Don't call him handsome."

"As always, your jealousy is unbecoming, Lark. And uncalled for, under the circumstances."

Lark crossed his arms and scowled. Anthony knew perfectly well how Lark felt.

"I have always found Rotherfeld to be timid and prudish, if you must know," said Anthony. "He's uncomfortable with himself and his proclivities."

"Do you think he offered for Louisa on false pretenses?"

Anthony frowned. "I found out about this engagement thirty seconds ago, and I can't know what's in Rotherfeld's head. Who knows why men do anything? Maybe he genuinely likes her. The news just surprised me because Rotherfeld is younger than we are and no one would have batted an eyelash had he postponed the inevitable and sown a few more oats first."

"All right." Lark looked Anthony over. "But let us speculate."

Anthony raised an eyebrow. "Very irresponsible of you."

"Well, now I think Rotherfeld's motives are not pure. It hadn't occurred to me to doubt his intentions until you shared this bit of information with me, but now I'm turning this over in my head. If he's ashamed of his own proclivities, he could be forcing himself to marry to prove something to himself. He could be marrying to save face."

Anthony nodded. "Indeed. I imagine, like us all, he has chosen Louisa because he must marry and wanted an intellectual equal and one the *ton* wouldn't see as surprising, although I suppose she is on the older side."

"Not like us all. I am not marrying."

"No?"

"Have we learned nothing? How could I pretend to love a woman when I am so obviously besotted with someone else."

"Besotted?"

"Anthony."

"You are too conspicuous with your besottedness. In the hour I've been here, do you know how many men have welcomed me back to the club and in the same breath mentioned how deeply you mourned my company, that you practically live in a bottle now because you are so miserable? Fortunately, everyone is too naive to suspect the true nature of our relationship, and they seem to think you are sad because you've lost all your friends to matrimony, including me."

"I did lose you to matrimony."

"You lost me because you left me," Anthony whisper-shouted. There was a harsh note to his voice.

"I do not anticipate that you will forgive me, and what's done is done, and I may have regrets and misery and all of it, but I cannot change it. And I have made you even more miserable than I could have anticipated, and I *do* regret that."

Anthony looked into his glass.

The thing was, Anthony's brightness had dimmed. Anthony had always been this beacon, a man who reveled in his fortunes in life, someone always funny and clever and practically glowing. It was one of the things that had attracted Lark to Anthony to begin with. And although Anthony was starting to come out of mourning—he wore all black tonight, granted, but he didn't seem as sad as he had been when Lark saw him a few weeks ago— much of that brightness was gone.

Lark had done that. Lark had pushed Anthony away and was

thus the catalyst for all that had come after.

"I'm sorry," Lark said. "This is… I should leave."

"No, don't."

"It's all my fault. What happened to you."

Anthony shook his head.

"It is. And I can't…that is…" Lark looked around. No one was near them. The crowd was thin tonight. "I am responsible for your…present state, and I have been miserable without you, so your unhappiness must be compounded, and I caused that, and I hate that I have made you so unhappy. And I've been wasting my time trying to drink away my memories, but I have made everything so much worse for you, and I…I cannot believe how much I've buggered everything, and I just don't…"

"It's all right, Lark." Anthony's tone was oddly comforting, and Lark hated it, because *he* should have been the one comforting *Anthony*.

"It isn't. It never will be."

Anthony frowned at him. "Did you have business here tonight?"

"I was hoping the gossip would distract me, but it's all politics tonight. I cannot sit at home or I'll drink."

"So you came to a club where most people drink? Are you no longer drinking?"

"Turns out when you try to destroy your brain with alcohol, you behave abominably in public."

"Lark."

"I have not yet ordered my staff to empty my liquor cabinet, but I suppose I must consider it to remove the temptation."

"I was about to say, if you have no business here tonight, come home with me, and I will keep you away from the liquor."

"Anthony, we cannot—"

"I am not propositioning you. In my home, we can speak candidly, and I can remove temptation. I would invite myself to yours, but I feel an obligation to be near my son, even though the nurse is with him."

"Your nurse will not grow suspicious that you have brought a friend home?"

"I find I am too tired to care. And before you lecture me, I am not bringing you home for an assignation, I am asking for your company and some conversation and nothing more. I will help keep you from the drink and you will keep me company for a few more hours, and then you will go home and not antagonize my nurse."

Lark decided to take the offer for what it was—a rekindling of their friendship. "All right."

"All right?"

"I shall keep you company for a few hours. We shall save ourselves from our worst impulses for a little while. Gossip more about the Rotherfeld-Louisa-Fletcher love triangle. Speculate wildly about men we do not know well."

Anthony smiled. "Yes. That is my intent."

"Then lead the way."

FLETCHER WAS AT the desk in his study, staring at his ledgers and finding some comfort in the simple act of arithmetic when his butler announced the Earl of Waring.

Fletcher's head was not focused on his work. He'd spent the night before at a perfectly nice dinner party at Rotherfeld's. He'd been seated at the other end of the table from Louisa, well out of her earshot, at dinner, something Fletcher expected was done purposefully. He'd spent a great deal of dinner trying to read her face—was she bored, distressed, overcome with lust?—but he'd found it impossible. She'd be good at cards if she ever decided to play. The whole night had been an exercise in frustration, though, with Hugh egging him on to go talk to her and Rotherfeld keeping him and Louisa apart in less subtle or convincing ways as the night went on. Louisa avoided Fletcher so assiduously,

Fletcher began to suspect that Rotherfeld was guarding her at her own instruction. So Fletcher had suffered through dinner—the food was good at least—and shared a cigar with the men, but had barely spoken to Louisa at all.

And now Lark darkened his doorstep. Fletcher stood and invited him to have a seat in one of the plush chairs across the room from his desk.

"How was the dinner party?" Lark asked.

"Dreadful. Rotherfeld has all the conversational skill of an old stocking, and Louisa and I argued over something ridiculous a few days ago, so she barely spoke to me all evening."

Lark tilted his head. "What did you argue about?"

"Normally I'd tell you to bugger off, but this is kind of your fault. I told her that if she was worried about remaining unmarried if she broke her engagement to Rotherfeld, I would marry her. She took this as me offering to marry her out of pity."

"Poorly done, old chap."

"How so? *You* suggested I offer her an alternative."

"But not like that. Did you tell her you love her? That you *want* to marry her?"

Oh. "No."

Lark raised an eyebrow. "You can see where she might have misinterpreted what you said. Louisa is proud, no?"

"All right. I will try again." Fletcher sighed and rubbed his forehead. How had he bungled this so badly? "Did you come here just to badger me?"

"No. I have some news."

"Good news or bad news?"

"Depends on what you want to happen next with Louisa."

"Is it about Rotherfeld?"

"It is. I learned something about him last night."

Fletcher couldn't decide what he wanted that to be. "Please tell me he's guilty of a crime. It doesn't need to be violent. He moonlights as a pickpocket, perhaps. Or he's in a great deal of gambling debt."

"No, no. He…how shall I put this? He's had relations with someone we know."

Fletcher slapped his hands on his desk. "That liar. He told Louisa he had no experience with women."

"Oh, no," said Lark. "He *doesn't* have experience with *women.*"

Fletcher's heart might have stopped. "With men?"

"With Anthony. Years before he and I got to know each other. I told Anthony last night that Rotherfeld was engaged to Louisa, and Anthony was shocked because he found it unlikely Rotherfeld was interested in women."

That would explain some things. If Rotherfeld wasn't attracted to Louisa, perhaps he *would* kiss her like a fish. "I don't know what to do with this information."

"I don't either, but I came here to tell you so that you can tell Louisa if you like. Perhaps it is another arrow in your quiver to slay Rotherfeld once and for all and win the girl."

"I'm not certain she'd listen to me." He couldn't imagine how he'd begin to tell her.

"You don't think this is information she needs to know?"

"I do, but…" But would she even believe him? "She was cross with me. Stormed out of my mother's house." Fletcher stood and started to pace. "*And* there's no reason to think Rotherfeld couldn't…perform marital duties." Saying that made Fletcher want to vomit.

"I take it from how pale your face just got that you are picturing it."

"He's all wrong for her, Lark. And I don't think that's just my jealousy talking. He's boring and proper and hadn't so much as even kissed Louisa until she practically begged him to. He thinks art is scandalous. He hates most things that she loves. And now I find out that he's interested in men? Not that…I mean, it's not a judgment, I just question whether he is a fit husband for Louisa. But if I tell her all that, she may misinterpret it, because apparently I am incapable of explaining that she should be with me without putting my foot in my mouth."

Lark stared at him. "Owen was right. You've got it bad."

"She *should* be with me. You agree with that, right?"

"I do. But if you are unwilling to mount a case for yourself…"

"It's not that. It's difficult to balance this. If I tell her I love her and want to be with her, but she doesn't feel the same way, that would be devastating, especially if she still wants to marry Rotherfeld. Not to mention, she'd have to break an engagement, something our peers are not exactly supportive of." Fletcher had been mulling this over for a few days. While he suspected that Louisa was unhappy in her engagement, that didn't necessarily mean she wanted Fletcher, especially not if he'd offended her by inadvertently implying he wanted to marry her out of pity. And, true, she wasn't married yet, but throwing over Rotherfeld to marry Fletcher—or not marry at all—would be a huge scandal.

"To the devil with what our peers think."

"Lark." Well, Fletcher didn't care much what others thought of him, either, but Louisa might, and her parents definitely would.

"No, I'm…I'm just so tired. I know you don't understand what Anthony and I are to each other, and I know you do not understand what it's like to desire those of your own sex, but I was so terrified of what society would do to us if they discovered our affair that I broke things off with Anthony, sent him into the arms of his now-late wife, and visited unspeakable misery on both of us. And I'm *tired*, Fletcher. I'm sick of trying to keep things proper and appropriate for the sake of a society that would just as soon see me hanged. I love Anthony just as dearly as you love Louisa, and I don't view that as sinful. And now I may never get the chance to be with him again because of the events of the last year, and…life is too short. If you love Louisa, you must tell her how you feel."

Fletcher paused to absorb all that. He had never heard Lark put it so passionately or succinctly. But Lark had a point. Fletcher let out a breath. "And what if she rejects me?"

"Then you can join me in the bottom of a bottle. I've still got a lot of good whiskey at home."

Fletcher sat with that for a moment. He'd been mealymouthed and equivocating when he'd tried broaching the subject with Louisa. He really had made a hash of things. No wonder she was cross with him. Clearly, what this situation called for was for Fletcher to lay out a case, to make an argument for why he was the man Louisa should choose. He should tell her how he felt. And if she rejected him, well, that would be terrible, but at least he would have put his full effort into it. If he kept acting foolishly, she could very well marry Rotherfeld and consign herself to misery, and Fletcher could not live with himself if he did not at least try to win her over.

So, he needed a new approach. No more dancing around things or trying to keep things proper. He should just lay it out for her.

"I will talk to her," he said.

"Good."

Something else occurred to Fletcher. "If Anthony told you all this, you must be spending more time together."

"We are, we are. I ran into him at the club last night. We got to talking. I don't know if a romantic relationship is in the cards, but it is nice to be able to speak with him again."

"That is something."

"Yes. But learn from my example. If you love her, you should act on it."

Yes. Of course. Because Lark and Anthony had once been in love and Lark had ended it and now look at them. Fletcher hoped to avoid the sort of misery that would send him to seek solace in a bottle, and he thought if he could just convince Louisa, he might avoid that fate. "I will, I will. I will speak with her as soon as I can."

Chapter Eleven

LOUISA RODE ALONGSIDE Daniel in the park. They took their horses for a slow walk. Daniel seemed content to enjoy the silence between them, but Louisa felt restless, especially after everything that had happened with Fletcher.

She was furious at Fletcher.

She was thus trying to overcome her doubts by spending time with Daniel, but riding horses through the park, even at a slow pace and side-by-side, was not especially conducive to conversation, especially not with Louisa's right leg starting to go pins-and-needles from being in the sidesaddle too long.

As a girl, she'd borrowed an old pair of Fletcher's breeches to ride astride. No one in her family seemed to think it improper, but here in London, with all of society looking on, she did not have that luxury. But whoever decided ladies should ride like this was likely a man.

Still, spending time with Daniel was likely the right thing to do. Even if she worried marrying him was the wrong thing, well, what was the alternative? If she ended the engagement, it would be a huge scandal, would it not? Not that she cared. She'd long been perceived as a bit odd, but her parents wouldn't like it. Still, she had to figure out how to make this situation work.

She looked around. She spotted Adele and Grace walking the distance. It was hard to miss them; Adele was taller than most women and Grace had shiny blond hair but seemed allergic to bonnets.

"Daniel?" she called out.

"Yes, my love?"

"Do you mind if I walk for a bit? I'd like to go greet my friends."

He looked up and must have also seen Adele and Grace. "Of course." He slid off his horse so that he could help her down from hers. She didn't really need his help—she'd been riding since she started to walk—but she indulged him. His firm hands on her waist probably should have made her feel…something. But they didn't.

"I can return the horses to the stables if it pleases you," Daniel said. "Then return in a little bit to escort you home."

"Oh, you don't need to—"

"I'm happy to, truly. You looked uncomfortable in the saddle."

"I don't love riding sidesaddle, truth be told. I *can* ride, but this leisurely pace over the uneven ground was making my leg sore."

"Oh."

"That is, I don't want you to think I'm uncomfortable with riding generally. Just…this particular ride was uncomfortable for me. I love to ride normally. I'm sorry. It's not your fault. I should have insisted on a faster pace."

He smiled. "No worries, my dear. I'll be back shortly." He took her horse's reins in his hand and then climbed back aboard his own mount. He walked the horses back toward the stables.

With a sigh, Louisa dusted off her thighs and then walked toward her friends.

Adele and Grace greeted her warmly. Louisa and Adele had grown especially close; Adele had been hidden away as a paid companion to an elderly countess before she'd married Hugh and had not known many in society, so Hugh had asked Louisa to help her integrate now that she was a duchess, and they'd become fast friends. Grace had been a harder nut to crack because she spent part of the year in Wales, but Louisa liked her a lot, and now it seemed she and Adele had bonded over being mothers. The three of them had spent a lot of time together the previous season, and Louisa genuinely liked both women.

Would Louisa join their ranks as mothers? It remained to be seen. If Louisa stayed with Daniel, she hoped the act of making heirs was more pleasant than kissing him was.

Lord, what a mess. To the devil with Fletcher.

"My friends, I am glad to see you," Louisa said.

"Was that Rotherfeld?" asked Adele.

"Yes. He is returning the horses, so I have a bit of time to talk with you candidly."

They began walking slowly.

"I'd hate to take you away from your fiancé," said Grace.

"You aren't. That is, I needed a bit of a break. We've spent time together nearly every day this week."

"Oh, that is nice. You must be excited for the wedding," said Adele.

Louisa recognized the empty platitudes for what they were. Adele was, of course, being polite and didn't know the whole truth, but Louisa did not want to pretend everything was fine right now. "Ladies, can I confide in you?"

Grace looked at her a bit mischievously. "Please do."

They formed a bit of a triangle. Not many people were out today—the air was crisp and the sky was overcast, not exactly ideal conditions for promenading in the park—so Louisa felt safe speaking to them. "I've had a terrible week. I need to talk to someone neutral about it."

"Oh, dear," said Grace. "Yes, tell us."

Louisa explained about how she worried she and Rotherfeld had little in common and how her attempts to engage him in conversation had not gone especially well, and the cold fish kisses, and then she explained what had happened with Fletcher.

"Wait," said Grace when Louisa was done. "Go back. You

kissed Fletcher."

"Yes."

"And?" asked Adele.

"It was amazing. I did not know kisses could be like that."

Grace made swooning noises. "Okay. So, you kissed him, and it was much better than kissing your actual fiancé, but then Fletcher offered for you, but only if you broke your engagement with Rotherfeld and couldn't find anyone else?"

"Yes. He'd pity marry me."

"Oh, Fletcher," said Grace.

Adele stared at her. "Oh, *Fletcher*? You mean *oh, Louisa*. What a dreadful thing for him to say! I'm sorry he said that to you."

"Fletcher's a fool," said Grace.

"I'll say," said Louisa.

"I see two possibilities," said Grace. "Either Fletcher feels sorry for you and has offered to marry you as a last resort because he cares enough to offer but not enough to follow through. He reasons that, even if you break things off with Rotherfeld, you'll find another husband."

"Easier said than done."

"*Or*," said Grace. "He cares for you and *wants* to marry you but didn't want to be presumptuous, so he tried to thread the needle and failed."

"I doubt it's that second thing," said Louisa. "He's never expressed any desire for me beyond friendship. But even if that were true, it's the silliest thing I've ever heard. He doesn't want to be presumptuous? Why do men not just say what they mean?"

"He may not understand your doubts about Rotherfeld," said Adele.

"I don't see how I could have been clearer."

"Men are foolish creatures," Grace said. "I love my husband, but he can be an idiot. We took the baby to visit my parents this week, and Owen tried to leave the house without the pram. When I explained to him that he could not, in fact, just carry the baby to my parents' house because Dafydd has grown quite heavy, Owen did not believe me."

"I hesitate to call my husband foolish because Hugh suffered a head injury from which he will probably never fully recover, and that is not his fault, but sometimes he mixes up the name of our son with the name of our dog."

"My father did that when I was growing up," said Louisa. "Called me Rosie, which was the name of our cocker spaniel. So that is not unique to Hugh."

"My guess?" Grace said. "I don't know Fletcher as well as you do, obviously, but he and my husband are close, so I see him a great deal, and I'd wager that Fletcher misspoke when he…offered to take you off Rotherfeld's hands. I know, for example, that Fletcher has been worried that your marriage will mean you will spend less time together."

"But even if that's true, I'm not sure Fletcher wanting to take me to the opera is a better reason to marry than Rotherfeld being rich and handsome."

"Fair," said Grace.

"But Fletcher cares for Louisa," said Adele. "They may not be in love now, but they could fall in love and be happy."

"The two of you seemed awkward at dinner the other night, and I suppose I know why now. Have you spoken since The Kiss?" asked Grace.

"No, not really. I was cross with him. I still am."

"Well, let me put it this way," said Grace. "If it were solely up to you, would you rather marry Rotherfeld, or would you rather marry Fletcher?"

"Fletcher." His name flew out of her mouth without her making a conscious thought, but she realized she didn't have to think about it. Given a choice between Daniel and Fletcher, especially after that kiss, her choice would be Fletcher. If he actually wanted her, that was.

"Then I think you should have a frank conversation with Fletcher and find out if he feels the same. Ask him if he truly wants to marry you or if he was just offering as a worst-case scenario."

"But if he does want to marry me, what of Rotherfeld?" Would they ever recover from the scandal? Would Daniel grow to hate her?

"He's a very good-looking man," said Adele. "I expect he'll have no trouble finding another wife. And he is coming this way so we should find a far less interesting topic of conversation. Needlepoint, say."

Louisa laughed. What a predicament she found herself in now.

Daniel approached their little group with a smiled. "Your Grace. My lady. It is agreeable to see you again."

"Thank you," said Adele, whose manners were more polished than Grace's. "Lovely to see you as well."

"Yes, nice to see you," said Grace. "We shall return your fiancée to you now."

"Much obliged. Will we see you at the Atherton ball a few days hence?"

Grace and Adele glanced at each other. "I suppose you will," said Grace. "I had quite forgotten about it, to be honest. My family keeps robbing me of my sleep and it is making me feel empty-headed, you see. My son has grown old enough to sleep through the night, or so the doctor tells me, but Dafydd does not seem to know that."

Daniel tilted his head like he didn't understand a word she'd just said.

"Swynford and I will be there," Adele said, nodding at Daniel. "Let me take the countess home now so she can sleep properly."

After they left, and Louisa and Daniel turned to walk back toward Louisa's home, Daniel said, "What was that about?"

"Grace told me once that she thought becoming a mother had robbed her of some of her faculties. She suspects it is because she does not sleep as well anymore. She has taken an…unorthodox approach to child-rearing in that she has a nanny but does not rely on her. So her son sleeps in an adjacent room and Grace wakes up when he does."

"What does Caernarfon think of this?"

Louisa fought back a physical reaction. Why should Caernarfon get a say? Instead, she said, "He allows it, I suppose, because he loves his family."

"Hmm."

"Did I know we were attending the Atherton ball?" Louisa asked.

"Did I not invite you? I plan to attend because a mate of mine from my Cambridge days will be in town, and I would be honored if you'd accompany me."

Louisa plastered a smile on her face. "Then I shall be there."

IT WAS NEARLY impossible to get a single woman to whom one was not engaged alone, especially once her parents began to suspect one's motives.

Two notes that Fletcher had sent to Louisa had been thwarted by her mother, who'd curtly told him Louisa was not available, but the third—which Fletcher hired a boy to deliver directly into Louisa's hand—was returned with a note from Louisa saying the best she could do was the Atherton ball.

It was the opposite of his request, which had been to speak to her in private.

He stared at the note and then pocketed it before he left for the club.

He asked his driver to let him out a few blocks from the club so that he could walk to clear his head. He'd spent the better part of the last day trying to mentally rehearse exactly what he wanted to say to Louisa, but maybe he needed something else to obsess over.

As he walked, he was struck by a memory from when he was a teenager.

Louisa must have been thirteen or fourteen at the time, and

Fletcher was home after his first year at Oxford. They were too old by then to play as they had as children, but he let Louisa challenge him to a game of chess. While she was setting up the game, Fletcher's mother pulled him aside and said that Louisa fancied him, which Fletcher had instantly dismissed. But then, when they were partway through the game, Louisa asked him who he was going to marry.

"I don't know," he said honestly. "I reckon that's something I can deal with after I finish school. It's not like there are many women at Oxford."

"You could marry me."

"You're too young."

She rolled her eyes. "I know that. I mean, when I'm old enough."

"Why?"

"Why what?"

"Why should I marry you?"

She shrugged. "We get along. We understand each other. I'm smarter than you."

"You are not!"

"I'm about to defeat you at chess."

"No, you aren't." He moved his rook. "Check."

"Fletcher." She moved her knight. "Checkmate."

He'd instantly forgotten the conversation and had never brought it up again, but he wondered now if it really was that simple.

And she was definitely smarter than he was.

He arrived at the club and found his friends. Owen handed him whiskey before he sat down.

Fletcher was so lost in thought he barely heard anything his friends said, but he sipped his whisky and then noticed that Hugh was clearly in his cups, swaying in his chair.

"Hugh?" Fletcher asked. "Is everything all right?"

"Adele is expecting," Hugh said, sounding dazed. "I found out this afternoon."

"He's a little overwhelmed," said Owen.

"I suppose I always knew we would have more children, but not so soon. I was just getting used to the first one."

"It'll be a little girl," said Lark. "Just to terrorize you."

"I will run every male under eighteen out of England if I need to," said Hugh. "Send them to Australia, I say." His speech was a little slurred, so Hugh was definitely drunk.

Fletcher laughed. "Well, all right, then. A healthy attitude."

Hugh sat back in his chair. He motioned for the discussion to carry on.

Owen looked at Fletcher expectantly. "Have you proposed to Louisa yet?"

Fletcher sighed. "No. Her mother keeps thwarting me. But Louisa promised to speak with me at the Atherton ball."

"Oh, that," said Owen. "Grace sent our acceptance, but I keep forgetting it's happening."

"I've never much liked Atherton," said Lark. "He's very loud."

Owen laughed at that. "Isn't his wife your cousin?"

"Distantly," said Lark. "She's got some charm. It runs in the family." He preened. "But he's like a walking headache. I think I accepted the invitation, too, though."

Hugh rolled his eyes. He turned to Fletcher and asked, "Why is Louisa's mother thwarting you?"

"I don't know." Although Fletcher suspected she saw him as a threat to Louisa's future marriage.

"Because Rotherfeld is younger, richer, better looking, and more connected than you are," said Lark. "Only the best for Lady Louisa, so she is doing everything in her power to make sure Louisa and Rotherfeld both show up at the altar."

"Younger, richer, *and* better looking? You wound me," said Fletcher.

"Am I wrong?" asked Lark.

Fletcher sighed. "I don't know for certain about him being richer, but you are probably right that Lady Petty will allow nothing to interfere with the wedding."

"Lady Petty wants only the best husband for her daughter, and on paper, Rotherfeld is very appealing."

Fletcher understood all this, but he wished Lark would not rub it in. "I know. But do I want to tussle with a mama of the *ton*?"

"Do you want the woman you love or not?" asked Lark.

"I do."

"Then you'll have to tussle."

"Wait," said Owen. "You plan to propose to Louisa at the Atherton ball?"

"No," said Fletcher. "I plan to apologize for saying something she…took the wrong way."

"Was offended by," corrected Lark.

"Yes. I said something that offended her, but I did not intend it the way she took it. I plan to apologize, and then possibly tell her that her fiancé is…of Lark's kind."

Hugh's eyes went wide. "How do you know that?"

"Beresford," said Lark.

Hugh nodded. "I suppose he would know."

"We should really have our own club," said Lark.

"I believe they call those molly houses," said Owen.

"Something more reputable," Lark replied. "Like this, but for men seeking other men, and not so seedy or full of young prostitutes as a molly house. There is a club that has an open policy of men being able to find whatever they desire, but I've always found it a bit…well, I wouldn't want to touch anything inside, let's put it that way."

"*Anyway*," said Fletcher. "I plan to talk to Louisa and tell her that I believe she and Rotherfeld are not well suited for several reasons, and that I love her and want to marry her if that's what she wants, too, and generally make the argument that I am a superior choice to Rotherfeld, but I do not plan to get on one knee or anything. That would be gauche, don't you think?"

"The way Rotherfeld announced their engagement?" said

Owen. "A little too loudly, I should add. Yes. Gauche. Not the done thing."

"I fear," said Lark, quietly, "that he is using Louisa to avoid being found out, and she deserves better than that."

Fletcher had come to think the same thing, which made him think Louisa was about to be trapped in a loveless marriage to a man she found dull. And every time he rehearsed his big apology speech, he ended up rambling, but he knew he needed to be more direct. He should just tell Louisa how he felt plainly. He loved her. Rotherfeld had ulterior motives. She should marry him.

"Lark?" said Hugh, cutting through Fletcher's thoughts.

"Yes?"

"You are being careful, right? I know you and Anthony are speaking again. I'd like for you to avoid that fate as well."

"I am always careful," said Lark. "And my relationship to Anthony is not dissimilar from Fletcher's to Louisa. I love him, but he's not capable of loving me back right now. I have not so much as touched him in more than a year."

"We are pathetic," said Fletcher.

"Indeed," said Lark, sipping a cup of tea.

Chapter Twelve

"WOULD YOU LIKE to meet Henry?"

Lark found the question an odd one—could one truly "meet" a human who was less than a month old?—but Anthony looked at him with such earnest hope that Lark said, "Yes."

Lark's mother had sent Lark to Anthony's house with a hamper of gifts—"I know you are friends, and he must be struggling with a loss like that," she'd said—so here Lark was. The hamper had a ham, several bags of sweets, and a great deal of tea. "The essence of life," Lark had joked as Anthony opened it.

And now Lark was following Anthony up the stairs to the nursery. When they reached it, Anthony dismissed Mrs. Church, telling her to rest for a bit.

The baby was awake, but quiet. Anthony picked him up and cradled the small boy in his arms. Something in Lark's chest tightened.

"I did not know my father," Anthony said. "He was much older than my mother, so perhaps he was more traditional, but during my childhood, he was just this man who lived in our house but who was generally to be avoided. And then he died when I was seventeen, and…well. Hard to miss a man I'd spoken with maybe a dozen times in my life." He looked down at the baby. "I decided, when Henry was born, that I would be a better father than that. That I would get to know him, and be available to him, and that I'd accept him no matter what he grows up to be. And when Matilda passed, I made a promise."

Lark steeled himself and walked behind Anthony so that he could get a better look at the baby.

"It's just me and him. We're our family. And I will always be here for him."

Henry had huge blue eyes and stared at Anthony as if he were the most fascinating thing he'd ever seen. Lark knew the feeling. Henry had a bit of wispy hair, with one big curl that looped around his forehead, and he had a scrunched up little baby face. He had a chin dimple like Anthony's, and a little button nose, and he really was very cute.

"He looks a bit like you," Lark said.

"Does he?"

"If you squint."

Anthony laughed softly.

Henry stretched and yawned, and it was one of the most darling things Lark had ever seen.

"Would you like to hold him?" Anthony asked.

"I've never held a baby before."

"I hadn't either until he was born. Here, hold out your hands."

Lark did as he was told.

"Hold his head," Anthony said as he passed the baby over to Lark. "That's the most delicate part of him, according to Mrs. Church. Then tuck your arm under… yes, just like that. See? You're a natural."

"He's very small."

"He's three weeks old."

Lark was changed in that moment. He'd never held a baby before and had never wanted to, but *this* baby was special. He seemed very small and fragile, but then he yawned again and looked so much like an old man that it made Lark want to laugh. Then the baby seemed to settle into Lark's arms and his eyes drifted closed.

This baby was Anthony's son. He was an important part of Anthony now. The same Anthony who had told Lark frequently that he didn't want children. This little boy existed primarily because Anthony's mother didn't want his title passed on to a cousin, and because Lark had ended their relationship a year ago, but holding Henry made Lark feel he'd done the right thing, because had it not been for his actions, this precious child might not exist.

"He seems like a miracle," said Lark.

"Yes. I think that constantly. And I feel…that is, since his mother is gone, I want to raise him well all the more. I'll have help, of course, but a child should have his parents. Or at least one of them."

Lark was impressed by Anthony's maturity, under the circumstances. Prior to all this, Anthony had been lighthearted; he loved fun and mischief and seemed to have few cares in the world. He'd never seemed especially grounded or responsible. But he'd taken to fatherhood.

"I'm in awe of you," Lark said.

"How so?"

"It would be easy for you to leave little Henry here in the arms of his nurse and return to your old life, but you've embraced being a father to this child. I admire that."

"Thank you."

Lark looked down at the baby again. He was fully asleep in Lark's arms. And some voice Lark's head whispered that, if he loved Anthony, then he'd have to love this little boy, too. That if they had a future together, then this child would be Lark's, in a way. Maybe he was getting ahead of himself, but he'd need to think about whether this was what he wanted.

"He's a sweet baby," Lark said, handing him back to Anthony.

"Not always. Sometimes he screams like the world is ending and nothing will console him. He keeps Mrs. Church up at night.

His nappies are among the foulest things I have ever smelled. You're lucky. He must have just eaten and his need to nap overcame his fear of strangers. Or he likes the look of you. Can't say I blame him." Anthony winked and then laid the boy back down in his cradle.

Lark could see the future, somehow. Of Anthony and this boy playing together. Of Anthony teaching him manners or the things he needed to be a man. Of Anthony and Henry having a friendship of a sorts.

Would Lark be a part of that future? Could this little boy be Lark's, too?

"You're thinking very hard," said Anthony.

"Would you want me to be a part of his life?" Lark asked, gesturing at Henry.

"Yes," Anthony said without hesitation. "I thought about asking you to be his godfather."

"Oh. Me?"

"I think it would depend a lot on the nature of our relation-ship, which is why I haven't asked, but if you want to be a part of his life, then yes, I'd like for you to be his godfather."

"If I am a part of your life, then I want to be a part of his, too."

Anthony smiled. "Good. I'm glad for that. I've been so busy with Matilda's affairs that I haven't scheduled the christening yet, but I must do that soon, at least according to my mother. I want you to be there for that."

"I will."

Mrs. Church returned. Anthony gestured toward the door. "Perhaps we should let him sleep."

As they walked back downstairs, Lark said, "I admit, all of this is a bit overwhelming and unexpected for me, just a fraction of what I'm sure it has been for you, but it's not terrifying."

A huff of laughter burst out of Anthony. "*I'm* terrified."

"I just mean, I've been thinking a lot about what I want my relationship with you to be in the future, and it's clear that if we're part of each other's lives, then I will get to know Henry."

"Yes. That is why I wanted you to see him. See how you felt about it."

"Honestly, my instinct is to gather all of you up and put you in my carriage and drive to Scotland where we can live anonymously on a farm far from other people, where no one would bother us. To the devil with London Society."

"Believe me, I've had the same thought. But this is all new for you. You should take the time to think about what you want."

"I will, truly."

"Good." Anthony led Lark into the sitting room. "Do you have plans tonight?"

"Not tonight. Tomorrow is the Atherton ball."

"Yes. Lady Atherton sent me a personal note with her invitation, saying she'd very much like to see me. I suppose I shall put on my weeds and attend."

Lark raised an eyebrow. "A personal note?"

"Her brother and I were school chums. I used to haunt their dinner parties regularly. She claims in her note to find me delightful company. I don't know if I can live up to that, but I wrote her back that I'd attend."

"I suppose rejoining society must feel good."

"It's a distraction, at least." Anthony sighed. "The rules of mourning are…difficult. I have no wish to cause a scandal, but I hate wearing black."

Lark chuckled. "You'll be back in your colorful waistcoats soon enough. Oh, I forgot, I brought you a gift."

"Another? Was that ham not enough?"

Lark walked over to the side table, where he'd left the box he'd brought in with the hamper. He handed the box to Anthony.

"What is this for?"

"I saw it at the tailor's shop and thought of you. Still appropriate for this period in your life, but perhaps not so boring."

Anthony lifted the lid of the box. Inside was a silk cravat, crisp white with thin black stripes. "This is very fine silk."

"I thought so, too."

"This is lovely. Thank you, Lark."

"It seems to me I missed your birthday during the period we were not speaking."

"I missed yours, too, but did not get you a gift."

"I expect nothing."

Anthony smiled. "Where has all your concern about getting caught and hanged gone? All those reasons you gave for why we should not be together?"

"I find that many of those reasons no longer matter. A year of utter misery has set me right, I suppose. If we should both perish, then so be it. I'd rather have you in my life than go on as I had."

"If that's the case, perhaps I should ask Swynford to be Henry's godfather."

"I can't tell if you're jesting."

"I can't tell if you are, either."

Lark laughed and shook his head. "I do want to be Henry's godfather, and I promise to take the responsibility seriously, but perhaps I've become a bit fatalist. If I'm to be charged with sodomy, then so be it. I couldn't mount much of a defense."

"I'd hire you the best solicitor money can buy."

"I'd do the same for you."

Anthony reached over and squeezed Lark's hand. "I hope you don't think me a tease."

"I don't."

"I feel like I've led you on a bit. We have this rapport, and I'm used to flirting with you, but I'm not quite there yet."

"There's no rush."

"The night of the funeral, you said you love me."

"I do."

Anthony nodded. "It still feels though a part of me is broken. I've hardly felt myself for weeks. My wife has been gone less than a month."

"I promise, I have no expectations."

"I do love you, though."

Lark smiled at that. "If we do this again, I want to get it right. Therefore, there will be no pressure. When you feel ready, speak to me. Until that time comes, I am here as your friend."

"And I appreciate your friendship."

"I will help ensure young Henry grows up to be a fine man. Regardless of what happens between us, I want to be a support to him."

"So soon? You just met him."

Lark shrugged. "Perhaps I've gone soft."

"Perhaps you have. Perhaps we both have."

Chapter Thirteen

"THE DUKE OF Rotherfeld and Lady Louisa Petty!"

It bothered Louisa still that Daniel had publicly announced their engagement at a well-attended ball and not quietly in the newspapers, because now everyone in the *ton* knew they were engaged. It made breaking the engagement more difficult, but Louisa was beginning to wonder if that was the idea.

Daniel escorted Louisa into the Atherton ballroom, and they greeted acquaintances on the way. Then she spotted the Earl of Waring speaking with the Marquess of Beresford, the latter in head-to-toe black.

Louisa had not seen Beresford in quite some time, but she knew Fletcher had gone to the marchioness's funeral. Seeing Beresford in mourning clothes was a bit jarring; he wore such colorful clothing normally.

"Let us greet the Marquess of Beresford. I have not seen him all Season."

"Oh. Ah, or we could dance."

"Do you not like Beresford?"

"We, er, don't know each other well. I haven't spoken to him in ages."

"Humor me. His wife just died. I believe this is the first time he's really been out all Season. I should like to pay my respects."

Louisa didn't know Beresford well, but she knew Lark, since

he was a close friend of Fletcher's. She saw no reason why she should not speak to them. She basically dragged Daniel over to where they stood.

She greeted them. Lark took her hand and kissed her knuckles. "Lovely to see you, Lady Louisa."

Daniel cleared his throat behind her.

"Lord Waring, Lord Beresford, I believe you know my fiancé, the Duke of Rotherfeld."

Lark raised an eyebrow and said, "Rotherfeld. Good to see you again."

Daniel put a possessive hand on Louisa's waist. "Waring." He turned toward Beresford. "Anthony. Condolences for your recent loss."

The use of Beresford's Christian name in such a formal setting struck Louisa as a little odd. Did Daniel know him better than he let on? And if so, why would he lie about that?

"Thank you, Your Grace," said Beresford. "I must say, I can't recall the last time we ran into each other. I have not been out much this season, but I don't recall seeing you in a few years."

"I spent a year on the Continent after the last time we saw each other. And perhaps we move in different circles now."

"Perhaps." But Beresford had a mischievous glint in his eye. "When is the wedding?"

"A fortnight. Saturday."

"Oh, that will be lovely. The weather is starting to get warmer, so it won't be too cold. I am fond of London at this time of year."

"Right."

Beresford seemed to be on a roll. "Oh, I've just recalled the last time we saw each other." He glanced at Louisa and winked. Winked! "The house party in Kent in '14. Was it at Lord Roscoe's estate?"

"It was," Daniel ground out through his teeth.

"That whole party was a scandal. Too much for this delicate lady's ears."

Lark stared at Beresford. "Do I want to know?"

"I assure you, you do not."

"A folly of my misspent youth," Daniel said to Louisa. "You do not want to know, either."

Of course, that only piqued Louisa's curiosity.

"My dear Lady Louisa," Beresford said. "Please save me a dance. I'd like the full experience of attending a ball and have not danced with anyone since my late wife."

"Oh. Of course, my lord."

Beresford claimed a dance on Louisa's dance card. Lark did, too, although she suspected he just did because he didn't know what else to do. Daniel grunted and escorted her away.

"You are much in demand."

"You'd be smart to claim the dance you want now, then." She held up her card.

Daniel claimed a waltz.

Louisa spent the next half hour dancing, mostly with Daniel, but also with Lark and with Hugh, and at last with Beresford, who took the opportunity to tell her, "I don't mean to create trouble between you and your fiancé."

"Somehow, I do not believe you."

"If perhaps I choose to highlight a few unsavory bits of Rotherfeld's past, it is only because Fletcher wants to antagonize him, and I am fond of Fletcher."

"I am fond of Fletcher, too."

"Perhaps not in the same way."

"No," she conceded. "Fletcher aside, I am confused, because either your implication about what happened in Kent is not what I think it is, or Rotherfeld lied to me."

"I will concede that the adventures at Lord Roscoe's party were perhaps not what you're thinking or anything you could conceive of, so it is perhaps not the sort of trouble you might have asked him about in the past. And truly, I exaggerated, it is not so bad. Mostly too much drink and young men behaving egregiously, as young men are wont to do."

"I cannot parse 'behaving egregiously.'"

"Perhaps Rotherfeld will share the details with you some day, but honestly, they are not important. And, anyway, I've always found Rotherfeld rather prudish, so it is possible *I* misbehaved and he was just…also there."

"That I believe."

"Ha." Beresford winked again.

As they walked off the floor, Louisa said, "I am deeply sorry for your loss. It must have been terrible."

"It was, it was. And I miss her dearly. But my baby son has been a bright light. Lark—that is, Lord Waring—has agreed to be his godfather. I can send you the details about the christening if you like, although you might be on your honeymoon by then."

"We are not leaving London until the end of the Season."

"Splendid. And you can leave Rotherfeld at home if he'd prefer not to attend a christening, although I should disclose that Young Master Henry is extremely adorable and he will make you want to have a brood of your own children as soon as possible."

Louisa laughed. "I look forward to seeing him, then."

"I could use something to drink and perhaps a card game. If you'll excuse me." Beresford bowed deeply and then left.

Louisa looked around. She spotted Daniel speaking with a man she did not recognize. They laughed together, and Daniel put a hand on the man's arm in a way that looked odd-ly…familiar? More than that. Not merely friendly. Flirtatious? Intimate? Was this the schoolmate he'd mentioned?

Louisa approached slowly.

"It was so muddy, and his boots were so thoroughly stuck, that when he walked forward, his boots came clean off, leaving him with just his stockinged feet in the mud," the man was saying.

"Oh, dear," Daniel said, still laughing. Then he spotted Louisa. "Richard, this is my fiancée, Lady Louisa Petty. Louisa, this is my dear old friend, Lieutenant Richard Hanley."

Louisa allowed her knuckles to be kissed, and then said,

"Hanley?" She searched her mental list of peerage names. "Any relation to the Earl of Chatterton?"

"My older brother," said Mr. Hanley.

"Richard serves with His Majesty's Army. He fought at Waterloo."

"Oh, indeed. That is remarkable. How heroic of you."

Hanley smiled and nodded.

"Do you still serve?"

"I do, although we are not presently at war. Mostly I turn up at a camp outside London every few months to march around and do drills."

"In case we do go to war?"

"Yes, although that is not currently a pending possibility as far as I know."

Louisa nodded and searched her mind for a topic. "You do not normally live in London?" Louisa could not recall ever seeing him before.

"No, I prefer the country. I generally stay at Chatterton House, which is well north of London."

"Are you married?"

"Louisa, you need not..."

But Hanley smiled. "It's all right. I am not married. Although I am afraid of the debutantes' mothers, so let's not spread that information too far."

Louisa smiled, mostly to be polite. "If you change your mind about that, put your uniform on. The women of the *ton* would swoon for you."

"I'll keep that in mind."

Daniel was giving her a look like he wanted her to shut up. Perhaps she had spoken too much or pushed too far, but Hanley did not seem offended.

Still. "Well, I will leave your gents to your conversation and go see if I can find some lemonade."

"Do not stray too far, my love," said Daniel.

"I won't."

She walked over to the refreshments table, wondering the whole way what the relationship between Daniel and Richard really was. Likely they were just old friends, but she'd never seen Daniel behave that way with anyone.

She was probably inventing things, drawing ridiculous conclusions, but as she poured herself a lemonade, she found herself looking around for Fletcher. They may be on the outs right now, but he'd be honest with her if he knew anything.

ANTHONY TOSSED HIS cards on the table after making a disgusted grunt. "Every last one of you cheats."

"Beresford is just mad because he forgot how to count cards," said Atherton, raking in his winnings.

"It's true. I am out of practice at fleecing you all out of your money." Anthony yawned. "Let me just say, though, that this one night of freedom has been a delight. Having an infant at home is no jest."

"Lady Atherton didn't get a good night's sleep for a year after our daughter was born," Atherton agreed.

"I worry constantly I will do something wrong, and my poor son will grow up to be, I don't know, an eccentric. A circus performer. An *accountant.*"

"Perish the thought," said Lark, counting his scant winnings.

Anthony stood. "Well, gents, now that you have all of my coin, I do believe it might be time to call it a night."

Everyone else followed Anthony's lead, collected their winnings and wandered off. Atherton moved to the next table and bought into the game happening there, but most of their party left the room.

Anthony stretched and yawned again.

"Did you walk here?" Lark asked.

Anthony nodded. He lived three whole houses away, which

was not worth the bother of his carriage.

"I believe I shall walk home with you. Make sure you avoid any ruffians lurking about in the bushes."

"I'd be grateful, I'm sure," said Anthony.

They left the card room, made their way through the ballroom to say their goodbyes, and then left the party.

It had been an interesting night. In some ways, Anthony was back in his element. Lark had spent a lot of the night in his orbit, and Anthony had been in his old self—charming, witty, self-deprecating. Some of the light had come back to him. It was an enormous relief to see Anthony looking so well. But Lark could also tell that Anthony was bone-deep tired, that some of his wit and charm was masking sadness and fatigue. The latter was subtle, and most who did not know Anthony well would not have spotted it, but Lark could see it.

"Did you take your carriage?" Anthony asked once they were outside.

Lark lived nearby as well, and walking was hardly a burden. "I did not. I find, especially in weather like this, I prefer to walk. It is a ridiculous show of wealth to take a carriage such a short distance when the weather is this fine. Perhaps if I were a woman with all those skirts and the little, delicate shoes that are fashionable right now…"

Anthony looked around and, apparently feeling satisfied with what he saw—which was nothing; there were no people or animals on the street—said, "So Rotherfeld is a piece of work."

"Anything aside from the obvious?"

"The house party in Kent that I mentioned—"

"It was one of Roscoe's affairs, you said? I went to one once. I can imagine." Lord Roscoe periodically held house parties at his country estate that were mostly an excuse to put a lot of beautiful people under the same roof so that they could have sex with each other in various combinations. It had proved too overwhelming for Lark, but he could picture a younger Anthony flourishing there.

"I was young," Anthony said with a shrug.

"Not *that* young. You said it was only four years ago."

Anthony grinned. Lark was happy to see it. Anthony said, "Well, let's just say, I was not interested in anything so conventional as a monogamous relationship until relatively recently. I've matured, you see."

"Of course.

They walked a few paces toward Anthony's house in companionable silence.

"That other fellow Rotherfeld was talking to, Lieutenant Hanley?" Anthony said.

"Chatterton's brother?"

"The same. He and Rotherfeld have been thick as thieves for a long time. Rotherfeld… he brought Hanley to our bed once."

Lark laughed. "Your life."

"I know, I know. I promise all that is behind me. I am just saying, that night, I felt a bit extraneous. I believe that Rotherfeld and Hanley have been lovers on and off for a very long time. That night they seemed to have eyes only for each other."

"In other words, Rotherfeld is about to do what I would not let you do."

When Anthony married, Lark had expected him to be faithful to his wife and said as much. Rotherfeld seemed to feel no such compulsion.

"Indeed," said Anthony. "The thing of it is, Rotherfeld and Hanley do not seem to require any sort of commitment or exclusive relationship, which is their prerogative, and I think it's because Hanley is so often overseas. Back in those days, when Rotherfeld and I had our brief affair, Hanley was serving in Wellington's army on the Continent. So it is likely that they do not require fealty to each other because they are so often separated by geography and Hanley's obligations to the army and, prior to Waterloo, the decent odds Hanley would meet his end on a battlefield. Thankfully, Napoleon has been dispatched with, so Hanley's life is no longer in danger. But that does not bode well for Louisa if she goes through with the wedding."

"Let us hope Fletcher follows through tonight, if that is the case."

They arrived at Anthony's home. Anthony said, "You may as well come inside."

"I thought you were tired."

"I am, although I was also starting to…well, let us just say, my social muscles have atrophied. I was starting to feel that I'd had enough of the ball. But I never tire of your company."

So Lark followed Anthony inside. The butler took Lark's coat, and all of this was achingly familiar. When Lark and Anthony had been meeting regularly for assignations, one of them always followed the other home after a ball or some other occasion. Lark did not think he'd be spending the night with Anthony, but that was all right. He'd settle for further conversation.

He'd seen the spark in Anthony tonight, like his old self was starting to break through again.

In the sitting room, alone again, Lark said, "I hate that my jealousy spikes when you speak of your past."

"You have nothing to fear. I have very little respect for Rotherfeld."

"Do you have regrets?"

Anthony appeared to consider it. "About my past dalliances? No, not really. Back in those days, everything was light and easy. I was young and stupid and fearless, so I did what brought me pleasure without much consideration of the consequences. I wish I still had a bit of that fearlessness."

"I feel like I'm the one who took it away."

"Perhaps, but I'd really rather nothing happened to me now. Henry needs me."

"That is true."

"And perhaps you need me."

That was definitely true, but Lark didn't say anything.

Anthony fiddled with the cart in the corner that held his

liquor but seemed to think better of it. Instead, he walked over to stand with Lark in the center of the room. "You've never judged me, you know."

"I definitely have."

Anthony smirked. "I mean, you don't judge my past indiscretions.

"It would make me a hypocrite."

"Lark, I think we should face the fact that we are two damaged people who have no business together and yet we are here, and I can't say I regret it. You still love me."

"Yes. I'll never stop."

"I've never stopped loving you, either."

Lark sighed and decided to take that in and savor it. He closed his eyes for a moment.

"You told me to marry, so I did. I did it for you and for my mother and to help Matilda. And I suppose I did it for myself, not for love but because I felt an obligation. That is a foolish reason to marry."

"And yet people have done just that for centuries."

"My point is just that I love *you*, you fool, and if I could, I would marry you tomorrow, but that is not the world we live in. At the same time, I feel so much pain and guilt and fear over everything that has happened in the last year and will happen in the next, and I don't know where to put it."

Lark took a few steps closer to Anthony, close enough to touch him. So Lark put his hands on Anthony's shoulders and then ran them up his neck to cup his cheeks. "Let me help you," Lark said.

Then Lark kissed Anthony for the first time in a year.

Anthony sighed into his mouth and put anchoring hands on Lark's waist. Lark parted his lips and tasted Anthony, and it was at once exciting and familiar. Kissing Anthony felt like coming home.

"You were right, you know," Anthony said after they parted gently.

"About?"

"Charlie Ingle."

Lark cursed. He of course knew the story of Charlie Ingle. Lark had known Charlie mostly by reputation. He was the youngest son of a baron, the scion of an absurdly wealthy if not especially politically powerful family. He'd run afoul of someone, was the way Lark had heard the story, perhaps won a bet against a vindictive man. Lark wasn't certain of the details. But all it took was one man going to the authorities to explain that Charlie Ingle was, in fact, one of London's most notorious sodomites for Charlie to be hanged. Lark had avoided the execution, although he'd heard after the fact that it was a spectacle.

Lark had thought society had grown more sophisticated than public executions, but apparently not if it meant hanging a sodomite.

In point of fact, the city had put more sodomites to death than murderers so far this year.

Lark and Anthony had some insulation due to their wealth, power, and connections, but Lark found, until recently, the constant fear that he'd run afoul of the wrong man to be a weight on his shoulders that felt too overwhelming.

But perhaps the fact that Anthony had, in fact, married and fathered a child won him some goodwill.

And perhaps Lark would rather die than live without Anthony.

He pressed his face against Anthony's shoulder. "I didn't want to be right."

"I know. And I want to be able to say that Charlie Ingle was reckless. I mean, everyone knew what he was."

"Did you ever—?"

"With Charlie? No. I don't believe I ever actually spoke to him. He stopped coming to society events years ago. But this is my point. I recognize the dangers, Lark, I do, but I also think Charlie Ingle acted in a way that was too risky. You and I, we can keep our relationship quiet and disclose it to only people we trust and… I've given some thought to leaving London, perhaps for good."

"You're not serious."

"A year ago, I never would have entertained the possibility, but Henry changes things. I'm all he has. I can't take risks that I used to feel I could. But at the same time, now that I know the unique misery of living without you? I can't do that either."

"Are we at an impasse?"

"No. I view it as a turning point. I will do anything to keep my family safe, and you, Lark, are my family. So if I have to leave London to keep us all safe, then so be it."

Lark kissed Anthony again. He had no intention of leaving Anthony again because he knew how miserable that would make him, but he'd do anything to keep Anthony and little Henry safe, too.

"I love you," Lark said.

"Mm. I love you, too. And I'd invite you to bed, but I believe I'll need to have a chat with my staff before I can allow that. Some of the staff came from my other house and are… aware of us, but I need to stop any gossip before it starts."

"So that's it. We're picking up where we left off a year ago."

Anthony frowned. "Not exactly. This is…whatever is happening here will be difficult to navigate. But I don't want to waste any more time doing what I *should* be doing. Life is too short. What I *want* to do is be with you and raise my son. I don't know how to make all that happen yet, but I am determined to try."

"And you forgive me for my unspeakable idiocy in pushing you away?"

Anthony nodded slowly. "Somehow, I do. I always understood why, I just disagreed with you. But then they hanged Charlie Ingle, and I thought, well, maybe Lark had a point. And I married Matilda, which meant that she spent the last year of her life free of her terrible family. I think she was happy, at least. And she gave me Henry, and I don't know how to express it, but I love that little boy more than I've ever loved anything—even you, no offense—and I am grateful for that. So some good things came of the events you set in motion when you kicked me out of your house."

Lark laughed softly. He put his arms around Anthony and pulled him close. "I'm so sorry about everything."

"I know." Anthony ran a hand up and down Lark's back, a gesture Lark found intensely comforting. "I know. I am, too. So let's make the most of the opportunity we have now."

"When did you get so clever?"

"Lord knows. Some kind of temporary condition, I think. I'm sure it will wear off."

Lark laughed into Anthony's shoulder. He loved this man. He intended not to let him go again.

BACK AT THE Atherton ball, Fletcher spoke with Owen and tried to pretend he wasn't looking for Louisa. He'd seen her dancing with Rotherfeld earlier but had since lost track of her.

"…but then Ardsley said he was writing a novel, so…" Owen was saying. Fletcher wasn't really listening. Owen had been telling some story about the Duke of Ardsley that Fletcher could not make himself care about.

Louisa appeared quite suddenly, as if she'd manifested out of thin air. "Greystone. May I have a word?"

"Yes, of course."

Owen frowned. "This is good gossip I'm giving you, and you haven't heard a word I have you?"

"I'm sure it was fascinating. Go dance with your wife. Tell me later."

Louisa led Fletcher out of the crush of the ballroom. "You men gossip more than we women do."

"Gentlemen certainly do. It helps us pass our idle time. But you did not come to me for gossip."

"No."

"I'd like to speak where we cannot be heard," Fletcher said, ignoring the barb. "Do the Athertons have a terrace?"

Just then, Lady Atherton appeared. "Oh, Lord Greystone. Lady Louisa. Have you seen my garden?"

Fletcher glanced at Louisa, who had a glint in her eye. "We have not."

"Oh, let me show you. It's magic at night."

It turned out to be serendipitous. Lady Atherton led them outside and gave them a tour of her small but quite grand garden. Gas lamps lit a path through the center, and a marble bench looked like a good place to have a conversation. And then, just as Fletcher was trying to work out how to get rid of Lady Atherton, a woman stuck her head out of the house and said, "Lady Atherton, I need your help at once."

"Oh dear," said Lady Atherton. "I suppose I must go then."

"Do you mind if we sit in the garden for a few minutes?" asked Fletcher. "I'm finding the cool air to be a nice relief from the crush of the ballroom."

"It's truly a lovely party," said Louisa. "We'll return in a few minutes."

"Oh, yes, of course. Stay as long as you like." Lady Atherton smiled. "Oh, I remember when you two were children."

"Oh," said Louisa, sounding startled.

"The two of you were always best of friends."

"Yes," said Fletcher.

"And now, Louisa, I hear you are marrying the Duke of Rotherfeld."

"Yes," said Louisa. "I imagine you must have received your invitation by now."

"Oh, yes, we did. I'm looking forward to it."

"I am as well." Louisa sounded like she was lying.

"I suppose I don't need to admonish you to behave, as you are adults now," Lady Atherton said. "But don't think I've forgotten that time you replaced the water in the birdbath with tea."

Fletcher chuckled. He'd been about eight at the time and had just wanted to see if birds liked tea. He'd pulled better pranks. But he appreciated that Lady Atherton remembered.

"Well, I must be off. Enjoy the night air." Lady Atherton went inside, leaving Fletcher and Louisa quite alone in the garden.

They both began speaking at once.

"I must ask your opinion," said Louisa at the same time Fletcher said, "I want to apologize."

Fletcher gestured toward the bench, and they both sat.

"You first," said Fletcher.

She took a deep breath. "I am still cross with you, but I need an honest opinion."

"Then I shall give one to you."

She nodded. "All right. I have some suspicions about Rotherfeld."

Fletcher held his breath. "What sort of suspicions?"

"I am probably imagining things, but I was with Rotherfeld tonight when we greeted the Marquess of Beresford, and…" She frowned. "I've spent enough time around them that I know Beresford and Waring have an unusual relationship."

Something in Fletcher warmed. Perhaps he would not have to break this terrible news to her. He'd been trying to work out how all night. "Yes," he said.

"They are…" Louisa shook her head. "They are lovers, are they not?"

Fletcher could tell by her body language that the idea made her uncomfortable. "Not currently, as far as I know, but they have been in the past, yes."

"I've heard that people who prefer their own sex are not uncommon."

"That is true. Not common, as such, but they exist." Fletcher was somewhat relieved he wouldn't have to explain this to her, and perhaps more relieved to let her into the small circle of people who knew about whatever was going on between Lark and Anthony.

"The idea of it…I don't quite understand it. Women do not appeal to me in that way."

"Nor do men appeal to me, but some people are just…built differently."

"Do you think it's a sin?"

"It's not really my place to say. I generally think people should make their own choices. And I've spent enough time with Waring and Beresford that I know how much they cared for each other. Or, I suppose they still do, but things are complicated because of Beresford's marriage and…anyway, it's not really my business."

"Right. Just, when Rotherfeld greeted Beresford tonight, he used his Christian name, which may not mean anything, but Rotherfeld told me they barely knew each other. If that were the case, he wouldn't feel comfortable calling Beresford 'Anthony.'"

Fletcher nodded. "Why would he lie to you about not knowing Beresford?"

"Exactly. And then, a little while later, we spoke with an old school friend, a Lieutenant Hanley."

The name rang a bell. Fletcher wracked his brain. "Ah…Hanley. A relation to Chatterton?"

"His younger brother."

"Yes, of course. What happened when you spoke to him?"

"It's not anything specific. Just something about Rotherfeld's posture. The way they spoke and touched each other. It seemed…intimate. Please tell me I'm imagining things."

Fletcher closed his eyes, hating himself a little bit. He didn't want to destroy her. But he said, "You are not imagining things."

Her eyes went wide. "I'm not?"

"I have been wanting to speak with you so I could tell you. Beresford confessed me that he and Rotherfeld were lovers many years ago."

Louisa gasped and put a hand over her mouth.

"I hate to be the one to tell you this. It's…awkward, no?"

"It is, but I want to know the full truth."

Fletcher hesitated. He couldn't decide how blunt to be, but if she was asking him for the full truth, he supposed he could give it to her. "I wanted to tell you sooner. I have no particular fondness for Rotherfeld, to be honest, but Beresford has become my friend, and I did not want to implicate him in anything, especially now that he has a child. So I couldn't tell you in a letter."

"No, of course not. Especially not because my mother has been intercepting my correspondence." She shook her head. "What a fool I have been."

"No. There's no way you could have known. By rights, you shouldn't even be able to conceive of this possibility. Ladies aren't meant to know about such things."

"Fletcher. Let me assure you, there are a lot of things we gently bred ladies aren't meant to know yet still know."

Well that was…useful to know. He wanted to ask about that, but he set it aside for later. "I just mean, you could not have known. The only reason *I* know is that Waring is one of my oldest friends, and we've discussed some of this at length, and even if I do not fully understand it, I understand that sometimes the heart wants what it wants. That desire and love are not always rational."

"That is one way to put it."

"I wanted you to have this information so that you might make an informed choice about whether to carry on with your engagement."

"My misgivings about Rotherfeld mount by the day." She stared into the distance before turning toward Fletcher. "But how do I confront him with this?"

"It could be that there is nothing to confront. Just because Rotherfeld and this Lieutenant Hanley are friends and seem close does not mean they are lovers. It does not mean Rotherfeld is stepping out on you."

"But it makes sense. The fish kiss thing, for example. He does not seem to desire me at all. Is it possible for a man to prefer *only* his own sex?"

"Yes, I do believe that is possible."

"Do you think that is the case for Rotherfeld?"

"I can't know what's in his heart or his head."

Louisa frowned and looked at the ground. "Let me think on it more. What else did you want to tell me."

Fletcher took a deep breath. Here he'd have to put his whole heart on the ground at her feet. He didn't think anything less would win her over. No more equivocating. No talking around things. He started with, "I wanted to apologize for how we left things."

"You said something cruel."

"I know. But I did not intend it that way. I misspoke."

"You misspoke?"

"I did not mean to imply that I'd marry you out of pity," said Fletcher, trying to keep the frustration out of his voice. He did not want to mess this up again. "What I *meant* is that all I want in this world is for you to be happy. If marrying Rotherfeld is what makes you happy, then I shall live with whatever comes next. But before you commit to him, I must tell you…" He sighed. He could not figure out how to say it in a way that would not make her run off again. "I'm making a hash of this again."

She looked up and met his gaze. "Keep talking."

"I *want* to marry you," Fletcher said. "I do. I offered because I meant it sincerely."

That seemed to take her aback. "But you said *if*."

"Yes, *if*. You should choose the man you believe will make you happy. I do not believe that is Rotherfeld, but if you do, then as I said, I shall live with it. I don't want to pressure you into marriage, though. Should you choose me, I would be over the moon. But I want it to be your choice." It didn't come out sounding as strongly as Fletcher felt. Maybe he should have put more emotion into that little speech. Maybe he should—

"You want to marry me? Why have you never said anything?"

"I wish I had. I wish I'd thought of this years ago and offered before you ever met Rotherfeld. But I didn't realize how I felt for you until you announced your engagement. I've been telling myself for years that I don't have romantic feelings for you. But it turns out I do."

"You do."

He had to just say it. To tell her plainly. "Louisa, you have long been one of my favorite people. We grew up together and we know each other well. You are clever and bold, and you make me laugh and you make me think. And you're beautiful. You're so brilliant and beautiful and I was a fool for not noticing it sooner. I have felt out of sorts since the moment Rotherfeld announced you'd consented to marry him and it's because…well, it's because I love you. I wish I'd realized it sooner, but I know it now like I know my own name."

"You love me?"

"This is a delicate situation. Obviously I'd be thrilled if you threw over Rotherfeld and consented to marry me, but like I said, it must be your choice. But I thought you should…you should have all the information. Make an informed decision."

Louisa stared at him. He couldn't tell what she was thinking, but he couldn't regret anything now. He'd said it all.

"Make an informed decision?" There was some wryness in her tone. Fletcher started to hope.

"Yes. Well, that sounds rather stiff and intellectual, but what I mean is—"

"Fletcher, how can you…it really took Rotherfeld proposing for you to realize how you felt?"

She sounded annoyed, which made him defensive. "I'm an idiot. Owen has been trying to tell me for a year that I had feelings for you, and I told him he was wrong, but of course he was right, and I was just denying it because…because I don't know. Part of me thought you viewed me as an older brother and I didn't want to interfere with that, and then you started courting

Rotherfeld and…truly from the bottom of my heart, all I want is your happiness."

"But you want to be with me?"

"I do." Desperately, now that he was voicing his desires, but he couldn't say that. She looked gorgeous tonight in the soft light from the gas lamps. Her gown was a dark blue, made out of some kind of shiny fabric and decorated with tiny beads. It hugged her figure in a way that made Fletcher want to touch her, or to rip the gown off so he could touch her skin. "I recognize how foolish that sounds. That I didn't realize it until Rotherfeld wormed his way into your life. But it's true. I, Fletcher Basildon, am a fool for not making you mine a long time ago, and now I fear I've waited too long, but you must know, Louisa, that I love you, I really do, and I never meant to imply that I want to marry you for any reason other than that."

She shook her head. "We're both idiots."

"Are we?"

"I did view you as an older brother, but I suppose lately that has changed a bit. You're not hard to look at, you know."

"I'm not?" Fletcher leaned forward, wanting to hear her say more.

She smiled. "Fletcher, you are a very handsome man."

"Lark told me you were marrying Rotherfeld because he's younger, better looking, and more powerful than I am."

"Perhaps younger and more powerful, but not better looking."

Something in Fletcher's chest swelled. Rotherfeld was universally acknowledged to be a handsome man, but Louisa liked Fletcher's looks better? That felt like victory.

But Louisa hadn't responded to anything he'd said. Did she not agree? Did she intend to go back to Rotherfeld despite everything?

He didn't want her to turn him down. He didn't think she would, but if he'd misconstrued this situation… "If you do not want to be together, it's better to tell me now. Let me down easy."

"Oh. Fletcher." She reached up and put a hand on his cheek. "I just didn't want your proposal to be pity. If you marry me, it's because you want to and we love each other. And I do love you. How could I not? But now I must figure out what to do about Rotherfeld, and I just don't know."

"There's still time. You could end the engagement."

"Yes. I need to think on it more."

Fletcher found that unsatisfying. He didn't want to push it, but he said, "Please don't marry Rotherfeld just because you feel obligated."

"No. I wouldn't. I need time to think of how to end things. And I was just thinking, I really want to kiss you, but if I do that, I'm no better than he is, assuming he is indeed spending his nights with Lieutenant Hanley."

"Oh." Well, that was disappointing. Fletcher wanted to kiss her, too. He wanted to drag her out of this party and straight to his bed.

She leaned over and kissed Fletcher's cheek. Fletcher caught her wrist and turned his head and their lips met. She wanted to know if he desired her? Of course he did. He hoped to show that through this kiss.

But she was right. She was still engaged to Rotherfeld.

"I am sorry," Fletcher said, pulling away gently. "We should go back inside."

"We should." But Louisa didn't move to stand.

"Don't marry Rotherfeld," said Fletcher.

"No. But he will be mad at me," she said.

Fletcher stood and held out his hand for Louisa. She took it, and he squeezed her hand before helping her up. "If you want me to be there when you tell him, I can."

"No. This is something I must do myself. Please… I'm with you, Fletcher. But I need some time to figure out how to do this."

"Not too much time. If you don't resolve this soon, you'll be standing at an altar with him." The wedding was less than two weeks away, and that ticking clock felt ominous now.

"A day or two. I've received quite a lot of shocking information tonight. I need some time to think it all over."

Fletcher nodded slowly. "All right." He wanted to give her the time she needed, and he imagined that this entire conversation had been a bit of a shock for her. But at the same time, this felt unsatisfying and unresolved. "It's just, I hear what you are saying, but I want…" But what did Fletcher want? A promise she wasn't prepared to give him yet?

"Cheer up. It's not a *no*. I need time."

"All right. I hear you. Let us go back inside."

Chapter Fourteen

THE NEXT AFTERNOON, Louisa found her mother in the sitting room, working on her needlepoint.

"Mother, I must speak with you."

"It's nearly time for tea. Let us speak like civilized people." She summoned a maid and requested tea be brought.

Louisa's mother had long relied on protocol. She liked things to be done in an orderly manner, in accordance with tradition. Her daily schedule was rigid. So Louisa had to wait for tea to be served before she could speak. Luckily, it didn't take long, possibly because Lady Petty had tea at the same precise time every day and the staff knew to anticipate it.

So Louisa bided her time while her mother poured tea and put a few biscuits on a plate for Louisa.

"What did you want to discuss, dear?"

She considered laying down her argument carefully, but what came out of her mouth was, "I need to call off my engagement."

"What? Why?" Mother already looked scandalized, so this would be a battle.

Louisa tried to brace herself. "I've learned some things about Rotherfeld that make me think we do not suit."

"What things?"

There was no way her mother—a sheltered, traditional woman who did not read much and had never been a gossip—

would understand the truth, so Louisa said, "Well, for one thing, he's very boring."

"Louisa. That is hardly a reason to call off an engagement. He's a husband, not a night at the opera. He's stable. There's no scandal attached to him."

"I wouldn't go that far. I think he may be…having an affair." There. That should put Mother off Rotherfeld.

"What evidence do you have for *that*?"

"I saw him talking to someone at the Atherton ball last night, and they seemed quite…intimate."

"Louisa. You must stop this nonsense."

"It's not nonsense! My concerns about Rotherfeld are sincere. I am near certain he is having an affair."

Mother shook her head. "You constantly do this."

That took Louisa aback. "Do what?"

"You've always been a rebellious child. You've read a few books about women's rights and now have decided you must be *strong* and *independent*." Mother's tone indicated these were negative traits. The disdain came across clearly. "You've been pushing off marriage since you came of age, and I know you are reluctant to do it, but you cannot push it off forever. Your father and I will not always be here, and the only way to set yourself up for the future is to marry. And in Rotherfeld, you've got a wealthy, powerful husband who will take care of you and your children."

Was that what she thought? That Louisa had read Wollstone-craft—which she had, granted—and decided to eschew marriage entirely? "I am not against marriage, Mother. But whoever I marry is someone I will have to live with for the rest of my days, so I want to marry someone I actually *like*."

"Women do not always have that luxury."

"It would not matter to you if my husband were stepping out on me? If he couldn't even find respect enough for me to be faithful during our engagement?"

"Men have affairs."

"Mother!"

Mother clucked her tongue and assumed a more formal posture. "Rotherfeld is a *duke*."

"And?" said Louisa.

"He's wealthy and powerful. His grandmother is close with Queen Charlotte."

"He's dull, Mother. He barely seems to like me. I'm starting to think he manipulated me into courtship and betrothal for his own purposes. And I don't love him."

"*Love,*" her mother spat. "Marriage is not about love. We women must marry to ensure our continued survival."

Louisa rolled her eyes at that. While it was true that women had few property rights, the Pettys were wealthy. Louisa could not imagine her family would let her live on the streets should her spinsterhood persist. "So you mean to tell me that nothing else matters but Rotherfeld's wealth and power? That if he were cruel or unfaithful, that these are things I must endure?"

"That is *not* what I said. But you are naïve if you think your husband can be this perfect angel of a man. And Rotherfeld is not cruel, I've never heard anyone say he is. And your only evidence for his unfaithfulness is that you saw him talking to a woman at a ball."

"But I don't want to marry Rotherfeld," Louisa tried, weakly.

"You've already committed, Louisa. You cannot tolerate the scandal it would cause if you were to jilt him."

Louisa was mildly worried about the scandal, but she said, "I hear what you're saying, but it's not like I'll die alone if I choose not to marry Rotherfeld. Should I end my engagement with Rotherfeld, I have another offer."

"From whom?"

"Greystone."

Mother balked. Then she shook her head. "I have been too permissive with you. Allowed you to read books I shouldn't have. You've had a taste of freedom and think you have autonomy. Did you think Rotherfeld's decision to court you was entirely his idea?

It wasn't. You've turned down too many proposals. After this season, had no one offered, you'd be on the shelf."

"What are you saying? Did you arrange things directly with Rotherfeld?"

"I had a hand in it. Your father has business with him. This was never intended to be a love match. It's a business arrangement."

That was a punch to the gut. No one had ever said that this was intended to be anything other than a courtship. How had Louisa not known this was arranged?

Because her own mother thought she was incapable of finding a husband.

"What's wrong with marrying Greystone instead of Rotherfeld? You like him. You've known him his whole life. He was like a second son to you, no? And he's just inherited a title and the wealth that comes with it. He'd make a fine husband."

"Greystone offered because he pities you," Mother said. "He showed no interest in you until Rotherfeld offered, so now he is telling you what you want to hear because he is your friend."

"That is not true." Louisa believed Fletcher now. She believed he loved her. And, truth be told, she'd been fantasizing about what marriage to him would be like for the last couple of weeks. It seemed far preferable than a dull marriage to a man who barely liked her. "Fletcher's offer was genuine."

Mother shook her head. "You cannot take his offer. There is a precarious business arrangement that will fall apart if you refuse Rotherfeld."

There was a *what*? "How can you have done this? Why did you not tell me?"

"It was not important to *you*. I suppose I should have expected your impertinence. But I assumed that, once you agreed to marry Rotherfeld, it was a done deal. And money and business are not the domains of women."

Louisa fought not to roll her eyes at that, too. This was completely absurd. "What kind of business arrangement?"

Mother waved her hand as if it didn't matter. "I know nothing of the details, and it shouldn't preoccupy you, either. What I know is that your father and Rotherfeld have entered into an agreement."

Louisa couldn't believe this. How could she have been so stupid? It was like everyone around her had manipulated her into agreeing to Rotherfeld's suit, and now that she recognized it, it might be too late. "And if I refuse to marry Rotherfeld?"

"Our family stands to lose a great deal of money, and you'd be shamed by the *ton*. Besides, Rotherfeld has a great deal of prestige. You'd be a fool to turn that down."

"And Greystone is a marquess who just inherited a fortune from his father. It's not like we'd live in poverty. If Father wants money—"

"You are naive and it is not that simple. Your father made a deal with Rotherfeld. The two of you suit. You will be closer to power, and you will not want for anything. You don't love him now, but he's friendly and handsome. You will grow fond of each other over time."

"I don't understand why I can't just marry Fletcher. You and father were great friends with the Greystones. You know him, you know he is a good man. I won't want for anything with him, either."

"Because the world is not that simple. Because we made an agreement with Rotherfeld that we cannot break."

"But Mother—"

"No, Louisa. You *will* marry Rotherfeld. I am done discussing this matter. Finish your tea."

Instead, Louisa left the room.

"I GAVE HER my heart. She said she had to think about it."

Fletcher was three servings of whiskey into his night at the club. He felt like he was swimming. The room was spinning. Everything was funny.

"All right, my drunk friend," Owen said. "Let's start again. You talked to Louisa."

"I told her I love her, and I want to marry her, and she said she has to think about it."

"In Louisa's defense, she *is* engaged to another man."

"She's going to marry that buggerer Rotherfeld, and I will die alone." He said *buggerer* with a couple of extra *ers*.

"So *he's* drunk," said Lark, sitting across from Fletcher.

"You won't die alone," said Owen. "You're a wealthy man with a title. If you made it known you wanted to get married, families would start throwing their daughters at you."

"But I want Louisa."

"What did she say, exactly?" asked Hugh, who had mostly been quiet through this conversation.

What had she said? It was a little fuzzy now, truth be told. "I told her I love her and want to marry her. I offered to go with her when she tells Rotherfeld their engagement is off, but she said she had to do it herself."

"That's promising," said Owen.

"But otherwise, her reaction was…understated. I told her I love her, and she treated it like a small matter. Like a small task to which she had to attend."

"I'm sure you're exaggerating," said Lark. "I saw you speaking together at the Atherton ball. She cares for you."

"She said so, but she didn't *act* like it. And she said she needs time. But there's no time!"

Owen rolled his eyes and took Fletcher's glass away. "No more whiskey for you."

"I recognize the wedding is less than two weeks away, but maybe she just needs a couple of days to sort out her affairs," said Hugh. "She needs to break the engagement, which is not always easy."

"Maybe."

Owen patted his knee. "You did the right thing. You made it clear how you feel. And it sounds like she intends to end her engagement to Rotherfeld, so you've won, my friend."

"I won't have won until she says she'll marry me."

"She will, my friend, she will."

Everyone else seemed to agree.

Fletcher wished he could have more faith that what everyone was telling him was true. He could see dozens of ways this could go wrong. Louisa could decide she loved Rotherfeld after all. Or she could decide she wanted Rotherfeld's wealth and power. That was very unlike Louisa, but stranger things had happened. Rotherfeld could decide not to end the engagement for whatever reason. Likely he needed Louisa more than she needed him.

He tried to tell himself everything would work out. Still, Fletcher spent the next hour swirling in his cups. Sobriety eluded him, especially once an attendant handed him another snifter of whiskey. He sipped it as his friends discussed whatever their own days had been like.

"Adele is in good spirits," Hugh said, "despite spending part of every morning, er, tossing up her accounts."

"Are you still afraid?" Lark asked.

"It just seems so unpleasant for her. I didn't want to have another child because I didn't want to put her through all this, but she insists it'll be all right, that it will pass and be worth it. I hope she's right."

"If the account tossing were not happening, would you still want another child?" asked Lark.

Hugh smiled faintly. "I will admit, I am a little excited. Although I was serious. If it's a girl, I will be locking her inside the house and running all the men off the island."

Lark laughed at that.

"Grace and I may return to Wales early," said Owen. "We have two more weddings to attend, but then we may slip away after the second one. Grace is anxious to get out of the city."

"Is one of the weddings Louisa's?" asked Fletcher.

"Yes," said Owen, a little sheepish. "But even if it doesn't happen, we're attending the wedding of Grace's friend Penelope Thistledown at the end of this month, so we must stay at least for that."

"And how do you feel about returning early?" Hugh asked.

"Honestly? I will miss my evenings with you all, but I prefer the company of my wife at night, and she loathes London, so if going to Wales makes her happy, that's what we're going to do."

"You really prefer her to us?" asked Fletcher.

"He prefers looking at her to looking at you," said Lark. "Plus she warms his bed at night."

"I won't apologize for having married the most beautiful woman in England," Owen said with a shrug.

Finally, Lark said, "Let me ask everyone's advice on something."

That got everyone's attention.

"Go ahead," said Hugh.

"Speaking of leaving London, I've had a notion to help Anthony raise his son."

Fletcher could make little sense of that. "Does he not have staff for that?"

"He does, but he asked me to be the boy's godfather, which is a responsibility I take seriously. I must give him spiritual guidance, right?"

"Sure, but have you seen your own godfather recently?" Hugh asked.

"He died when I was seven, so no, but I think Anthony asked me because he wants me to play a role in the boy's life, and given how unorthodox our relationship is, I had thought to… I hesitate to say the role is as a spouse, as I could be no replacement for a mother to the boy, but… I don't know. Perhaps this does not and cannot make sense."

Hugh nodded, though. "You seek a marriage of sorts to the person you love, and that person has a child, and therefore, you want to be…a stepfather, perhaps."

"Yes. That is the sum of it."

"I almost miss having Beresford around," Fletcher said, still drunk. "He's entertaining."

"Less so these days," said Lark, "but I think his current malaise will pass eventually. He's been very sad, but I keep getting glimpses of his old self. This loss was difficult for him, despite what you all might think, and it will take time to recover, but he will get there."

"And you're not worried about all the things that made you end the relationship to begin with?" asked Hugh.

"Oh, I'm still worried about all of it. I find I care less now, though. I'd rather have a short time with him than a long life without."

"Love," Fletcher said, "is stupid."

"I am going to have to hide the rest of the whiskey in this place, aren't I?" asked Owen.

"It *is* stupid," Lark said to Fletcher, "but wonderful, too. The best and worst thing you will ever experience."

Fletcher groaned.

Chapter Fifteen

LOUISA HAD THOUGHT her parents would be overjoyed that she wanted to marry the son of their closest friends. In London, they were literally close; until a few years ago when Fletcher's father's failing health had inspired him to move to the family's country house permanently, the Greystone family had lived in the house behind the Pettys'. As a girl, Louisa occasionally slipped out her bedroom window, climbed down a trestle, and across the garden and snuck into the Greystone house via the kitchen. Their cook never locked the back door. As an adult, Louisa suspected that everyone in the house knew what she'd been up to, but at the time, she'd really thought she was getting away with something. She'd sneak through the quiet house and into Fletcher's room, and they'd talk or play chess until she got tired and snuck back home.

To sneak out of her house now, she didn't need the window; her parents adjourned for the night on the early side, and by the time Louisa had donned a cloak and decided to sneak out, the staff had all gone to sleep, too. Louisa left through the front door.

Fletcher lived in a town house a short distance from her own home, and she arrived at his door in a matter of minutes. It was a modest home, not one befitting the kind of wealth and stature that Fletcher possessed, but he'd never been showy. Families like Fletcher's, who had been wealthy and titled for several generations, tended to think conspicuous wealth was gauche and not done.

The street was quiet. No one was about. She knocked on Fletcher's door and was let in by the butler, who installed her in a sitting room and went to find Fletcher.

Fletcher himself walked into the room a few minutes later, wearing a very fine blue dressing gown that went to his ankles.

"What the devil are you doing here?" Fletcher asked, sounding sleepy and irritated.

Louisa decided to get to the point. "I think we should elope."

Fletcher's eyes went wide. "You...what?"

In one burst, Louisa said, "I told my mother that I wanted to end my engagement to Rotherfeld, and she told me that I could not because Rotherfeld has a business arrangement with my father, and even if *you* are willing to marry me, that is not good enough, so I think we need to go to Scotland. Tonight."

Fletcher just stared at her, his expression incredulous. "I'm sorry. I have a terrible headache. Can you slow down? Your mother will not let you break the engagement?"

"Rotherfeld is in business with my father. I do not know the extent of their agreement, but apparently it is contingent on my marrying Rotherfeld. If I don't go through with it, my family stands to lose a great deal of money."

Fletcher frowned. "Oh. So why are you here?"

"You must help me. I want to marry you, Fletcher."

"You do?" Fletcher looked pained and confused, but a smile briefly peeked through.

"I've been thinking about it since the Atherton ball."

"You have." He rubbed his forehead and looked dazed. Like all of this was confusing him, but Louisa thought she'd been clear.

"Fletcher...I can't tell what you're thinking. *You* said the night of the ball that you *want* to marry me."

"I do. But you seemed...well, not especially enthusiastic about the idea."

"There's just so much..." But she frowned. Perhaps Fletcher

misread her the way she'd misread him. They were both idiots. "Fletcher. I intend to marry you and not Rotherfeld, because I love *you*. So if my mother will not let me out of my engagement, then I think we should elope. People do that, right? Get married in Scotland?"

"Yes, but…" Fletcher rubbed his head again. "We cannot simply… Louisa, think about what you are saying."

"I have given this a great deal of thought."

"You cannot simply throw over one of the most powerful men of the *ton* and not expect some kind of retaliation. Not to mention your father's business deal. If it's true that if you don't marry Rotherfeld, your father could lose money, what condition will that leave your family in? There must be a way out without us eloping."

She made a frustrated grunt and said, "Fletcher, you are being too practical."

He rubbed his temples. "Too practical? I went out tonight and got very drunk because your reaction to my marriage proposal seemed faint at best, but now you tell me we must elope right now, when I've barely had time to process what you've just said to me. And you have no consideration of the consequences! We'd be shunned by society, and your father could potentially lose a lot of money! Is that what you want?"

"No, but I won't marry Rotherfeld."

Fletcher sighed. He looked tired and sad. "Please hear me when I say that the last thing in the world I want is for you to marry Rotherfeld. I want you to marry *me*. But we need to take a minute to think this through."

"You love me."

"You bloody well know I do."

"I kind of like Cranky Fletcher."

He frowned. "My head is pounding so much I can hear it. I can scarcely think. I'd prefer to discuss this on the morrow. But I suppose, since you are here, we must discuss it now."

He sat on the sofa and rubbed his temples. Louisa sat next to him. She was sympathetic to his headache, but she felt what she thought was a reasonable amount of panic at the current situation. She needed help. Running off to Scotland had felt like a good solution an hour ago, but Fletcher was right, there would be fallout from such an act. She didn't much care for what happened to Rotherfeld, nor to her own reputation, but she did care about her father.

"What must I do?"

Fletcher turned to look at her. His eyes were bloodshot. "I think you must talk to Rotherfeld and tell him the whole truth about what you know, and then ask for him to break the engagement. I suppose I can go to your father and find out…whatever this financial deal is, and also formally ask for your hand. That might grease the wheels."

"Or you can fight Rotherfeld for my honor with pistols at dawn."

"I truly hope it does not come to that." Fletcher let out a ragged breath.

"Are you ill?"

"Too much drink." He bent over and put his head in his hands.

"Because of me?"

"I was upset. I felt like I had given you my heart and you seemed to lack what I thought was the requisite enthusiasm."

"Fletcher."

"I hope you know, I would not be marrying you as a favor or to keep you away from Rotherfeld. I'll marry you because I want to, because we belong together. Because I love you."

She splayed her hand on his back. His body was hot beneath the fine fabric of his dressing gown. "I am sorry. This situation is vexing."

"It is."

"I'd be marrying you not to escape Rotherfeld, but because I want to. Because Rotherfeld is dull, but when you and I kissed, I felt…excited. Because I do love you, Fletcher. I think you might be my best friend, but you are also handsome and clever, and I know you'd defend me to the death. You've been trying to do right be me all this Season, even though it must have pained you to do so."

"I just want you to be happy."

Louisa smiled. "And that is how I know that you love me. You want what's best for me, not what you most want. If I told you right now that I loved Rotherfeld and I planned to marry him no matter what, you would let me, even though it broke your heart. And you'd hold your tongue about how you felt about it."

"To you, yes. Then I'd go meet my friends at my club and drink a significant amount of whisky."

"Rotherfeld doesn't love me. I've grown convinced he offered for me to salvage his own reputation and is likely determined to see it through, which is why he must have made a nice offer to my father, something my father didn't feel he could turn down. Rotherfeld is acting selfishly."

"Yes."

"Fletcher, you have been at my side my whole life, and it's a true shame that we never understood what we really meant to each other, at least not before now. We didn't have an opportunity to explore what's between us, and now we've arrived at a crisis point."

"I do not believe the situation to be that dire. We still have a week and a half until the wedding." Fletcher offered her a weak smile.

"You think I'm beautiful."

His expression softened. "I do. I've thought so for a long time. I did not recognize my own feelings about it, though, and I regret that I've been so foolish for so long. I could have saved us both from all of this anguish."

"I don't see why my father should turn down your suit."

"We shall see, I suppose."

So resolved, Louisa knew she should leave. They had something of a plan, but Louisa found she did not want to leave

Fletcher's company. In fact, she wanted stay.

"Fletcher, I..."

"You should..."

She kissed him. She ran her hand down his back and nudged him closer and opened her mouth to let him in. He let out a huff of surprise, but he kissed back, moving his lips against hers and then tentatively licking into her mouth. He put a hand at the base of her neck to hold her there, and he kept kissing her. Louisa's skin began to tingle and something warm spread across her chest. She wanted more, was suddenly insatiable, and she put her arms around him and pushed him back onto the sofa.

He laughed when he hit his head on the arm of the sofa, but he kept kissing her, putting his arms fully around her and holding her close. Louisa lay on top of him, and she couldn't remember her body ever feeling this alive. *This* was what people made such foolish decisions about. *This* was what she wanted. Not Daniel's cold fish kisses.

She ran a hand down Fletcher's chest, surprised by how hard and muscular he seemed. His big hands pressed into her back and pulled her to him. They writhed together for a moment, and then she gasped because she thought she could feel—

"Oh," Fletcher said.

"Oh?"

"I just realized, you are fully dressed, and I am in nought but my nightshirt."

He gently eased her away. His dressing gown had come untied to reveal a soft blue nightshirt that looked like it had been washed many times. He hastily pulled the dressing gown closed, concealing what was happening below his waist, if anything.

"You want to stop?" Louisa asked.

"No, but I am barely dressed, and you are engaged to another man, and so we must."

Louisa touched her lips, which still tingled from his kisses. They may not have done much more than kiss, but Louisa felt like she had a notion for the kind of pleasure she would find on her wedding night, assuming she married Fletcher and not Daniel.

"I don't want to stop, either."

Fletcher stood, adjusted his dressing gown so that it covered his body again, and then held out a hand to Louisa. "If all goes to plan, we'll have years and years to explore each other. But for now, you should go home."

"I don't want to."

"I know. But you must. The rest will come in good time." He leaned over and kissed her lips briefly again. "I love you. I can't keep myself from saying it. But we've got a week and a half to get a wedding called off, so we best get to work."

"I love you, too. Thank you for…everything."

"I can't believe you snuck out of your house."

She shrugged and adjusted her cloak.

"I'm going to make one of my footmen escort you home so that I know you made it back okay."

"You don't have to."

"Yes, I do. And I'm guessing that marriage to you means I shall never have a dull moment again. Sneaking out of your house like we're children again." He shook his head.

"As I recall, you snuck out of your house a time or two. *Someone* certainly left sweets on my bedroom windowsill on my birthday every year."

Fletcher grinned. "I'd do it again if I thought I wouldn't get caught. I bet I could find increasingly clever places to hide sweets on your birthday from here on."

She grinned back at him. "I'm sure you will. After all, who wants a dull life?"

"Not me. Not at all."

Chapter Sixteen

Before Anthony's marriage, it had been common for Lark and Anthony to drop by each other's homes. At the time, Anthony had owned several London residences and had set the most discreet aside for his romantic trysts, although he and Lark saw so much of each other, Anthony mostly lived there. It felt instinctual to pop over to Anthony's house on a whim, but times had changed. Anthony's more formal home—he'd sold the rest of his London properties recently; he'd told Lark he'd put the money into a fund for Henry—was widely known to be his home. So Lark had to be more careful about his impromptu visits, and he had yet to spend a night here. Anthony refused to be parted from his son overnight, so they hadn't had time or opportunity for trysts. A few stolen kisses made up their romantic relationship right now.

Lark didn't know how to behave anymore. He thought to throw caution to the wind, but he didn't know how well he trusted Anthony's servants.

He left his home during regular calling hours. He stopped to buy a newspaper and a scandal sheet and scanned both as he walked. He cared little for the actual news—Sir Walter Scott had written a new novel and also found some ancient artifacts in Edinburgh Castle that were on display now; some old theater had been renovated and was reopening in South London; another of the king's sons had succumbed to matrimony; it was all enough to put a man to sleep—but there were a few good items in the scandal sheets. A certain Lord D—had been caught canoodling with Lady C—at the opera, while Lady C—'s husband was on the Continent for some kind of business opportunity. Lord D—could have been anyone; Devonshire, Donegall, Derby, Lark wasn't sure. Next, Lord S—was having an affair with an actress, but that was referring to Swansea and Lark already knew about it. Then there was a Miss R—who had jilted Lord M—at the altar, which Lark was surprised he hadn't heard about yet. It must have been a wedding with a limited guest list. Probably just as well. Lord M—could have been Marlborough, whom Lark had seen around town chasing skirts all Season. Rumor had it he planned to marry soon.

Lark loved this kind of nonsense. It was a nice distraction from how fraught everything in his life felt lately.

Of course, Lark was just as high profile as any of these men. Lark was a direct descendant of Edward III's son John of Gaunt, and thus a descendant of William the Conqueror, and he was somewhere deep in the line of succession. His father was the powerful Duke of Beaufort, a kind but strong-willed man whom Lark was fairly certain would outlive everyone. Thus Lark had yet to inherit the title he knew would come to him and that he felt a certain amount of obligation toward, but he also had a younger brother who would happily give the title to his son.

It meant, though, that all of society knew who Lark was. His family was prominent enough, and enough of his cousins were married to minor royals, that he could probably get away with more than he thought, that his money and his title could make a lot of accusations go away. He just didn't want the attention or risk. He didn't want to be made an example of. He didn't want to be Charlie Ingle.

Society knew that Lark and Anthony were friends. It wouldn't be odd for him to call on a friend.

He walked up the stoop of Anthony's town house and rang

the bell. The butler let him right in and murmured, "My lord is in the nursery."

Lark took that to mean he should go up there. Lark had been here enough recently that he knew the staff and his way around his house, so he took a deep breath and ascended the stairs.

He found Anthony sitting in a rocking chair with his back to the door. He didn't appear to hear Lark approach, despite the creak in one of the boards at the top of the stairs. Instead, he was rocking the baby and singing softly.

It would never cease to surprise Lark that Anthony had taken to fatherhood this way. A year ago, this man had wanted children even less than he wanted to get married. But now, here he was, singing to his infant son.

Lark took in the sight, since he had at least a moment before Anthony noticed he was there. The problem with all of this was that Lark loved this man, and loving this man had changed the entire trajectory of his life. Lark had pressured Anthony into getting married because he didn't have the strength to commit to a marriage himself, not when he loved Anthony as much as he did. It wasn't a matter of his sexual proclivities; he was attracted to women as well and had always imagined he'd marry one. But he couldn't do that now.

So what would he do instead? It wasn't like he could move in here, or marry Anthony, or even let word of this affair leak out to the public. He supposed they could carry on in separate residences, and Anthony might be more willing to spend nights together when Henry was older.

Or they could go somewhere more discreet.

Anthony had an entailed estate in the countryside, in Kent, and it was far enough from civilization that no one would think it odd if Lark accompanied him, perhaps to assist with his business affairs—they were friends, after all—or even because a child could always use another father figure. A kind uncle who taught him…manly things. Lark wasn't sure what those would be. How to ride a horse, perhaps. How to dance. How to treat a lady.

Was Lark actually contemplating leaving London so that he and Anthony could raise Henry together?

Well, Lark was clearly losing his mind. Enough woolgathering. He cleared his throat.

Anthony started and turned around.

"Lark. How long have you been standing there?"

"I don't know. A few minutes. Long enough to hear you sing."

Anthony used his legs to rotate the chair to face Lark. He remained seating and continued to rock the baby. "I'd be embarrassed, but you've heard me sing plenty."

Lark walked into the room. "Indeed. At breakfast when the conversation lulls. In the bath. When you're puttering around your house and think no one is listening. And, apparently, to your son."

"He seems to like it. It calms him down when he…grows ornery."

"Ornery?"

"Sometimes, he gets this fierce look on his face right before he lets out a yowl that will pierce your ears, and even when you make sure all of his needs are attended to, still he screams. It takes a lot to get him to calm down. I find rocking and singing helps."

"An important discovery." Anthony seemed to be alone. "Where is Mrs. Church?"

"She's having dinner with her family. I gave her the afternoon off."

"I'm amazed you have not hired a legion of staff to attend to the baby."

"I gave that some thought, and I decided that, because he's my family, I wanted to try to be as good a father as I could. My father wasn't around much, but I want to be here for little Henry."

"That's admirable."

"Admirable and stupid. You were not here a half hour ago. This little man has a good pair of lungs on him. I had no idea what to do. Mrs. Church should be able to take time off as needed, but I need another person here to help when she does."

"Funny you should mention that."

"Do you perhaps have a nanny in your pocket?"

"No, but I've been thinking."

"That sounds dangerous. What have you been thinking?" Anthony rotated his neck. "Sorry, I've been sitting at a weird angle. I have a kink in my neck."

"Get up," Lark said. "Give me the baby."

Anthony hesitated, but then he stood and handed Henry to Lark. Lark cradled the boy in his arms while Anthony stretched his shoulders.

Little Henry smelled a little like spoiled milk, but it was oddly pleasant. His little body fit nicely in the crook of Lark's arm. He cracked open an eye as if to ascertain whether the new man in his immediate presence was friend or foe and seemed to decide on the former. He closed his eye and seemed to fall back to sleep.

Lark's heart ached with how darling this little child was, but he supposed he had missed the wailing.

"I had a thought," Lark said.

"About the staff?"

"About us. Maybe when the Season is over, we should go somewhere…less crowded. As a sort of trial for whether us living in close proximity will lead us to bliss or murder."

"Ah." Anthony nodded. "I had been considering the same scheme. It's odd, having spent less time among Society this season, I find I don't miss it as much as I expected. I love it, don't get me wrong. I love the balls and parties and the ritual and all of it, but I find that I don't need it the way I once did. Perhaps it's a sign of aging."

"In other words, the social whirl of London does not have the same anchor on you as it once did."

"Correct. And perhaps the thing to do would be to take Henry and Mrs. Church and her family and hie off to the country for the summer and live as a married couple might. Did I ever drag you to my estate in Kent?"

"No, I can't say I've had the pleasure."

"After my father died, I took everything out of the master's chambers and bought entirely new furniture. There's an adjacent chamber for the mistress of the house, and the decor there is a bit more feminine, more to Matilda's taste, but we can alter it however you like."

"Or I can just sleep in your bed."

"You could. I don't know where you will keep your trousseau, however. My dressing room is usually quite full."

"Of course it is."

Anthony smiled. "I imagine I could make room for a few pairs of trousers and your appallingly dull waistcoats."

"Apologies for not festooning my body in whatever riotous colors are fashionable right now."

Anthony grinned. "'Tis a good idea, us going to the country for the summer. I think we should. And if we survive a few months without one of us doing violence to the other, perhaps we have a future."

"Would you want my help, seeing to the rearing of Young Master Henry?"

"Oh, certainly. There are some matters you are smarter about than I. I can't think of what they are right now, but I'm sure there are some." Anthony winked.

Lark rolled his eyes. "Shall we let the young master sleep?"

"Yes. You can place him in the cradle. Gently."

Lark carefully placed the baby back in his cradle. Henry stretched and sighed and then went back to sleep.

As Lark stood up from bending over, Anthony placed an arm around him. "I haven't spent a summer in the country since I was a boy. What does one do there?"

"I imagine we will find things to occupy our time. Surely you also have some business to attend to when you are not singing to your infant son."

"I do indeed. But I'd just as soon spend my days in bed with you." Anthony kissed Lark's temple. "If I have not said so, Lark, I am enormously grateful to have you back in my life."

"I feel foolish for pushing you out."

"You did what you felt was needed. And I don't know that our circumstances have changed except that I have given my mother the grandchild she…well, craved is the wrong word. The grandchild she wanted for status reasons and has, since his birth, basically ignored. She plans to spend the summer in London, by the way. She and some of her friends are doing some charitable works, primarily building a lending library for the poor. It seems very important to her that she take a hands-on approach."

"Good to know, I suppose."

"She won't be at the estate, is my point. It would be just you and I and Henry, our funny little family. Well, and the Churches, whose discretion I will pay for if need be. But I don't think we need worry much. Despite her name, Mrs. Church does not seem especially religious."

"This plan of ours is mad."

Anthony grinned. "My schemes generally are. But one day at a time, my love. One day at a time. We shall spend a summer in the country and if we survive it, then we will work something out for the next season. There's a rumor Lord Dwindle next door is interested in selling his house and decamping for the coast."

"Oh?"

"Lord Dwindle is approximately seven hundred and three years old and brings up the restorative sea air at least three times whenever I speak with him. I know moving three whole blocks from your residence to his would be an undertaking, but we could build a secret passage between the houses, and think of how fun that would be."

"You're right. All your schemes are mad. A secret passage? Are you eight?"

Anthony laughed, and Lark was delighted to hear it. Then Anthony seemed to remember the sleeping baby, and he immediately stopped laughing. He retreated to the corner of the room, further from the cradle. "It can be a normal door between the houses, but that is so boring. Imagine a bookcase with a hinge that—"

"I get the idea," Lark said, following him to the corner.

"Something to consider."

Living in the adjacent house would make keeping their affair discreet easier, that was for certain. "Is it a nice house next door? Have you been inside?"

Anthony nodded. "It's the mirror image of this one. Built by the same architect. I can't speak to all the rooms, but the first-floor footprint is nearly identical, just reversed."

"I'll consider it, then. This house is a little larger than mine. I'll just say I wanted more space for…my frolicking bachelor ways, and since we are friends and you are friendly with your neighbor because you're friendly with everyone, it made a certain amount of sense."

"That's the spirit!" Anthony kissed Lark's cheek. "And if it's awful, we can adjourn back to the country whenever we like."

"Well, as you said, one day at a time."

"I love you, Lark."

Lark smiled. "Despite everything, I love you, too."

Anthony put his hands on Lark's shoulders. "Despite everything? My more irritating qualities are the parts of me you love the most."

Lark sighed because it was true. Anthony had a big personality, when he wasn't in mourning, and he liked to antagonize people by joking around. Anthony had once been an even bigger gossip than Lark. And, yes, those were the parts of Anthony that Lark missed the most.

He glanced at the baby, who was still asleep, and then leaned over and kissed Anthony. He put his arms around Anthony's shoulders and sank into Anthony, who held him by the waist. They kissed like the world was ending.

"Oh." Anthony said suddenly.

"What is it?"

"I hope this won't affect how you see me and my, er, masculine virility, but for the last month or so it has been difficult for me to…" He gestured below his waist. "To arouse myself. I attributed it to grief, but apparently I just had to kiss you for longer than three seconds."

Lark looked down. "Congratulations."

"Not that I can do anything about it now. I don't want to traumatize the poor boy, but we should stay within earshot in case he needs something. Here, come with me next door."

They walked out of the nursery and into an adjacent sitting room.

"Mrs. Church's chamber is on the other side. This is I think meant to be a space for children to play once they've gotten a little older than Henry is now."

"You think?"

Anthony shrugged and sat on the sofa. He patted the seat beside him as if he were summoning a pet, so Lark rolled his eyes and sat next to Anthony.

"I did not design this house," said Anthony. "I spent time here as a child, but my father mostly left me in the countryside with my mother, which perhaps is why I was long so reluctant to leave London. And Father would not allow me to do anything so disruptive as playing or being loud, so for my whole life this room has always been kind of a stale sitting room. But I believe the architect's intent was for this entire floor to be devoted to the children of the house." He looked around. "Perhaps I should festoon this with toys. What do boys play with these days? Rocking horses? Little soldiers?"

"I've no idea."

Anthony smiled and snaked an arm around Lark's shoulder. "So you will likely be completely useless when it comes to rearing a young boy."

"I imagine I can figure it out."

"Mmhmm. Now. Where were we?" Anthony leaned forward to kiss Lark.

Lark put up a hand and pressed his fingers to Anthony's lips. "I thought we were keeping an ear out should Henry need something."

"We are. The room is right there. I'll hear if he cries."

"Is your nurse not due back?"

"Not for another hour at least. I believe she and her husband have gone to have dinner with his mother in Bloomsbury. That's almost clear across town; it'll take her some time to get back. I'm not suggesting we commit any acts that shall not be named right here on this sofa, but I do believe I would like to spend the next few minutes kissing you."

Bloomsbury was only clear across town if one had a very limited idea of where in London it was acceptable to go, but Lark decided not to comment on that. Instead, he put his arms around Anthony and said, "You've thought of everything."

"I'm very clever."

"All right, all right." Lark *had* missed this part of Anthony, the part that never took anything seriously. It was frustrating at times, but it was fun, too, and so Lark kissed Anthony and decided that whatever happened, he'd deal with it.

Chapter Seventeen

L OUISA DIDN'T HAVE to wait long for her confrontation with Daniel. He called on her the next day.

"I apologize for not coming to see you sooner, my dear," he said as he sat with her in the drawing room. Louisa's mother winked—*winked!*—on her way out the door.

"I saw you two nights ago at the Atherton ball," Louisa pointed out. "So it is not as though you and I have been separated for a great deal of time. Although I am quite anxious to discuss something with you."

"It's just that I promised your mother we would get to know each other better before we got married so as to assuage your fears. She mentioned you were having second thoughts."

Of course her mother had meddled. Father had still said nothing, but Mother seemed awfully invested in making sure this wedding happened. Louisa wasn't sure what to make of it— beyond the business deal, what was her motivation?—but she decided to set that aside for now.

"I am indeed having second thoughts," Louisa said. "It is why I wanted to speak with you. And what I have to say…it's a bit…delicate."

Daniel frowned. "All right. What are your second thoughts?"

"Well, first of all, I know…" Louisa frowned. How to say this? She glanced at the door. There was no shadow or anything to indicate her mother was lurking there, as though she *wanted* Louisa to put herself in a compromising position. Well, that wouldn't be happening. "Look, let's be honest with each other. We don't really suit."

"What are you talking about? I think we suit each other well."

"We have so little in common. We often must go awkwardly digging for topics of conversation because we share so few interests. You don't care about any of the things I'm passionate about, and I don't care about any of the things you are. I suspect, once married, we will quickly become bored with each other's company. We both deserve better than that."

"Surely that can't be true, though. We must have common interests that either we do not yet know about or that we will discover once married. I don't care for opera, and you are not interested in birds, but…travel, say. I love to travel. Do you?"

"I haven't done much travel, to be honest."

"Well, see? That could be something we have in common. Once we're married, I'll take you to the Continent."

Louisa shook her head. "It's not just that, though. That is just the most easy-to-explain reason why I don't believe we should get married."

"How many reasons are there?"

Louisa closed her eyes and counted. "Four." When she opened her eyes again, Daniel was staring at her with open shock. "Daniel. Surely you must be aware of some of the reasons."

"I suppose that depends on what you think your reasons are."

Louisa did not appreciate his patronizing tone. "Well, let's see if you find any of these reasons persuasive. We have nothing in common. That's one. The second is that you…prefer the company of your own sex."

"What? Why, the very accusation—"

Louisa sighed. She had anticipated this reaction. "Let us calm down with the histrionics. I saw you speaking with your friend at the Atherton ball, and with the Marquess of Beresford, who, as it happens, is friends with some of my friends, and who let slip that you and he had an affair years ago."

Daniel stared at her. He said nothing.

"I don't judge you, to be clear. I'm also not naive. I know some men prefer their own sex. Greystone has a close friend who does, as well, and even though I don't completely understand it, I don't view it as wrong or sinful. What I do think, though, is that, again, you and I will not suit. I want…I want more than what you can offer. I want to be loved and desired, not just tolerated."

"I could learn to love you with time."

"*Could* being the operative word."

"Louisa, I—"

"Do you want the other reasons?"

He grunted affirmatively and threw his hand aside, as if he understood protest was futile. "Please."

"The third is that my mother told me that have a business arrangement with my father that hinges on me marrying you. That does put me in a complicated spot because I do not wish to harm my father or his business prospects, so I don't know what to do with that, aside from asking if it's true."

"It is true that your father and I have a business deal that is contingent on our wedding actually happening."

Louisa was disappointed to have that confirmed. "I'm sure my delicate female brain is too weak to understand it," she said with a raised eyebrow, "but that is something I intend to revisit later."

"Then tell me the fourth reason." Daniel's tone had grown testy, and he crossed his arms now.

"If you must know, I love another, and he has offered for me, and I'd like to be free of this betrothal so that I might marry him instead, because I think he and I *do* suit, and we'd be very happy together."

"Greystone," Daniel said flatly.

"I suppose it would probably surprise you to know that, until about a week ago, I didn't know any of this. I didn't know about your affair with Beresford until a couple of nights ago, in fact, although after the way you spoke with Lieutenant Hanley at the Atherton ball, I had some suspicions. And the one time you and I kissed, it felt… I felt nothing. There's no connection, no passion between us. So I had begun to suspect you felt no lust for me, which I take no offense to, by the way, as I am old and plain and…well, it doesn't matter. But I didn't know I had romantic feelings for Fletcher—for Greystone—until recently, either. And now I'm rambling."

"Do you find me so horrid that you must concoct all these reasons?"

"Concoct? No, not at all. I meant it when I said yes to your proposal. I wish you had not announced it so publicly, but it's in the past. I thought the two of us would get on well. You're very handsome and you have some charm. I thought we'd grow to care about each other over time. But it seems our engagement has unlocked all of this other information, and now that Fle— Greystone, now that Greystone has offered to me, I find myself contemplating the future. I am sorry. But surely this is a relief to you, too."

"On the contrary," Daniel said. He sighed. "You're right, I do prefer my own sex. And I thought marrying might be a cure for it. I do genuinely like you, Louisa. You're not plain. You're very pretty. And you make me laugh."

"Thank you, I think. But you know as well as I do that we will likely never mean more to each other than friends do. You don't love me, and you never will. And so we are at this impasse, because I want to end our engagement, but my family will not let me, I suppose because of this business deal. And I think marrying Greystone would make me happy. I guess I can't know that. He and I have always regarded each other like siblings. But he says he loves me now, which is already offering me something you can't give me."

"You haven't…had relations, though, right?"

"With Greystone? No." She decided to omit that they'd kissed. "He won't so much as touch me while I'm still engaged to you. He is a gentleman, after all."

Daniel frowned. "You've put me in an awkward position, Louisa."

"I know. I know, Daniel, and I'm so sorry to be doing this to you, but I want out of the engagement, and I know of no way to make that happen without being upfront and honest about why. Surely you see my logic."

"I do. But you must also understand my position. Breaking the engagement will make us both look terrible, it will be a huge scandal. I need a wife so that it does not become more widely known that I have had dalliances with my own sex, and…"

"Wait." Something horrible suddenly became clear to Louisa. "You offered for me because of my proximity to the shelf, didn't you?"

"No, I—"

"It makes sense. I am, after all, too old to be a debutante. I'm practically a spinster. Several suitors have told me I'm too clever for my own good, or they distrusted my relationship with Greystone, which I guess they were right to, but at any rate, I have arrived at this present moment rather old to be a new wife and so I must have been desperate, right? I would have said yes to your proposal because I needed to or I risked social ostracism. And then you made the deal, whatever it is, with my father to further incentivize the marriage. Because Greystone is not exactly poor, and his family and mine have known each other for decades, so he is a more logical choice of husband now that he's come to his senses. But I'm trapped."

"You aren't trapped."

"But you do not intend to let me out of the engagement."

"I don't."

"This is hardly a strong basis for the beginning of a marriage."

"Please try to see it my way, Louisa. And now that you know why I want to get married, we are being honest with each other, are we not? Honesty is a sound basis for a marriage."

"Yes, but if you can't love me, then it is not enough."

"Marriage doesn't need love. It's not much more than a business partnership."

"A business partnership in which one of the partners has no power or freedom."

"Oh, here we go with the Wollstonecraft business."

Louisa bristled at that. Had he been talking to her mother? She stood up. "Am I wrong? The woman in a marriage has no power. She is basically a broodmare for her husband to produce heirs and look pretty. That's all you want of me, isn't it? And perhaps that is enough for some women, but it is *not* enough for me, and I don't see why I should subject myself to it, especially when I have a better offer."

"And what will you do when I *ruin* your family, Louisa?" Daniel stood. "What then?"

Louisa couldn't tell how serious Daniel was being. Could he really ruin her family? Why would he do such a thing? "Surely you can find an unwitting debutante who is too empty-headed to uncover your schemes. You don't really need me."

"I could do that, but you've already said yes. And I have no intention of ending our engagement. The wedding is still happening. You'd do well to get used to the idea. I believe we'd make good companions for each other, and I think with time, you will see that." He stood and put his hat back on his head. "Good day, my lady."

With that, he stormed out of the room.

Louisa took a moment to gather herself. She was so angry she wanted to hurl the precious ceramics her mother collected at his departing figure. Several figurines were on the mantel, and wouldn't it feel so satisfying to watch that ceramic cherub break into pieces against the floor?

Before she committed any crimes against ceramics, her mother walked back into the room. "Louisa, what happened?"

"I tried to break the engagement and he refused."

"Well, of course he did. Why would you do anything so foolish?"

"Mother, he and I do not suit. We have little in common and he seems not to have much respect for me. If he's not stepping out on me now, I can guarantee he will in the future. How can I marry him?"

"Louisa, I'm not having this argument again."

"He said some pretty cruel things to me. He only offered for me because of my advanced age because he wanted someone desperate enough not to say no, and then he made the deal with Father to keep me trapped."

That seemed to give her mother pause. But then she said, "Don't be dramatic, Louisa," and swept out of the room.

Not knowing what else to do, Louisa let out a scream, ran to her bedroom, and threw the door shut.

LORD PETTY KEPT an office on Bank Street, so Fletcher went there hoping to catch him without his wife or daughter around. He was pleased when Lord Petty's secretary said he was in and would see Fletcher when he finished with his current meeting.

Fletcher spent his time waiting in the hall trying to mentally formulate what he would say. How did one broach a subject like this? *Your daughter is desperate to break her engagement to the man you have an important deal with. Would you mind disclosing those details?*

Obviously that would not do.

The secretary showed Fletcher in as a man Fletcher didn't recognize walked out. Fletcher couldn't remember exactly the sort of business Petty most frequently did; real estate holdings, he suspected. England's most profitable asset was its land, after all, and Petty was a fairly wealthy man.

"Ah, Fletcher," Petty said as Fletcher walked in. "Good to see you, son. How many I help you today?"

"I want to discuss something delicate with you, my lord. So I thought I'd start by reminding you of how fond you were of my father."

Petty regarded Fletcher warily. "Yes. I miss him a great deal."

"As do I," Fletcher said.

"Have a seat."

Fletcher sat, still not entirely sure what to say, beyond, "It's about Louisa."

Petty nodded as though he expected this. "What is it?"

"Sir, I need you to know that Louisa came to me because she is in some level of distress. She wants to end her engagement to Rotherfeld, having determined that they do not suit. I can't say I blame her. I made an attempt to befriend him, and it did not go well." Which was putting it mildly. Fletcher's loathing of Rotherfeld expanded each day like weeds in an untended garden.

"Oh. What was your impression of him?"

"Candidly? I found him unspeakably dull."

Petty grimaced. "Not the most scintillating conversationalist, I will concede, but—"

"Please let me finish." Fletcher felt like he had to lay it all out quickly. He'd spent the carriage ride here practicing what he'd say, but now it all left him. His heart pounded. He'd known Lord Petty his entire life, had always thought him a friendly, respectable man, but talking to him about Louisa was personal in a way that made Fletcher's stomach flop. "And please also know how uncomfortable I am having this conversation, but I made a promise to Louisa, and I have a great deal of respect for you. I have always known you to be a kind and rational man."

"Well, thank you, son, but—"

"Louisa came to me because she does not believe you and her mother are listening to her distress regarding the wedding. When Louisa asked her mother if she could end the engagement—and please know, it is not only Rotherfeld's temperament but some other factors, too, that are rather salacious and that I'd prefer not to explore too much—but when Louisa talked to her mother, Lady Petty said that Rotherfeld had a business arrangement with you that was contingent on the wedding going through, and thus Louisa, no matter her distress, could not end the engagement without risking losing a great deal of money for you."

Recognition dawned on Petty's face. "I see."

"I suppose my question is two-fold. Is there a business deal? I need not know the particulars, but the second part of my question is if there is anything I can offer that would entice you to break the agreement with Rotherfeld."

Petty regarded Fletcher for long moment. Fletcher couldn't interpret the look on his face.

"You seem rather invested," Petty said at length.

"As I said, Louisa asked me directly for help."

"And I appreciate that, but it seems out of character for you to meddle in business affairs. I know you are now managing your father's investments, so maybe that's changed, but you've never seemed especially interested in this sort of thing. Unless you have some other motivation."

Fletcher nodded. Perhaps Lord Petty knew Fletcher better than he thought. He was reluctant to play this card, but he said, "Well, my lord, should the engagement with Rotherfeld end, I intend to offer for Louisa's hand myself." Once it was out, Fletcher braced himself for Petty's reaction.

That seemed to surprise Petty. "You do?"

"I know this may seem sudden, but—"

"No, my boy, you misunderstand me." He sighed. "What a pickle. I would happily throw over Rotherfeld tomorrow if I could. You're right, he's a bore, and I have my own suspicions about him that you've all but confirmed, but he's wealthy and has a fine reputation, so I didn't hesitate when he offered for Louisa. But you are like a son to me, and I would happily welcome you to my family…had you asked three months ago."

"So there is a business deal?"

"It's a mess. It's all a grand mess."

"I don't mean to pry the details out of you, but perhaps I can be of some assistance. My business acumen is not as well-honed as my father's, but I have spent the better part of the last year being advised by the best advisors in London."

Petty nodded. "You really would marry Louisa? She has always insisted that the two of you felt like siblings and had no interest in marrying each other, and she's been on the shelf so long now that I suppose I thought—"

"I believe it took her prospective marriage to Rotherfeld for us to both come to our senses."

Petty smiled. "I can understand that. Lady Petty and I circled around each other for a bit before agreeing to marry." He sighed. "All right. This all started about six months ago. We spent the summer at our estate in Bristol, and Rotherfeld came to visit for a few nights. I figured it was part of his courtship with Louisa, but one night over cigars, he mentioned that he was in Bristol in part on business because he'd recently come into some land not far from my estate. He wanted us to go in on the farm there together and share in the profits."

Fletcher's knowledge of Bristol was not encyclopedic, but something about that tugged at his memory. "The Cadwallader sheep farm?" It was an extremely profitable farm that sold wool to one of the textile factories Fletcher's father had invested in. It had come up in one of the many business meetings Fletcher had sat through in the last few weeks.

"The same. After Mr. Cadwallader passed away last year, Rotherfeld claimed, the deed passed through a circuitous route and landed with Rotherfeld, and Rotherfeld wanted my help as a local to figure out the best use for it. Long story short, I invested some money on renovations of the house there and hired a staff to see after the sheep. The wool is supplying several textile mills in the region, and—you know what, the details are not of import. The moral of the story is that I invested the money on the understanding that Rotherfeld and I would share the profits from the farm. We didn't sign a formal agreement because we were to be family, after all."

The lack of a written agreement was a problem, and all but ensured that Petty would see none of the profits should the engagement end. Thus there'd be no possibility of recouping his investment. At least Fletcher had a better understanding of the issue now. One detail snagged in his mind, though. "You knew of Rotherfeld's intention to propose to Louisa six months ago?"

"Indeed, it was one of many things he asked me for on that visit. And I admit, I was rather charmed by him. He's dull, yes, but he has a good head for business, and I suppose I figured, he wouldn't renege on this deal because he'd be at every Sunday dinner for the rest of my life, so why did I need a written agreement?" Petty made a disgusted sound and shook his head.

Fletcher summarized the predicament: "The deed is still in Rotherfeld's name. And he intends to take it with him should the engagement end, meaning you'd have lost your investment, which I'm guessing was substantial."

"Precisely."

Fletcher swallowed a colorful oath.

"You see the bind I find myself in. It is a great deal of money I stand to lose. On the other hand, I hate to think of Louisa unhappy. Is she rather desperate to end the engagement?"

She'd sent Fletcher a note this morning to say she'd failed to persuade Rotherfeld directly. "I believe she is. Some information has come to light that—"

Petty held up his hand. "I suspect I know what you are about to say. I overlooked my suspicions for the sake of the business deal and Louisa's happiness. I did think she was happy. She told me she wanted to marry Rotherfeld. You know that, right?"

"I do know that, and I thought she was happy, too, sir. She didn't start having misgivings until a couple of weeks ago."

"And now it is all falling apart."

Fletcher didn't think Petty would disclose how much money he'd invested in the sheep farm and how much he stood to lose, but that was all right. Fletcher had other ways to figure it out. He wondered if he could just buy out Rotherfeld.

"You'd be wise to stay clear of this matter," Petty said. "I see the wheels turning in your head."

"All I want is Louisa's happiness. And she has told me she

does not want to marry Rotherfeld, so I am doing what I can to see that she gets her way, but this is not an easy situation. Surely you can see the problem here. Rotherfeld needs a wife, regardless of the reason. He likely chose Louisa because she is old enough that he thought she'd be desperate to marry, and he got involved in business with you so that you could not send him away if she got cold feet. I've a letter from Louisa this morning saying she tried to ask Rotherfeld directly to end the engagement, he refused, and now she feels trapped."

"Yes, I fear I do understand."

"Please know, I am not trying to lose your money."

Petty smiled faintly. "I was foolish not to put things in writing."

"But you believe that my only motive here is Louisa's happiness."

"I do believe you, because I've known you since you were a boy and I've seen what a good man you've grown up to be. If a marriage to each other is what both of you want, then I want that for you, too. I've always had a soft spot for Louisa. I'd rather lose the money than have her be miserable."

"But it is a great sum, I take it."

"Do you plan to try to buy out Rotherfeld?"

"I'm considering it."

"You recently sold some of your father's business."

"It was too much for me to manage on my own. But I did make a tidy profit from the sales. I can put at least some of that toward the sheep farm in Bristol."

"I don't think Rotherfeld will sell, but you are welcome to try."

"Why wouldn't he sell?"

"Some men are motivated by more than money, and Rotherfeld has a reputation to maintain."

So Petty understood the situation they were all in as well. Fletcher was a little surprised that Petty was so insightful, but perhaps he'd seen what he wanted to see until recently, too.

"Well. Now that I know the situation, I suppose I must talk with him," said Fletcher.

"Godspeed." Petty rubbed his forehead. "I admit, I am at a loss about what to do. I don't want you to lose money or get entangled in this mess, either. Your father just left us, and you must have enough to manage."

It didn't seem like Lord Petty would be much help. "I will consult with my advisors, I suppose."

"Let me give you some advice, son," Petty said, standing to escort Fletcher back out of the office. "Always trust your gut. I had an inkling that something was amiss when Rotherfeld first came to me, but I had no evidence that anything was not as it should have been, and Louisa seemed happy. I should have trusted my instinct rather than go into business with Rotherfeld, and I shall regret this decision for a long time to come, I imagine. When you have those kinds of inklings, listen to them."

Fletcher nodded. He really hadn't been listening to his gut lately, but maybe if he had a year ago, Rotherfeld would never have become a thorn in his side. "That is good advice, thank you."

"I do hope you are triumphant in your quest. But Louisa is more important to me than money, so if you are unsuccessful—"

"I shall endeavor to succeed."

Petty nodded but looked unconvinced. "If you are unsuccessful, I'll lose money. As I said, Louisa is more important to me. So we will figure something out." His sadness at this prospect was palpable.

So Petty had already given up. Fletcher understood that Rotherfeld might prove to be a substantial foe. And he only had a week to figure out how to vanquish him.

Chapter Eighteen

"I COULD LEAK something to the scandal sheets," Lark said at the club that night. "A rumor that a certain Duke of R—is having an affair with a Lieutenant H—that would bring them both down, and yet they persist..."

"Subtlety, thy name is a scandal sheet," said Owen.

Fletcher sat in his usual seat in the club and enjoyed his friends' attempts both to strategize and cheer him up.

Hugh leveled his gaze at Lark. "You don't think Rotherfeld would retaliate?"

Lark shrugged. "I'm not saying I thought it through."

"I have to buy him out, right?" said Fletcher. "I have to push a giant pile of money at Rotherfeld, buy the farm for more than it's worth, and go into business with Lord Petty, who would then become my father-in-law."

"Sure," said Lark, "you could make some kind of deal in a smoke-filled room, out of the gaze of the public, *or* you could bring the man down in the papers. I've got an in with *Talk of the Town*. He'll never track the rumor back to me."

"You're in a suspiciously positive mood," said Hugh. "And possibly have a death wish."

Lark shrugged. "Things are looking up. Although perhaps not for Fletcher, if he is about to be parted with a large sum of money."

"I don't want to own a sheep farm," said Fletcher. "I can barely handle all of my father's holdings as it is."

"Hire someone to oversee your part of the investment but let Petty run it otherwise," Hugh suggested.

"This is all seeming a bit…" Fletcher struggled to find the word. "I don't know. Unseemly. Like I'm bribing Lord Petty into letting me marry Louisa."

"Normally it's the other way around," Owen pointed out.

"I don't understand why money must be involved at all," said Fletcher. "Why do we make marriage into a business arrangement? Don't answer that, I know why, I just… Louisa does not want to marry Rotherfeld, I am trying to rescue her, but now I might have to buy half a sheep farm, and it all seems absurd."

"What's your plan?" asked Hugh. "You're real plan, not Lark's plan to tarnish his reputation."

"I don't know. Talk to Rotherfeld, I suppose."

"Are you having second thoughts?" asked Hugh. "About marrying Louisa, I mean."

"No." And he genuinely wasn't. "But I thought I had the solution. No doubt, if she breaks the engagement, there will be social fallout, but it will blow over, especially since it's not like this will render her unmarriageable. I plan to marry her, after all. And then we can leave town until next season, when everyone's attention will have moved on to something else."

"That's a good plan," said Lark.

"But only if Rotherfeld agrees to give up on the engagement. Unfortunately, it sounds like that is something he is unwilling to do, and he's basically bribed Louisa's father to keep him from ending things."

"Did Petty say how much his investment in the farm was?" asked Owen.

"No, but this afternoon, I dropped a hint with my man of business that I was interested in finding out, so he's probably got half of Scotland Yard combing through public records. I fear it is a large amount, though, or Petty would not be so reluctant to part with the money."

"So, what now?" said Hugh. "Is it expected that Louisa just say *yes* at the wedding if Rotherfeld does not relent? If you want to marry her, why not just elope?"

"I want to do this right," said Fletcher. "I'm not marrying her just to rescue her from Rotherfeld. I'm marrying her because I love her."

"And that's noble," said Owen. "But sometimes marriages are not love affairs."

Said a man whose marriage was arranged after he was caught kissing his now-wife.

Fletcher sighed. "I am running out of time. I may have to be that man who shows up at the wedding and objects to the union."

"That would keep tongues wagging," said Lark, sounding delighted.

"Larkin Woodville," said Hugh. "What has gotten into you?"

Lark shrugged. "It's good that everyone is making summer plans, because it looks like I won't be staying in London this summer, either. Anthony and I will head to his country estate to hide for a bit. See if we can make a go of things."

This was not met with the enthusiastic response Lark was probably expecting.

"Are you sure?" asked Hugh.

Lark laughed ruefully. "No. I'm not really sure about any-thing except that I love him. Maybe us spending a summer in close proximity will inspire enmity. That feels likely, in fact. Or perhaps we will discover that we are in fact well-suited, and we'll spend the rest of our lives together, albeit not publicly. That little boy is precious and deserves all the love in the world now that his mother is gone, and I can contribute to that."

"What an odd, untraditional assortment of men we turned out to be," said Hugh. "My mother didn't approve of my wife. Owen planned to install his wife in Wales so they could lead separate lives and fell in love with her anyway. Fletcher has to rescue his love from a nefarious duke. And Lark is going to build a family with a man who, until a few years ago, we all found irritating."

"Your mother still doesn't approve of your wife," Lark pointed out.

"And even so," said Hugh, "the next Duke of Swynford is walking around and sassing his grandmother, so I feel like I got the last laugh there."

"Sassing her? Really?" said Lark.

"Mother came for luncheon a few days ago and wanted to visit with her grandson, who told her, repeatedly, that she was old and boring."

"Isn't he two? Does he know the words *old* and *boring*?" asked Fletcher.

"He knows a frightening number of words. Some of them are nonsense, but he's stringing sentences together now and it's both adorable and alarming."

"I hope you know what you're in for, Lark," said Owen. "The nursery is directly above my bedroom, and I woke up this morning to the sounds of the nanny running after my son. Like this." Owen drummed his hands against his thigh to demonstrate. "For a half hour. Until Grace woke up, too, and went up there to see what was going on. The nanny suggested we let the boy run around the garden during the day. To let him outside like we would a dog, basically."

Hugh nodded. "You need to let them tire themselves out sometimes."

"Having anything to do with your children is… Is it a new development for this generation?" asked Fletcher. "I imagine if you'd asked my father what I was like as a child, he wouldn't be able to tell you."

"It's likely not normal," said Hugh. "I don't think it's the done thing for fathers to be so…hands-on. Nor to talk about their children over whisky like this. But as I've established, we are…outliers."

"I regret that my father and I were not closer," said Fletcher.

"So I understand why you are behaving as you are. It just struck me as odd, but maybe it shouldn't have."

"Perhaps the key to becoming an adult is that you realize you don't have to do things the way your parents did," said Lark. "My own parents have stopped asking me when I'm going to get married. They have, perhaps, given up."

"My mother hasn't," said Fletcher. "Since Father died, she's been somewhat relentless. But I haven't wanted to tell her about Louisa until I know how everything will be when the dust settles."

"The dust settles where?" asked Anthony, suddenly appearing.

"Ah, you made it out after all," Lark said.

"I was going to go mad if I spent any more time glaring at the wallpaper in my sitting room," said Anthony, settling into the chair an attendant brought over. "Mrs. Church, little Henry's nurse, insisted I leave the house for my own sanity, so here I am. But I promise to try to be the most delightful company. What are we discussing?"

Fletcher gave Anthony an appraising look. He'd cut his hair shorter recently and he wore all black, making him look decidedly not like himself, but he had a familiar glint in his eye.

"Well, darling," said Lark, "we are discussing Fletcher's impending nuptials, or not."

"Oh, right, the business with Rotherfeld." Anthony leaned forward as though he were interested in these proceedings.

Fletcher assumed Lark had already filled Anthony in, but he said, "There is a precarious financial transaction at the heart of all this."

"How foolish we have been as a society to make something so intimate into a business transaction," Anthony said.

"Or, how foolish of modern society to make a business transaction about love and intimacy," said Lark. "For decades, our royals, for example, have married European princesses but carried on affairs with the women they truly cared for or were attracted to. Are we moving into an era in which men choose wives they truly love instead? It seems to me it makes married life far more pleasant."

"Each generation wants their lives to be better than their parents," said Anthony. "But I believe we've arrived at a turning point in history, no? Radicals agitating for women to have more freedom, for society to be less buttoned up, our notions of what marriage could or should be shifting, machinery is making the things we buy, our clothing has become a little less restrictive, and so on and so on. New freedoms lurk around the corners, gents. And though perhaps we as individuals are not the tip of the spear for change, you can't deny that change is happening."

Fletcher just stared at Anthony, not really appreciating this philosophical turn. Anthony was right, but this was hardly the time. "Yes, change is an unyielding tide and all that. I don't see how that helps my current predicament."

"Maybe what you should do is go to the wedding, object when appropriate, and then give Rotherfeld a swift kick to the gut," said Lark. "Push him out of the way and marry Louisa yourself. I mean, your family will be in attendance, will they not?"

"My mother was invited, yes. And several cousins, actually."

"Then they cannot object to you getting married without their presence."

"Lark, I know you're giddy in love and all that," said Hugh, "and I'm very glad your melancholia has passed, but your delight in scandal and the misery of others is going to take a moment to get used to again."

"Giddy in love!" Anthony said, laughing. "Is that what you are?"

Lark rolled his eyes, but he was smiling. "I'm just making suggestions."

"And fine as they may be," said Fletcher, "I don't intend to create a scene if I can help it."

"None of you are any fun."

"Marlborough's mistress has gifted him with an illegitimate heir," said Anthony.

"And?" said Fletcher.

"Just sharing gossip. And, I suppose, feeling a bit put out that this news has mostly been greeted with yawns—a young duke fathering a child before he marries, something that has happened since the first duke was created—but so many less significant things are considered scandalous. And I could easily take this to a dark place, so let us ignore me and carry on brainstorming how to get Fletcher out of his predicament."

"Well, what do you suggest?" Fletcher asked Anthony.

"Money fixes everything." Anthony shrugged. "I share in Lark's delight in the possibility of a scene at a wedding. Were any of the rest of you at Mitford's wedding, when he was left at the altar? Couldn't have happened to a bigger cad."

"I only heard about that," said Lark. "If I recall correctly, the scandal sheets reported he'd been regularly spending nights with a lady of the night, and indeed, spent the eve of his wedding with this woman he was paying."

"I don't blame his would-be bride for avoiding syphilis and ending that whole charade," said Anthony.

Fletcher looked back and forth between Lark and Anthony, who were leaning toward each other as if this were the most fascinating conversation they'd ever had. He cleared his throat.

"Oh, right," said Anthony, grinning. "My point was, I understand why you would perhaps not want to make a scene, much as I might enjoy it. But this might be one of those cases in which you might deploy your substantial power and fortune in order to orchestrate the outcome you most desire."

"I had already come to the same conclusion," Fletcher said, "although it may be a great deal of money. There's a sheep farm in Bristol that—"

"Is this much ado about a sheep farm?" Anthony asked Lark.

"It is. But it's a famous and quite profitable sheep farm. Your coat may very well have been made with wool from said sheep farm."

Anthony looked down at his black wool suit coat and ran his

hands over the lapels. "All right. Someone spell out the particulars for me."

Anthony sat patiently as Fletcher described the situation again. When Fletcher finished, Anthony said, "All right. I've got an idea."

Fletcher listened and found it oddly reasonable. "I'll take that into consideration." He wasn't willing to commit to a plan, but Anthony's idea was better than anything he'd come up with so far.

"It is nice to see you out here, solving our problems again, Anthony," said Hugh.

"I am nothing if not unerringly practical."

"Ha," said Lark.

Anthony cut Lark a wry look, but said, "I do enjoy your company, gents. Many of my friends have abandoned London in recent years and I am grateful that Lark introduced me to you all."

"Just don't let Lark be hanged," Hugh said. "That's all I ask."

"I spend every day trying to determine how best to ensure no harm comes to him."

"This is an odd situation we all find ourselves in," said Fletcher.

Owen held up his glass. "Let's toast to Lark's and Anthony's happiness. And Fletcher's, too."

All five men clinked their glasses together.

LOUISA FROWNED AT the pink blob that was supposed to be a flower in her embroidery project. She must have miscounted stitches. But then, of course she had; her mind was elsewhere.

Her father appeared in the doorway of the sitting room, which surprised her. He was rarely home at this time in the afternoon.

"There you are," he said, as though he'd been looking all over for her.

"Hello," she said. "Did you need something?"

Father walked into the room and sat next to her on the sofa. "Let me speak with you about something."

"Please do."

He frowned. "Fletcher Basildon came to speak to me today."

Louisa's pulse sped up, but she felt somewhat gratified that Fletcher had abided by his half of the bargain. "And?"

"Do you really feel trapped in your engagement to Rotherfeld?"

Lord George Petty had long been a bit soft, something Louisa had always appreciated. He was ruthless in business, but kind and empathetic with his family. The way he said the word *trapped* made Louisa believe that he'd understand her plight in a way her mother didn't.

"When Rotherfeld first started to court me last season, I was open to him," Louisa said, deciding to start at the beginning. "He is very handsome, after all, and he was kind to me, and he was always a perfect gentleman. That all impressed me. It wasn't love, but I know better than to expect love, at least right away. When he proposed, I couldn't think of a reason to say *no*, and I imagined that, over time, we'd get to know each other and grow fond of each other and have a perfectly agreeable marriage. However, this season, as we have gotten to know each other quite well, some…new facts have come to light."

"Yes, Fletcher mentioned. But why don't you tell me yourself?"

Louisa wondered how much Fletcher had told Father. "I did tell Mother, and she essentially told me I was being foolish, and I did not have a choice in this matter." She sighed. "As for Rotherfeld, I don't think we suit, is the main thing. I find him dull. He thinks my interests are frivolous. Often when we spend time together, we run out of things to discuss. And perhaps that is something that can be overcome, but I…" Louisa felt tears sting her eyes. These were petty reasons not to marry. She was reluctant to talk about Daniel's affairs with men, but she didn't know how else to convince her father. "And I believe he's having an affair with someone else. I suppose I don't have proof, and I am just operating on a gut feeling I have, but I'm certain I saw him with someone at the Atherton ball, and… Well, it doesn't much matter. I confronted him yesterday, and he didn't confirm my suspicion about the affair, but he didn't deny it either. So I asked him to let me out of the engagement, and he refused. And he was honest. He wanted a wife. He as much as admitted that he chose me because I'm old enough to be on the shelf and he figured I'd be desperate. I *wasn't* desperate, but he seemed like a nice man, and who was I to turn that down? But now he's got this business arrangement with you, and I just think… I think he and I will make each other miserable. Neither of us wants to be married to the other, but Rotherfeld feels that he must marry, and so, yes, I find myself trapped."

Father looked at the floor for a long moment. "There have been some unsavory rumors about Rotherfeld in the past. I ignored them because he seemed like such a good-hearted young man when we spoke. And when he came to me with this farm deal, I thought he was acting as my future son-in-law and introducing me to a good business prospect. I didn't realize he was putting me in a position where I could not say no to him."

"I don't think he's a bad man. But I don't want to marry him."

"Fletcher offered to marry you."

So he'd really said it all. "Did he?"

"This cannot be a surprise. I take it you and he have been discussing it."

"I… yes. He hasn't formally proposed, but he told me he'd marry me if I ended my engagement to Rotherfeld."

"Do you want to marry Fletcher?"

"Yes," Louisa said, suddenly overcome with her emotions. The longer she stared down this situation, the more clear it was to her that she very much wanted to marry Fletcher. She could practically see their whole future together, laughing and teasing each other and making good on the promise of a few stolen kisses. She knew she would cry now, frustrated as she was with Daniel, and she hated it. She wanted to show strength. But the predicament she found herself in now weighed on her. "Yes, I want to marry Fletcher. I wish either of us had realized how much we meant to each other sooner than a month ago, but here I am now. Rotherfeld and I are not married yet. Please tell me it's not too late."

"Oh, my dear. I hate to see you cry." Father reached over and wiped away an escaped tear with his thumb. "I do not believe it is too late, but it's possible Rotherfeld intends to ruin me financially if you don't go through with it. Which is not my way of saying you must marry Rotherfeld, but I do not know what I will do if you don't."

"Fletcher can help, surely. He just inherited his father's business holdings."

"I don't want to ask that of him. Financial entanglements with one prospective son-in-law should not be cured with entanglements with another. On the other hand, I've always liked that boy." Father shook his head. "I know not what to do about any of this."

"In other words, you won't force me to marry Rotherfeld, but there could be serious consequences if I don't."

Father sighed and nodded. "That is about the sum of it."

What a mess. Louisa had no idea what to do. And there was less than a week to go until the wedding.

Chapter Nineteen

FLETCHER MET LOUISA in his drawing room. At least it wasn't the middle of the night—she'd arrived at his home in the early afternoon—but it was probably still inappropriate. She braced herself for Fletcher to say as much, but she didn't care anymore.

Maybe propriety didn't matter anymore.

"What are you doing here?" he asked, even though must have known.

"I told my mother I was calling on Lady Adele, and she allowed me to walk outside without taking my maid."

"Foolish of her." But a small smile played across Fletcher's lips.

"Indeed. But I needed to speak with you."

He sighed. "I don't have much to report. I spoke with your father."

Louisa sat on the sofa and motioned for Fletcher to do the same, but he stood. Every emotion seemed to be displayed on his face at once. He shot Louisa a sad smile, like maybe he was happy to see her but unhappy about the circumstances, but he also looked distressed, like he thought the meeting with Louisa's father had been futile. But it hadn't, at least not from Louisa's perspective.

"I know you talked to Father," Louisa said. "He told me."

"I want you to know, I feel terrible that you feel trapped in the engagement, and I believe that it's not too late as long as you aren't legally wed to Rotherfeld, but I walked away from the meeting with your father convinced that the only way to end the engagement is for me to spend some money. So I spent the morning trying to find out how much that would cost me, and I finally just got word that it's a hefty sum."

"You mean father's half of the business arrangement. Do you intend to buy out Rotherfeld?"

"That's an option on the table. That is, I could pay Rotherfeld's half of the farm that he invested in and go into business with your father. It was my initial instinct to do that."

Louisa hadn't known it was a farm. Father invested in a farm? An expensive one? "But it's a lot of money," she reiterated.

"It is. Not an unsurmountable amount, but enough that I'm hesitant to part with it. I have my man of business looking into it now, though. He's also investigating a few other options. Beresford, of all people, had an idea about what I could do instead, but it still involves spending some money."

"I don't want you to have to buy me." Louisa could not understand what the men in her life were about. "I'm a woman, not a parcel of land or a fancy trinket."

"I understand that, and I agree with you, but I can't see another solution. Can you?"

Louisa was angry and frustrated and she stood so she could pace back and forth across the room. In point of fact, she could not figure a way out of this, hence feeling trapped. "I didn't know Rotherfeld was so…nefarious. I had no idea."

"I know you didn't."

"I feel like a fool."

"You shouldn't. You couldn't have known. He fooled all of us." Fletcher tracked her with his gaze as she paced. "And I don't think he's a bad man. He's just not the man for you."

"He tricked me. Made me think he could love me. But I wasn't much more than a mark to him."

"So maybe he *is* a bad man. It's not too late to, I don't know, leave a snake in his house. Preferably a poisonous one."

"Fletcher. Be serious," Louisa said, although she giggled. She was angry, though.

She stomped across the room. Fletcher stood in the middle and stared at her as she paced. She was mad at him, too, angry that he didn't speak up for her sooner, sad that they'd missed an opportunity by being fools about each other and not recognizing their own feelings. If she could have married Fletcher a year ago, she wouldn't be in this predicament.

"I hate this," she said. "I hate that I as a woman have no power to choose who I marry because I happen to be a little older than most women are when they get married, I hate that Daniel took advantage of my need to find a husband, I hate that it took my engagement to make *you* realize you had feelings for me, if you even do or if you're just saying you do to rescue me as a friend, and I—"

Fletcher grabbed her arm, and she abruptly stopped pacing. "I do have feelings."

"And I hate that I have to keep you at arm's length because of my engagement to Daniel, because all I want to do all the time is kiss you."

Fletcher stared at her for a long moment, his expression unreadable. "Louisa."

"I hate that Daniel is preventing me from starting the rest of my life because *he* needed a bride."

"I can't change the past," Fletcher said, sounding like he regretted that fact.

"I want it to be you at the church Saturday. I don't want to see Daniel ever again."

"I'd marry you tomorrow if I didn't think Rotherfeld would retaliate by ruining your father."

"Fletcher, I—"

Suddenly, he swooped over and kissed her.

This was what she'd wanted. Fletcher's lips were warm and

firm, he tasted a bit like tea, and kissing him made her chest warm and her skin tingle. Fletcher put his hands on her waist and pulled her close, and she was reminded that he had experience with women, but she had no experience with men. She trusted him, though, trusted him to show her what to do, trusted him to care for her and not to hurt her. He'd know what to do on their wedding night, though, something she looked forward to experiencing, especially since kissing him was so good. She put her arms around his shoulders and kept him close to her so they could keep kissing.

"We shouldn't," Fletcher said when he pulled away slightly. "Rotherfeld…"

"To the devil with Rotherfeld."

Fletcher chuckled softly. "I quite agree, but I don't mean to cuckold the man."

Louisa took a step back. "On my growing list of resentments of Rotherfeld is the fact that I want to kiss you and see what comes next, but you keep stopping me because of my engagement."

"Trust me, if I had any less integrity, you'd be naked on my settee right now, but I am trying to be a gentleman."

"I wish you wouldn't."

"Louisa." His tone was reproachful but amused.

"You truly want me?"

"More than anything."

Louisa frowned at him. "Do you think I'm beautiful?"

"Yes." No hesitation.

"Have you always thought so?"

"Perhaps not when you were a child, but especially since we started attending the opera together? Yes. I noticed you were beautiful. You have that yellow gown you wear sometimes, the one with the little flowers embroidered on it?"

Louisa was surprised Fletcher had noticed her that much. "What about it?"

"When you wear it, it shows of your… bosom, in a quite

appealing way. Since the first time you wore it, I wondered about that. I didn't want to leer at you, but...yes, I find you very attractive. But I also thought we considered each other siblings, and what sort of lech lusts after his sister?"

"The one who is not actually related by blood."

"Fair. But for me, half the fun of going to the opera with you, or going to garden parties or dinner parties or balls, is your company. I would like the opera far less if you didn't attend with me. I would enjoy other social occasions far less if we could not gently mock the other attendants together. I always enjoy myself more when I am with you. That is how I know we will have a very good marriage, if that is what you are worried about."

"I think you are very handsome. You like to wear your breeches in a way that is...clingy."

He raised an eyebrow. "Clingy?"

"As in they cling to your thighs in a very appealing way." She felt heat flood her face, but she pushed forward. "And I like your hair now that you've grown it a little long."

"Oh." He touched the edges of his dark hair.

"And I am staring down a wedding to a man who does not desire me, but do I not deserve to be desired?"

"Yes, you absolutely do."

"I desire you, Fletcher. Do you desire me?"

"Like a man on a hot day desires a glass of water."

And then they were kissing again, despite Fletcher's protestations.

He was fully dressed for the afternoon, wearing a crisp white shirt, beige waistcoat, and a black jacket and trousers. And even through all those layers of fabric, Louisa could feel the heat of his body when she put her hands on his shoulders.

Heat. She felt hot everywhere, but she welcomed it.

Fletcher pulled away again and sighed. "You're really testing me." Then he pulled her close. He placed a hand on the side of her head and gently pressed her against his chest. He was quite a bit taller than she was, so her ear pressed just below his shoulder.

He held her there for a long moment.

She trusted Fletcher implicitly. She felt safe with him. They'd never really touched this way before, but something in Louisa understood that he would never push her farther than she was willing to go, and that he'd take care of her if she needed it. Hell, he'd been doing it their whole lives.

"You remember when we were children," Louisa said, mostly into Fletcher's shoulder. "Some summer in Cornwall, the Earl of Courtland was visiting, and he had a daughter who was about my age. So we were playing outside, but she was really mean. She kept calling me ugly and skinny and we ran out to the pond."

"Oh, I remember this," Fletcher said. "She tried to push you in the pond."

"Said I belonged with the other toads. And you saw her chasing me, and you ran out to intervene. You talked her down and you took me out of there. You saved me."

"Not my greatest feat of strength."

"Perhaps not, but it meant a lot to me at the time. Especially when you *accidentally* stumbled and sent her into the pond instead." She smiled at the memory. "Or the time you told Amelia Featheringworth where she could put all the ostrich feathers in her hair when she said my gown was hideous the night we went to see *Die Zauberflöte*."

"She was just being petty. As I recall, the shade of green she wore that night was reminiscent of mushy peas."

"My point, Fletcher, is that you always come to my rescue and you always defend me, and I think those are admirable traits in a husband. And when I kiss you, I feel all…hot and bothered. Kissing Daniel is cold, nothing like the heat I feel with you."

Fletcher hugged Louisa closer. "Never speak of kissing Daniel again."

"Are you jealous?"

"Unspeakably."

Louisa laughed softly and put her arms around Fletcher's torso.

"I want you to know," Fletcher said, "that money is no object. There are a lot of things I will do to make sure you marry me instead of Rotherfeld. I'd pay a fortune. I'd fight a duel. Hell, I'd fight a war."

That warmed Louisa. She knew Fletcher was not kidding because he'd been her protector and defender for years. "Thank you. Let us hope that it does not come to that."

"What if he says no?" Fletcher asked, stroking her hair. "If I offer him the money and he won't sell? It may come to a war. I don't run very fast or punch very hard, but I'm a pretty good shot."

"Please do not commit a crime on my behalf. I can't imagine it will come to *that*. Can it really be worth it to keep me captive? Surely he can find some desperate heiress to be his wife. I'd far prefer some kind of civil agreement before it escalates to violence. Because you may be a good shot, but it's possible Daniel is, too."

"He may not like getting jilted right before the wedding that he announced so publicly."

"Do you see how he's been laying this trap?" Louisa pulled away from Fletcher so she could look at his face. "He announced the engagement publicly to discourage me from ending it, because everyone at the Rutherford ball, who is basically everyone who matters, knows about it. He made the deal with my father so my father wouldn't let me out of it. But I won't be trapped."

"No. I daresay you'd rescue yourself if you could."

"I'll say no at the altar if it comes to that. I won't marry him. Or I'll run off to the Continent. I have a little money. How much can a ticket to France cost?"

Fletcher laughed softly. "Take me with you to France, if that is the case."

"I thought you wanted to do this right. You didn't want to elope."

"I don't, but we might get desperate. Let us exhaust all the other options before we restage Waterloo and have to raise armies to end it."

Louisa laughed. "This whole situation is absurd."

"I know." Fletcher reached over and pushed a strand of hair behind Louisa's ear. "We will figure it out, okay? I've got a few tricks up my sleeve that I hope will work. I was kidding about needing to raise armies, but I am just saying, if that's what it takes, when all other options are exhausted, I'll do it."

"Thank you, Fletcher. I love you."

He kissed her forehead. "I love you, too."

FLETCHER FOUND ROTHERFELD at one of the lesser gentlemen's clubs. It took most of a day of investigating where Rotherfeld had memberships before he made this discovery. The man couldn't have just spent his evenings at White's; that would have been too easy. And Rotherfeld had apparently been making the rounds—his regular club was still under renovation—so it had been a real challenge to track him down. Fletcher finally got a break when one of Beresford's friends happened to know where Rotherfeld had been spending his evenings and on which nights all season. On Tuesdays, Rotherfeld had landed at this particular establishment, which seemed run down and the sort of place where one did not want to touch anything.

Lark had warned him that this particular club was known to harbor men who were interested in other men, although the membership was not that exclusively. It seemed to be a club mainly for men who wanted discretion, and there were a few women about, too, although Fletcher suspected they were paid for. Feeling out of his depths, Fletcher had begged Lark to come with him, so now they were walking around a dimly lit room.

Fletcher hated every part of it. The space made his skin crawl, although he could not put a finger on why. Perhaps it was because Lord Whitney was holding court in the club's main room; Whitney was known to use his power and money to get very young women into bed with him. No respectable peer would have anything to do with him, but apparently Baron Dabney, an extremely wealthy man with a questionable reputation, had no compunction about laughing and smoking cigars with the man.

The goal now was to get in and out as quickly as possible. Why was Rotherfeld here? To find other men to bed? To engage in other nefarious doings?

"So what is your plan exactly?" Lark asked.

"If I ever had one beyond forcing Rotherfeld to talk to me, it has fled my mind. You don't frequent this place, do you?"

"No. I would prefer not to know what my peers get up to in their spare time."

Fletcher had to laugh at that. "You lie. You're single-handedly keeping the scandal sheets in business."

"All right, I like gossip, but I don't need to see it with my own eyes."

The only saving grace was that the inside of this club was so dimly lit and smoky that it was difficult to see much.

So now Fletcher peered through the cigar smoke and was glad to have found Rotherfeld sitting in a corner, speaking with a young man. Fletcher held Lark back to observe them for a few moments. Rotherfeld had his hand on the young man's thigh, and then he leaned forward to…either whisper in the man's ear or nip at his chin, it was hard to tell from this angle. But the placement of Rotherfeld's hand was a giveaway. Then Rotherfeld moved, briefly rested his lips against the man's, and leaned away slightly.

Fletcher's first instinct was to look away because he had no business looking upon so intimate a moment, except now he had unambiguous proof about Rotherfeld's proclivities.

"That's Epperson's son," said Lark, gesturing toward the young man.

"You know unsavory things about him, don't you?"

Lark pressed a hand to his chest, clearly offended. "Not

firsthand. I've been besotted with a certain marquess for several years now, so I do not pursue other men, and anyway, the younger Epperson is barely out of short pants. What do you take me for?"

"He's, what, twenty years old? What do you think?"

"If that. Too baby faced for my tastes. Apparently not for Rotherfeld's, though."

Anthony suddenly appeared. "Lark, my darling friend, this place is a scandal."

Fletcher rolled his eyes. Lark had invited Beresford to tag along, apparently because as soon as Lark mentioned he would be coming to this club tonight, Beresford had expressed interest. "Curiosity," Anthony had insisted.

Lark glared at Anthony. "If you so much as look at any of the other men here tonight…"

Anthony laughed and threw an arm around Lark. "No need for jealousy. You have nothing to worry about. This place reeks of desperation."

"And spilled whisky," Fletcher said. "What would possess someone of Rotherfeld's stature to join such a club."

Anthony stepped away from Lark. "I'd think that would be obvious. To cater to his own sexual desires since he won't find them at home."

The "with Louisa" was implied.

Fletcher cursed.

"My, my. Language." Anthony grinned. "How much do you want to punch him right now?"

"A lot."

"Here, Lark and I will distract Young Master Epperson while you talk to Rotherfeld. I implore you to try to avoid dragging him to pistols at dawn."

"I'm a better shot than he is," said Fletcher, not knowing if it was true.

"Oh, I have no doubt. But I have no intention of getting up early enough to be your second."

Fletcher blew out a breath. He let Lark and Anthony drag Epperson off, and Fletcher slipped into the empty chair. He perched on the edge of it, wanting to touch the fabric of the chair as little as possible.

Rotherfeld looked startled. "Greystone."

"I suppose you know why I am here," said Fletcher.

"Lady Louisa. Did you seek me out here?"

"Much to my chagrin. I can't wait to leave." Fletcher struggled to remember what he intended to say. This whole situation made him uncomfortable, but for Louisa, he would push past every qualm he had about it. "But Louisa has enlisted my help. So I'll appeal to you at this level. She feels you've trapped her in a marriage she doesn't want. And if you go through with the wedding, that resentment will only grow with time. Is that truly what you want? Surely there's someone else you can trick into marrying you."

"She feels trapped?"

Fletcher didn't believe Rotherfeld's disbelief for one minute. Rotherfeld had, after all, engineered the trap. He made a show of rolling his eyes. "Louisa is a lot smarter than you gave her credit for. She knows why you announced the engagement at a ball. She knows why you made the deal with her father. And she's furious because she doesn't feel like you listened to her."

"So she sent you?" Rotherfeld's voice dripped with disdain. "You are not but the little dog at her feet hoping she'll drop some scrap of food on the floor. You are trying to steal my fiancée from me, so you're putting ideas in her head and—"

"I believe your presence here only emphasizes the pile of lies you were about to push toward me. I'm not planting ideas in her head. I told her the truth. I *saw* you caress that young man."

Fletcher regretted coming here tonight. He wished they could have this conversation in the light of day and not in a seedy club. But he'd tried Rotherfeld's home during regular calling hours and was told by the butler that he was not home. Given the way the sand was draining out of the hourglass, Fletcher had instead launched this ridiculous crusade to find wherever

Rotherfeld was in the city tonight. Everything about this situation now felt uncomfortable, unclean, and unsafe. But Fletcher persisted for Louisa's sake.

He considered his approach. He leaned forward. "I know who and what you are. I know why you want to marry Louisa, but she deserves more than being trapped into a marriage. She's a passionate woman with her own wants and desires, and she's smarter than you'll ever be. As a woman, she may be powerless, but I'm not."

"She sent you to do her dirty work."

Rotherfeld was really angering Fletcher now. "No. She confronted you herself first and you didn't listen. So let me make this clear. *I'm* marrying Louisa. You will not be. And there's a lot I'm prepared to do to make sure that happens."

"Such as?"

"Lord Petty is like a second father to me, and I will not allow his financial ruin."

That seemed to take Rotherfeld by surprise. "Are you offering me some kind of remuneration?"

Fletcher hesitated. Buying the farm was his last card. But he said, "Not yet. I was hoping we could reach some kind of settlement. But if buying you out is what it takes, it's not off the table."

"Let me think on it."

"You don't have much time. The wedding is due to occur in a number of days."

"You don't think I realize that?" Rotherfeld huffed.

A headache was starting to bloom at Fletcher's temples. He looked around. This place really was quite sordid, only a gentlemen's club insofar as Fletcher recognized several men who could be considered gentlemen. Probably he was not doing his own reputation much good by sitting here and talking to Rotherfeld.

Lark and Anthony looked like they were about to eat young Epperson for lunch, though.

"Think fast," Fletcher said, standing. "My offer is limited. As we speak, I have my men looking into ways around the predicament you've put the Petty family in." Fletcher felt good about that. He hadn't made a promise, and Rotherfeld likely didn't know that Fletcher had managed to discover the true value of the farm. He might settle for less than its full value. And if not, well, Fletcher could afford to bail out Lord Petty if he made some easy sacrifices. He didn't care about a dowry or any of that. He just wanted Louisa.

"You're leaving? You come in here and make accusations and dangle money and leave?"

"I've said my piece, and the cigar smoke here is heavy enough to choke on, so if you don't mind, I intend to inhale some less thick air outside. If you're interested in my offer, I will be at home with my man of business during regular calling hours tomorrow." He handed Rotherfeld a card.

"All right."

"Louisa won't marry you. Let's find a way out of this that will cause the least stir."

"It may already be too late for that."

Fletcher nodded. "The blame for which I put entirely on you."

Fletcher turned on his heel and walked toward the door. He grabbed Lark by the collar on the way.

"Say goodbye to your little toy, Anthony," Lark said as he was being dragged away.

"Enchantée, monsieur," said Anthony. "But, alas, my darling friend has insisted we leave. Rotherfeld is available again, but I've heard he has a small member, so proceed accordingly."

As they walked outside, Lark said, "You've heard no such thing."

"What are you talking about?"

"The thing you said about Rotherfeld."

"About his small member? No, I made that up. But would it really be so bad if that rumor spread?"

"I hope it spreads like a persistent rash," said Fletcher.

Chapter Twenty

FLETCHER HOPED THAT, when his butler announced that the Duke of Rotherfeld had come to call, Rotherfeld had come to his senses.

Alas.

Fletcher had been holed up in his office for most of the morning with Richard Cox, a capable accountant and business manager who had taken over the management of the Greystone estate and business holdings after the previous marquess's death. He met with Fletcher regularly to make reports and ask for final decisions. Fletcher had sold a few of the estate's holdings, and Mr. Cox informed him that he did have enough on hand to buy out Rotherfeld's share in the Shropshire sheep farm—"Say *that* five times fast!" Fletcher had joked, but Mr. Cox did not appear to appreciate this—but Mr. Cox had also been digging into Anthony's idea for how to thwart Rotherfeld financially, and also found it sound.

But now Rotherfeld stood in Fletcher's study and said, "I heard what you said last night, but I'm not interested."

"You came all this way to say you're not interested?" said Fletcher, not believing him. There was no reason to have come all the way to Fletcher's house if the answer was a flat no. Fletcher figured Rotherfeld had come to negotiate.

"The reputational damage—"

Fletcher wanted to grab Rotherfeld by the embroidered lapels of his very expensive jacket. "Let me put this more plainly," Fletcher said. "You think this is a negotiation, but it is not. You will not be marrying Louisa. You can come to the church if you like, but she'll refuse you, or not show up at the church at all. You can threaten Lord Petty if you like, but I'll buy Petty out of his share of the farm, and then you will have to do business with me. And let me warn you, I may seem mild-mannered, but I am willing to fight to the ends of the Earth for the people I love. And I love Louisa. So if you carry on with the wedding, or if you touch so much as a hair on her head, I will make you regret it."

Mr. Cox sat at the desk and made a *tsk* sound. Fletcher didn't care for his judgment. He needed Rotherfeld to understand he was opposing the wrong man, and that Fletcher's patience for this nonsense had run out.

Rotherfeld's face paled.

"The way I see it," Fletcher went on, "you can end the engagement quietly now, we'll all agree that things just didn't work out, and Louisa and I will marry in a small ceremony at the end of the season. We won't call attention to it, people will forget it ever happened. But if you persist in this delusion that Louisa is somehow the answer to your problems and not a flesh-and-blood woman with her own wants and desires, then I will ensure myself that your humiliation is maximal."

This seemed to, finally, chasten Rotherfeld. "What do you plan to do?"

Fletcher shrugged. "Not me. Louisa plans to jilt you. Would you really like for that to happen in front of rows of society's finest, sitting in pews in a church?"

Rotherfeld frowned.

"You forget also," Fletcher said, "that I know your secrets. I saw you at your club. I don't know if you are still having an affair with Lieutenant Hanley, but I know you did. There were several prominent witnesses to your trying to woo young Epperson. I am not above having a friend leak something to the scandal sheets.

You want to talk about reputational damage? What will happen to you if the *ton* finds out Louisa jilted you because you're a sodomite? What would happen if I told Lord Petty? If I told the whole *ton*?"

Fletcher hadn't intended to go so hard. He hadn't intended to be brutal. But he was tired of having this debate with Rotherfeld. He wanted it to be made clear that Fletcher had all the cards here.

Rotherfeld didn't say anything. He stared at the ground. He seemed to be thinking.

"Have you nothing to say?" Fletcher asked.

"You threaten me with this?"

"I don't want to. Like I said, my preference would be for us to end the engagement quietly. Louisa will send your regrets to the wedding guests. Louisa and I won't say anything publicly. We'll have a small wedding six weeks hence, no one will remember any of this come next season. We don't need to make this a whole to-do, unless you fail to see reason. Let Louisa go, and all of this goes away."

Rotherfeld nodded slowly. "And what of my investment?"

"As soon as you leave," Fletcher said, "I am going to go to the Petty residence and offer to buy Lord Petty's half of the farm. Maybe he can't afford to lose the money, but my man Mr. Cox here assures me *I* can. I'd prefer not to, but Louisa is more important to me than the money, so I've removed that bit of leverage. You and I can do business perhaps, or you can buy me out and we have nothing to do with each other again."

"I see."

"The rest is all your reputation. So we can handle this quietly now or publicly on Saturday."

Fletcher felt he'd done all he could here. He didn't want to be half-owner of a sheep farm, but he'd make the most of it if he had to. If the farm were profitable, which it seemed to be, perhaps Rotherfeld would buy out Fletcher's half anyway. Buying out Petty instead of Rotherfeld had been Anthony's big idea, and Fletcher liked it because it gave him all the leverage now.

"So, let me sum up," Rotherfeld said. "You will buy out Petty's half of the investment. And you will likely try to make my life as hard as you can financially. And if I don't end the engagement, Louisa will jilt me at the altar, and you will leak my affairs to the scandal sheets. Do I have that right?"

"You do. And if you agree today to end the engagement with Louisa, none of that happens. Well, I will still own half a sheep farm and we can further negotiate that, but everything else stays quiet."

"I see."

"Have we reached an understanding?" Fletcher asked.

Rotherfeld dropped his head and stared at the ground again. Then he looked up at Fletcher. He nodded. "We have."

"Perhaps while I speak with Lord Petty this afternoon," Fletcher said, "you can speak with Lady Louisa."

"Perhaps I should."

"I knew you'd see reason."

LOUISA WAS NOT normally one to succumb to despair, but she tossed aside her ruined embroidery and nearly cried. She was glad she had not actually cried, though, when the butler announced that the Duke of Rotherfeld and the Marquess of Greystone had arrived.

That was odd enough, but then only Daniel darkened the sitting room doorway.

"Did you do away with Greystone on your way here from the door?" she asked.

"No," said Daniel, looking affronted. "He is speaking with your father."

"Oh." What did this all mean? "The two of you arrived together."

Daniel looked down. "Greystone has given me an ultimatum.

He has told me either I must end the engagement with you in private now, or he will publicly humiliate me at our wedding. And frankly, I'd prefer to avoid public humiliation."

Louisa's heart warmed. He'd held up his end of the bargain. He was going to do whatever it took. She assumed he'd gone to talk with Father to sort out the details.

"I suppose," Daniel said, "I did not realize the extent to which our continued engagement was distressing you."

"I did try to tell you."

"You must understand the position I'm in."

Something in Louisa snapped. She hoped her mother was not in earshot for what she was about to say but couldn't risk closing the door if this engagement was about to end. "Here's what I know," she said, in a hiss of a whisper. "As a woman, I have almost no power to choose who I marry, nor do I have a way around the fact that I must marry if I want any semblance of independence from my family. My father has never put pressure on me to marry and likely will continue to support me for the rest of my life if I need that, but I don't want that. I want more freedom of movement than that. So I knew that, when you offered for me, it was a step toward independence."

"I can still give you that."

"No, you can't. Not with what I know now. That you view me as a means to an end. Well, Greystone and I may have acted foolishly, but I know, at least, that he views me as a person, and that if we marry, we'll be true partners, and that is what I want for myself."

Daniel frowned.

Louisa took a step closer. "I know also," she said as quietly as she could, "because my friends are terrible gossips, that there are others in society like you. It's not my place to disclose their secrets, and I can't know your specific circumstance, but there's no reason I can see why you and, say, Lieutenant Hanley could not live a perfectly satisfactory life away from the social swirl of London."

"Satisfactory," Daniel spat. "You know nothing, Louisa."

"Perhaps not about that, you're right. But the truth under everything is that I know I cannot marry you and I do not want to. I know that if we end our engagement, Fletcher will have me, and I know that, if a wife is truly what you want, there is another woman out there who will have you. And I think Fletcher's right. It is better to quietly end things away from the gaze of our peers, rather than waiting for me to publicly jilt you."

Daniel frowned, but then he nodded slowly. "You talk a great deal, did you know that?"

"People have mentioned."

"When Fletcher is done, I will speak with your parents. If you agree that this is what you want, I will end the engagement."

Louisa tried not to let triumph show too much on her face. Her relief was palpable. "Thank you."

"I do like you, Louisa. I think we could have made something of our lives. Although perhaps not if you are in love with Greystone."

"As I said, he and I were fools not to recognize it sooner, and if we had it would have saved a lot of grief, but here we are. I'm sorry, Daniel, that things did not work out, and I truly hope you find happiness in the future, but it cannot be with me."

"Well, thank you for that. I am sorry, too, for what it's worth."

She didn't believe his sincerity, but she asked, "What made you change your mind?"

Daniel just shook his head. "Your Greystone can be quite persuasive when he wants to be. I believe I underestimated him. He is rather more...cunning than I expected."

Louisa couldn't help but smile at that. Fletcher often played like he was a happy-go-lucky, idle member of the *ton*, but he could be ruthless when the occasion called for it. Louisa had witnessed it herself in all the ways he'd defended her when she'd gotten herself into trouble as a child. And it seemed he'd done it again.

Fletcher always came through for her. She didn't need to know what he'd said to Daniel, just that whatever he'd done, it had persuaded Daniel, finally, to let this go. And for that, Louisa would always be grateful to Fletcher.

"I should…I should go speak with your father," Daniel said, beginning to back out of the room.

"Goodbye, Daniel."

He waved his hand but then left the room.

Louisa spent the next period of time—it could have been twenty minutes, it could have been three hours, she was too nervous to find out—mostly pacing or sitting on her hands or stabbing at her embroider project.

When at least Fletcher appeared in the doorway, she felt such an immense relief that she launched off the sofa and into his arms. He let out a huff of laughter as he caught her but then, with his hands firmly on her waist, he picked her up and placed her a foot away from himself.

Louisa's parents arrived a moment later.

"The Duke of Rotherfeld has departed," said Father.

"This is quite a turn of events," said Mother. "He's a *duke*."

"Yes," said Father, "but we've known Fletcher his entire life, and we know him to be kind and trustworthy, and I am not at all certain Rotherfeld shares those same traits. And I'd much rather our Louisa be safe and happy than to worry about her status."

"Yes, but…a *duke*."

"And Fletcher is a wealthy marquess."

"Is he less wealthy now?" Louisa asked. She worried he'd had to make a big financial sacrifice to free Father from the commitment to Daniel, and she hated that possibility and hated Daniel a bit for engineering it.

But then Father said, "No. I sold my share of the farm back to Rotherfeld for a good price. It took some persuasion, but he finally agreed. We left Fletcher out of the transaction entirely."

Louisa wondered what that persuasion entailed; she wondered if Fletcher had found some evidence of wrongdoing on

Daniel's part to use as leverage. She couldn't imagine Daniel would so easily part with his money otherwise.

"I hope," Fletcher said, "that you do not need a big wedding, because part of the agreement was that you and I shall marry in a small ceremony at the end of the season so as to not draw an exclamation point at the end of the broken engagement with Rotherfeld."

"I care not at all as long as we marry," Louisa said.

Fletcher smiled. "Then that is what we shall do."

Louisa looked at her parents. "So that's it? Everything with Rotherfeld is over? Fletcher and I can marry?"

"Yes, my dear," said Father.

Louisa could not keep herself from letting out an excited squeal. She grabbed Fletcher's hand. He laughed, perhaps caught upon her enthusiasm.

Mother sighed. "All right. We must write some letters telling people not to come to the church on Saturday. Perhaps you will help, Louisa."

"Of course." It would be unpleasant work, but worth it in the long run.

Louisa was free now. And she'd marry Fletcher, and the two of them would be happy together for the end of their days. The only downside was that she'd have to wait until the end of the Season for the rest of her life to begin, when she wanted it to begin right now.

She wanted to spend the rest of the day with Fletcher, planning their future, making plans, or just spending time in each other's company. But it was not meant to be.

Fletcher leaned over and kissed her cheek. "Forgive my haste, but I left my man of business pacing in my house, and I must give him the news that we will not need to part with a great deal of money after all. And that I think, perhaps, I should like to take my soon-to-be-wife on a spectacular honeymoon instead. Perhaps to Vienna. Or Milan."

A thrill went through Louisa's chest. "Oh, I have always

wanted to see La Scala!"

She wanted to tell Fletcher she loved him, but not in front of her parents. Instead, she smiled at him. And she began a new scheme.

Chapter Twenty-One

FLETCHER WAS ABOUT to fall into bed after a very long day— although he couldn't say he was upset at all about the way the day had turned out—when someone knocked on his bedroom door. It turned out to be his valet, who said, somewhat sardonically, "There is a lady here to see you."

Louisa.

"The lady is now my fiancée, so I suppose you will have to make yourself used to her presence."

"Yes, my lord, although need I remind you that you are not married *yet*."

"You are dismissed, Reeves."

"Indeed."

He turned and left. A moment later, Louisa, wearing what Fletcher had come to think of as her mischief cloak, appeared in the doorway. Fletcher, once again, found himself wearing a dressing gown in her presence.

"I suppose I should make myself adjust to the constancy of your presence in my vicinity at night," Fletcher said.

"That was a lot of fancy words to explain that we shall soon be living together."

"Yes, but not for another month or so. I promised your former fiancé that we would wait so as to not embarrass him."

"Very sensible of you."

"You shouldn't be here." He both wanted her to leave and for her to stay, and it was a terrible position to be in. He wanted to honor the commitments he made to Louisa's parents, but he also wanted Louisa and didn't want to wait much longer. Having her standing here was the worst sort of temptation because, he suspected, if he made a move, she wouldn't say no.

"What can anyone do?" Louisa asked, sounding defiant. "Force you to marry me?"

Fletcher sensed this was not an argument he'd able to win. "Very well. Why have you come?"

"I was supposed to be married a few days hence, and although I have less fondness for my prospective groom now than I did a few weeks ago, I was still...no, let me not frame it that way."

Fletcher suspected he knew where this was going. "I don't mean to be prudish," he said, "but I do not think this is appropriate."

Louisa made a determined face, standing tall and clearly ignoring Fletcher. "I believe we should be together. Physically. Tonight. Do you not want to be with me?"

"What I want does not signify." Fletcher truly did not want to mess this up.

Louisa shot him an admonishing look. "Then what does?"

Fletcher felt his will unraveling. He didn't know if Louisa knew what she was doing or not—he suspected she knew the effect she had on him at least in part—but she removed her cloak reveal she was wearing the yellow gown Fletcher had mentioned he liked. And there were her breasts, straining against the fabric, on display and begging for him to touch them. He hesitated to make a move. She seemed to be pulling at him with some invisible force that made him want to put his hands on her, but he couldn't... Not yet.

"Apologies, but it is quite warm in here. I am at least not wearing my stays."

He groaned. "You are a wicked woman."

She draped her cloak over a chair and walked toward Fletcher, kicking his door shut on the way. "Fletcher, let me make this plain. I came here tonight because I cannot wait any longer, because I am tired of the promise of kissing being snuffed out because of my existing engagement. That engagement is over now, and you and I are betrothed, and I see no reason to wait longer."

"Your father would have my head if he knew you were here."

She waved her hand as if this were of no import. "I'll be home before morning, and they will never know. And, again, I repeat, what's the worst that will happen? They will force us to marry sooner? That is fine by me."

"You are reckless."

"I am *determined.*"

Fletcher laughed, overwhelmed by her. "You don't know what you're asking me."

"I wish people would stop assuming that I'm an idiot."

"I don't think you're an idiot. I think you are inexperienced."

"Well, that may be true, but I have this feeling. It is…unsatisfied, I suppose. Itchy, a bit. You are standing there in your dressing gown, and I keep thinking about what your body must look like under it, and I feel like I am crawling out of my skin."

Fletcher knew something about that feeling. "Louisa…"

"We are to be married, Fletcher. I do not see a problem with…getting ahead of ourselves." She stepped forward, close enough to Fletcher to touch him.

"But—" Fletcher said, although his heart was not really in the protest. Here was the woman he loved, propositioning him, and he was trying to say no… Why?

She put her hands on his shoulders and leaned up on her toes to kiss him. Fletcher gave up; she was determined, and he was constitutionally incapable of pushing her away. He put his hands on her waist and kissed her.

She really wasn't wearing stays. He was so used to grasping

her and feeling the boning under her gowns that being confronted with the softness of her body surprised him. He moved his hands up her back to pull her closer.

"Show me, Fletcher," Louisa said. "Take me to bed."

She deserved everything, all the pleasure in the world. She started fiddling with the collar of his dressing gown, which was tied closed tightly, but he wore nothing beneath it, intending to sleep in the nude that night. Being this close to her, with such little clothing, sent a tingle up Fletcher's spine. He wanted to touch her everywhere, to watch her fall apart, to have her writhing in his arms. And even though everything told him he needed to wait until they were truly married, having her here, her body under his hands, dissolved any resolve he had.

As he felt the tie at his waist loosen as he and Louisa pressed together, he began to undo the buttons at her back.

"Are we to be naked?" she asked, in what sounded like a scandalized whisper.

Fletcher fought not to laugh. God, he loved this woman. "I thought that's what you wanted."

"It is. I don't know what to expect entirely. That is, my mother sometimes speaks of marital relations as something to endure."

"No," said Fletcher.

"No?"

"Relations between men and woman can—nay *should*—be pleasurable for both partners, and never something to merely endure, and I know you have your own strong desires. I look forward to hearing you tell me all about them."

"I do. I profess to my first desire to be seeing what you are wearing beneath your dressing gown."

"Nothing," he said, kissing her neck.

"Nothing!"

"You did intrude on me as I was about to go to sleep, and I did not have time to put on other clothes and make myself more presentable, not that it matters if the aim is to be naked together."

She gasped when Fletcher nipped the exposed skin of her shoulder now that her gown was slipping.

"Take this off," he murmured, tugging at her gown.

She stepped back, and Fletcher saw the war on her face. She wanted him, but she didn't know what to do. He enjoyed that contrast. And he'd succeeded in undoing all of the buttons at her back, so she was able to let her gown fall to her feet with minimal effort, despite the stiff fabric. Beneath the gown, she wore only a shift tucked into a petticoat, and the latter was loosely tied and already falling down her hips. But the key thing was that her shift was nearly transparent, and Fletcher could see her hard nipples poking at the fabric.

Fletcher pulled her close again. He kissed her again and knew his arousal would be plain now, but he cared not. This was *Louisa*, a woman he'd been wanting for weeks if not longer, and their relationship was about to take a significant turn.

Louisa's petticoat slid to the floor. Fletcher picked her up and carried her over to the bed.

"This will change how things are between us," Fletcher said. "Are you certain this is what you want?"

"I've never been so certain of anything."

FLETCHER'S DRESSING GOWN was coming undone at the waist, and the knowledge that he wore nothing under it was the most tantalizing thing Louisa had ever experienced. It was all she could do not to tug at the belt on his dressing gown, but she wasn't sure if that would be the right thing to do. Instead, she wrapped her fingers around the lapels.

"The thing about nudity," Fletcher said in a low, quiet tone, "is that it does help with excitement."

"Oh. Is this a scientific observation on your part?"

"It is."

"You of course having experience with women of a more…daring disposition."

Fletcher paused, his hand raised as though he were about to touch her. "Are you jealous?"

"On the contrary, I'm glad one of us knows what to do."

"I want to see your body in the good light," he said, gesturing toward the lamp on the side table.

"All right," she said, unable to breathe.

Fletcher started at her calf, where her shift ended. He slid his hand up her leg, her shift catching on his wrist as he moved. She'd opted not to wear drawers, either, and this whole situation felt rather scandalous, but her plan had been hasty and driven by instinct more than anything else.

She helped him peel off her shift, and she thought she'd be embarrassed to be so…nude…under his gaze, but instead, as his eyes darkened, and he seemed to like what he saw, and she suddenly felt beautiful and powerful.

Fletcher kissed her. He used one hand to prop himself up and the other to cup her breast. He tweaked her nipple, and it felt like rocky waves went through her body. She let out a gasp.

"Yes," Fletcher murmured. "We're alone. You can be as loud as you need to be. I want this to feel good for you and I want you to *react*."

"I want you to feel good, too."

"I already do."

She didn't believe him. She pushed his dressing gown off his shoulders and looked down at where the tie at his waist came undone. "Let me see you," she said.

He helped her take off his dressing gown and was completely naked underneath, which was as big of a shock. She only ever saw Fletcher with many layers of clothing on. She had no idea that his arms were muscled that way, that his chest was carved like the statues she'd seen except that it was dusted with dark hair. And unlike every nude statue she'd ever seen, the appendage between his legs was…quite large.

"Oh!" she said.

"I know you've seen art, but flesh-and-blood men are a bit different."

"They look so small and manageable in art," she said, gesturing at his member.

He laughed. "And often they are. But when men are aroused, they grow larger."

"And *that* is supposed to fit inside me?"

"It will. But this is why we touch and kiss and leer at each other first. It creates arousal."

She already ached between her legs. How much more aroused should she be?

Out of curiosity more than anything else, she wrapped her hand around Fletcher's cock and stroked it. It was harder than she expected, but his skin was soft and warm. He hissed as she stroked him, which she took to mean that what she was doing felt good. She kissed him and kept stroking until he put a hand on hers and nudged her away.

"Did I do something wrong?" she asked breathlessly.

"No, but I am so wound up that if you keep doing it, all of this will have ended before I'm ready for it to."

"Oh."

Fletcher put a finger under Louisa's chin and nudged it up so that she was looking at his face. "Louisa?"

She just stared at him.

He smiled. "You're beautiful. Probably the most beautiful woman I've ever seen."

"Probably?" she said, sounding affronted even though she flattered.

He laughed. "Definitely the most beautiful woman I've ever seen. You, my darling Louisa, are my favorite person on this planet and I am thrilled to be here with you tonight and I cannot wait to start our lives together, as evidenced by the fact that you are in my bed right now and we are both naked."

"You're the most handsome man I've ever seen. I had no idea

you were so…strong."

"Oh?"

"Are you a pugilist, or—"

"Let us not discuss this right now."

"Shall we not talk during…relations?"

"We can talk as much as you like. I love the sound of your voice, and I love talking to you. But I don't want to get into my exercise regimen when we're about to—"

"Oh! Of course, I—"

Fletcher kissed her, probably to shut her up.

She sighed into his kiss and put her arms around his back, pulling him on top of her. She spread her legs, more because of instinct than anything else, and he seemed to fit right there between her legs.

Then he touched her there.

The shock of it sent more cascades through her body, but she liked how it felt and shifted her hips to meet Fletcher's fingers. He slipped a finger inside her, which felt strange, but also good. Some weird, unholy noises came out of her mouth as he pressed his thumb against a spot that felt *very* good.

"Have you never…touched yourself here?" Fletcher asked.

"A few times, but it's different when… Oh, do that again."

Fletcher chuckled. It sounded smug. Louisa wanted to give him an admonishing look, but she was too caught up in what he was doing.

He slipped a second finger inside her and pressed against *that spot* with his thumb. Louisa moaned. This was too much, it felt too good, it was making her body twitch and tingle.

"Is this all right?" Fletcher asked.

"Yes," she said shakily. "It feels good."

He kissed her. "This next part may hurt. Tell me to stop if it does."

Louisa's heart picked up, but she trusted Fletcher and knew he'd stop the moment she told him to. She felt something blunt at the entrance to her body and understood what was happening.

She grasped at Fletcher's shoulders and held him there as he began to push inside her. It did hurt a little, but she was determined, and the pain was short-lived. Suddenly, whatever Fletcher was doing felt so good, Louisa groaned and dug her fingers into Fletcher's shoulders.

Fletcher groaned, too, and his face was beginning to lose its control. He put a hand under one of her knees and pressed it up and then began to move within her.

"Oh!" she said.

"Are you all right?"

"It… I've never felt anything like this."

Fletcher paused. "Is that good or bad?"

"It's good! It's good. Keep moving!"

Fletcher sighed and began thrusting in and out of her, and Louisa felt something within her building. Parts of her body ached, but in a very good way. And when Fletcher pressed his thumb against *that spot*, right above the entrance to her body, her whole body jolted with pleasure. *Yes*, she thought, *more of that*, but she couldn't make her mouth form the words because she was so absorbed in *feeling* and taking whatever Fletcher wanted to give her.

He groaned again. "How are you—?" he started to ask.

If he finished the sentence, she didn't hear him, because something crashed over her whole body. She threw her head back and groaned and let this sensation wash over her.

She knew it was a sexual peak—she'd made herself get there before, but it felt so much better with Fletcher's arms around her, with him inside her.

Fletcher kissed her and kept pumping his hips, but his rhythm became more erratic.

"I wanted to last," he said, "but…" Then he groaned and jerked away from her abruptly. Then she felt him spill on her belly.

He rolled onto his back, panting. He breathed heavily for a long moment, as Louisa felt her own heart rate slow down. "Was that all right?" he asked.

"It was more than all right."

After a moment, he slid out of bed and walked across the room to his washbasin. Louisa took a moment to admire his bare backside. He really was a splendidly put together man.

He came back a moment later and used a cloth to clean up her belly and between her legs. He sighed and said, "This is all so new, this thing between us. We've never talked about children. I don't even know if you want them."

"Is that why you…?" She gestured at her belly.

"Yes. That, and we're not married yet, and I didn't want anyone to do the math."

She rolled onto her side and took his free hand. He stood next to the bed, and she gave him a very thorough once over. "We'd make very cute children," she said.

He laughed. "I suppose."

"Well, let me answer your question this way. I felt ambivalent with…my former fiancé," she said, not wanting to say Daniel's name when she was naked with Fletcher. "But with you? Yes, I want children. I want to watch them grow up and be little terrors at your estate in Cornwall where they'll catch frogs and hide salamanders under teacups the way you did one time."

"I was ten years old," Fletcher said, but he laughed.

"But yes, I want that, Fletcher. I want that future with you."

He tossed the cloth vaguely in the direction of his washbasin, missed by a couple of feet, waved his hand as if this were of no matter, and then lay down beside her, on his side, facing her. He said, "I want that, too." He pressed his head against hers. "We were unholy terrors as children, weren't we?"

"I think we were…normal children."

"Our children will *definitely* be unholy terrors."

"Probably."

Fletcher laughed. "Then I look forward to having them with you."

She smiled and ran a hand through his hair. "Was this strange to you? Being with me like this?"

"No," he said. "It felt like the most natural thing in the world. It went…a little faster than I would have liked, but we have our whole lives to perfect it."

Louisa smiled at him. "I love you, Fletcher."

He kissed her forehead. "I love you, too, but you'd better get back into your clothes and out of here before someone at your house notices you're gone. And I'll be sending one of my footmen with you to make sure you make it there. And you will not sneak over to be with me again until we're married."

"You can't possibly expect me to abide by that last rule of yours now that I *know*."

He sighed. "Perhaps, *you're* the unholy terror."

"If I am, I learned from the best." She sat up, preparing to get out of bed and do as he asked. "You love me."

"More than words can express.

Epilogue

THE WEDDING WAS a quiet affair at the end of the season, held in the garden behind the Petty house with just their close friends and family in attendance.

After the wedding, Fletcher and Louisa spent a month on the Continent together, seeing some of the finest opera houses—and operas—in the world. They both had a wonderful time, touring museums, looking at art, making love both at night and at odd hours of the day when they were idle and alone and the mood struck.

Fletcher could not remember ever being this happy. How had he been so foolish as to not see that Louisa was his perfect partner in everything?

When they returned, they were invited to a house party at Beresford House in Kent. Also in attendance were the Duke and Duchess of Swynford and their son, the Earl and Countess of Caernarfon and their son, a friend of the Marquess's named Baron Edgmont, and of course Larkin Woodville, Earl Warning, and the Marquess of Beresford's son.

Lord Edgmont was a bit of a curiosity; Fletcher had never met him before. It seemed he was a childhood friend of Anthony's who didn't spend much time in London, but who kept up a lively correspondence with Anthony still. He'd been a vicar at a small church a few miles from Beresford House before coming into his title and deciding he'd rather tend to some land he'd inherited, but he jested when he and Fletcher just met that once a vicar, always a vicar, and that made Fletcher wonder if he should perhaps be on his best behavior, and if Edgmont knew the true nature of Lark and Anthony's relationship.

Still, it seemed like a fairly normal house party on the first day. Beresford House sat on a sprawling estate that allowed for horse riding and long strolls, something Fletcher took advantage of with his new wife. The manicured gardens off the back of the house proved to be a lovely place to take a walk and engage in casual conversation and steal a few kisses.

The two boys who could ambulate, Edward and Dafydd, took off running across the path in front of where they walked one afternoon, one of the nannies hurrying after them.

"There are too many small boys about," Louisa said.

"There are three, and the third barely counts because he is not yet big enough to walk," Fletcher pointed out.

"That is too many."

Fletcher laughed at that. "It is kind of fun having children about. I've not had many opportunities to spend time with them."

"I hope our first child is a girl."

"I could see that." Fletcher froze. "You don't...that is, do you know something..."

"Oh, no. I am not expecting. I'm just saying that when I do, I hope it's a girl."

"We did have fun in Europe, though. It would not surprise me if—"

"All in good time, my love."

In the evening, Anthony generally eschewed formality. They all had dinner together in his formal dining room, but wine and conversation flowed freely. After the meal, the genders didn't segregate themselves. Instead, Anthony had everyone gather after dinner for conversation and some casual games. He explained the rules of whist to Louisa, who took to it the way she'd taken to chess and quickly swindled several of Fletcher's friends out of the wooden tokens they were using instead of money.

The gratifying thing was that everyone enjoyed each other's company. No one felt the need to exile the women because they were able to keep up their ends of conversation. Anthony refrained from breaking out the cigars, mostly for Adele's sake because, now that she was expecting, many smells—cigar smoke, roasting chicken, Anthony's cologne—made her nauseous, but Lark did pour wine for anyone who wanted it.

So Fletcher was having a great time with his friends and Louisa and couldn't think of a more pleasurable house party he'd ever attended.

The party took a turn on the third day. That was when Anthony announced that they would be doing something a bit unusual that afternoon. He led everyone out to the gardens, where seats were arranged in a semicircle around a display of flowers. Lord Edgmont walked over and stood in front of the display. Edgmont looked like a vicar about to preside over a wedding ceremony.

When everyone was seated, Lark said, "Thank you all for coming. We wanted you all to be here because Anthony and I have decided to do something a bit unusual and we wanted our close friends as witnesses. We are going to have a ceremony, led by Lord Edgmont, in which Anthony and I declare our commitment to one another."

"Is this a wedding?" asked Grace.

"Something like it," said Anthony. "Lark and I wanted to state before our friends and God that we are committed to one another and promise to be faithful and love each other and raise Henry together. We know it's a bit unorthodox and you may have moral objections. If that's the case, you may leave."

No one stood to leave.

Lark smiled. "Then let's do this."

It was a lovely ceremony. Lark and Anthony stood facing each other and holding hands and Lord Edgmont gave a beautiful speech about love and commitment. Perhaps because Lord Edgmont was no longer a vicar, this ceremony had no formal status, but it hardly mattered. What mattered was that Anthony and Lark were in love and making a promise to each other, one that everyone bearing witness would honor. Fletcher held and squeezed Louisa's hand throughout the ceremony, deeply moved. And, as with any wedding, Anthony and Lark kissed at the end of it. Fletcher marveled that this was taking place at all, but at least they had the privacy of Anthony's estate to have this moment.

That night, Anthony hosted a feast with a string quartet playing music, so Fletcher got to dance with his wife as Anthony and Lark danced with each other, too. It all felt very much like a wedding, and the unspoken consensus seemed to be to treat it as such.

Fletcher confronted Lark near the refreshment table about halfway through the dancing. "Congratulations are in order."

"Thank you. I feel a little bad for luring you all here under false pretenses." Lark grinned. "Except I don't feel bad at all."

"What are you planning to do now? Will you stay here in Kent?"

"Before we left to come here, I bought the house adjacent to Anthony's in London from his elderly neighbor. It will take some time to clean up the place. I still have to sell my old house and move all my things. But it's basically our pretense. I shall live with Anthony but keep the adjacent house for appearances, basically." Lark shrugged. "Anthony wants to cut a door to attach our houses. Or build a secret passage."

Fletcher smiled at that. "Oh, you should definitely build a secret passage. If he wants help with that, I volunteer my services."

Lark laughed. But then he said, "I have no idea if any of this will work. I do hope to be in London for at least part of the season so that I can see all my friends, but we're safe here in Kent, too. The staff is all familiar with the situation. Anthony gave everyone a raise, which I'm sure smoothed over any ruffled feathers."

"Likely true."

"We're probably doomed, but… I love him. So here we are."

"Well, good luck. And thank you for inviting us. This has really been a wonderful three days. I can't think of a more fun party I've attended."

"I'm glad. I didn't see the need to stand on ceremony and tradition since we have all been friends so long and I've never been much for tradition anyway."

"If only all house parties were this informal."

Lark smiled. "If only."

As Fletcher and Louisa went to bed that night, they chatted about the day. Anthony had put them in a lovely room that was a bit ostentatiously decorated. The four-poster bed with a damas canopy over it was not to Fletcher's taste, but it seemed in character for Anthony, who didn't seem to do anything by half measures.

Louisa said, "It really was a lovely ceremony. I'm so happy for Lark and Anthony."

"I am, too, though it's going to be difficult for them. They will have to keep their relationship a secret. They may spend less time in London during the Season." That was one thing Fletcher felt sad about. He and his closest friends were all married and starting families now and would likely have less time for each other. He hoped they would, at least, continue to meet at their club in London during the season. He cared a great deal for his friends and their families and would hate to lose that.

"Promise me something, Fletcher," Louisa said, turning down the bedding.

"Anything."

"If we have a child who prefers his or her own sex, we will love that child unconditionally."

Fletcher walked over and kissed the top of Louisa's head. "Of course. We will love all of our children unconditionally. They will not want for anything." He found it suspicious that she kept bringing this up. "Are you certain you are not—"

"I don't *know*. It's too soon to know anything. But I have a suspicion."

"Do you?"

"It may just be in my head, which is why I didn't say anything. But we did…have relations…well, *frequently*, while we were on the Continent, and I suppose I suspect that… But I don't actually *know*, so it's all just speculation at this point."

"We could, you know, have relations right now. Just to make sure."

Louisa laughed and put her arms around Fletcher's neck. "I love you."

Fletcher grinned. "I know. I love you."

THE END

About the Author

Kate McMurray writes romance novels. She likes creating stories that are brainy, funny, and of course sexy, with regular guy characters and urban sensibilities. She advocates for romance stories by and for everyone. When she's not writing, she edits textbooks, watches baseball, plays violin, crafts things out of yarn, and wears a lot of cute dresses. She lives in Brooklyn, NY, with a bossy cat and too many books.

Instagram / Threads: @katemcmurraygram